IN A
RAVEN'S
SHADOW

PETER BROWNING

Tellwell Talent
www.tellwell.ca

ISBN
978-0-2288-4922-3 (Hardcover)
978-0-2288-4921-6 (Paperback)
978-0-2288-4923-0 (eBook)

Für Elyse

ACKNOWLEDGEMENTS

My sincerest thanks to Jane and Barry. Without your knowledge, guidance and, most important of all, your encouragement, this would not have been possible.

*For Nicole,
I hope you enjoy
the read.
Cheers!
Peter*

"In torment, there was release.
In the darkness, there was light.
In solitude, there were companions."

—C.C. Humphreys, *Vlad: The Last Confession*

PROLOGUE

The overgrown road wound through the old cut-over forest, lined on both sides by wild shrubs full of snowberry and rosehips. The air was fresh and clean from the rain the night before; raindrops hung from the clover and other weeds that filled the ruts where years ago logging trucks had hauled the trees to local mills. It was mostly a young aspen forest, no more than thirty feet tall, that had grown in after the fallers had finished. Over the rolling site, a handful of taller fir veterans that had survived the chainsaws stood watch like guardians over the thriving trees.

The boy was twelve years old now and stood motionless in the middle of the road. His brown hair was uncombed. He wore a denim jacket, grey T-shirt and denim pants. An old worn pair of black sneakers covered his feet, but the holes in them revealed his dirty blue socks underneath. After a few minutes, he began walking slowly and quietly along the road, stopping regularly to watch and listen. It was his favourite time of year. The aspen was just beginning to turn colour. It would only be another month before all the leaves were red and yellow. But it was the shrubs he was most interested in. He carried a small gauge shotgun. It was loaded—with the safety on—and held across his body, the barrel pointed slightly up to his left. The grouse would be here. If he was patient, he knew he could bag at least four or five of the "wild chickens" before the day was over. The birds loved to gorge on the berries that hung from the shrubs. They would also need to dry off after last night's rain, so he was sure he would see them looking for the sunny breaks in the forest canopy that splashed warmth onto the old road.

He was by himself, and he wanted it that way. The old man would be two or three miles away, sitting in a larger clearing and waiting with a rifle for the mule deer that might stray into the open. The old man was his father, but he never referred to him as "dad" unless he had to address him as such. Even at this age, the boy knew that a father should take an active role in rearing a child in the hopes of helping his boy become a decent human being. But the old man was simply a supply of genes and the dispenser of discipline once the boy was born. By being alone, the boy could enjoy this time without the fear that hung over him whenever the old man was close. But there was a bonus to living in a household with a temperamental ogre—his wits were keen, and his reflexes fast. By planning ahead and sensing the moments that might invoke rage, it was possible to avoid childhood mistakes, or at least as many as possible. Whenever a broken dish or spilled milk initiated a slap to the side of his head, he moved fast, blocking the blow with a raised hand or ran fast enough to let the old man's anger fade. This upbringing had honed his instincts, sharpened his senses, and when a target presented itself, he could shoulder his shotgun in a flash and shoot with the very best.

Hunting was a skill the old man believed every male should learn and embrace. When the boy was eight, it was his job to field strip the weapons, then clean and oil each one before presenting them for inspection. Perfection was acknowledged with a rare smile; it was one of the few times he actually felt like a son. At ten, he was brought to walk beside the old man when hunting and was made to learn every nuance, either by observing or listening to instruction only given once. The conversations that other sons and fathers enjoyed were rare, usually entailing how life had screwed the old man over instead.

But today was his day, and the forest solitude was a benediction that gave him strength. The gun in his hands was an extension of his being; holding it felt as natural as any craftsman holding his tools. He had no fear of the woods. His sense of direction was keen and without fail. So he took another breath, deep and full, then walked another ten steps to stop and wait and watch and listen.

CHAPTER

1

The best part of growing older is each day, you have less to lose. The teacher embraced this thought daily, and it always brought a wry smile to his face. Knowing that the important things in life were now the simple daily pleasures, not the vast array of material garbage that he, like everyone else, had spent so much energy chasing in his youth, served to reinforce this truth. It was not as though his past was a waste; certainly not. But now, his life valued knowledge, reflection, and most of all, peace of mind. As he approached middle age, the bitter realities of each year set their limits as well. Every morning when he looked at himself in the mirror, he realized that time was eroding his physical being and the vibrancy within. Eyes that were once bright and blue had now faded to a dull grey colour. They often reminded him of a dying fire, a warning of ebbing vitality.

Today was no different. He strolled along the sidewalk just as he did most days, making his way home. With his briefcase in hand, he watched the world go by. He was dressed as was his usual style, although style was not a part of his everyday vocabulary.

Khaki slacks, a plain blue shirt and tie, a dated corduroy jacket, and well-worn oxfords were the choice today. Such attire was comfortable, cheap, and easily interchangeable with four similar outfits in his bedroom closet. As he walked, no one noticed him or, if they did, paid much attention. He preferred it that way. Being innocuous was easy, as it allowed him to evaluate each day and the life that went with it without bother.

He was a teacher, and it was the job that gave him a reason to get up each morning. No, it was a career. Jobs were for those who didn't like what they did. But teaching gave him life and meaning. Children were the essence of innocence. They marvelled at the slightest classroom trick or story that highlighted the day's lessons. Words such as malice, malevolence, or evil did not apply to the students he taught. Life had not yet crafted an ugliness in them that was so prevalent in adults. Sure, he had his share of boneheads who wasted their time and were minimalists at best. But as a group, they could laugh easily, explore their imaginations without criticism, and play without hostile intent. With this, teaching was the best part of his day, and their acceptance gave him the energy to live on as happily as he could. It was his refuge.

The rest of the world was a different story. Traversing the minefield of mankind was arduous, painful, and unforgiving. And it had only gotten worse. It was apparent that humanity had lost its way and every medium glorified greed, vanity, and excesses of every kind. Years of this had made the teacher cynical, and he offered no apologies for this. His smiles were a façade. The idle banter of meaningless conversations was used simply to survive amongst others. For the most part, interactions with those he was unfamiliar with were conducted cautiously. He left no openings for anyone to exploit.

But he did have friends. And those, he could count on one hand. These relationships had survived the test of time. Trust had formed with all of them, and they could be counted on when things were at their worst. They did not question his lifestyle, passed no judgement on his thoughts or comments, and he did the same. Contact with them was infrequent as he preferred to be alone for the most part. It made no sense to become a bother. They had lives of their own, but it was always good when visits or social settings brought them together. Like all good things, he knew it was best to savour these occasions sparingly.

As he walked the last few steps to his townhouse, he brought out his keys and opened the door. As was his custom, he placed his briefcase near the coat rack, removed his shoes, and hung his jacket on the nearest hook. The interior was furnished sparingly and quite plain with the faint odour of last night's supper hanging in the air. The walls still had the faded pale blue paint from years past and supported several pieces of cheap art and a framed Rolling Stones poster that reminded him of more carefree times. There was a kitchen/living room area with the standard appliances, flat-screen television, an old oak table and chairs, and an ugly floral print sofa that he had purchased from a second-hand store. He surmised that it probably came from a retirement home as no one with their original teeth would have purchased such furniture new. The remaining three rooms were, of course, the bathroom and two bedrooms. One was his, the other a guest room that might have been used once, but he couldn't remember. Nor did he care.

Alone with his thoughts, he reflected on the past. He had been married for a while once, and like for many, it hadn't worked out well. But life was easier this way. Time, being a precious commodity, could be spent as he pleased. There were no more arguments over inane issues or obligatory visits to boring relatives. Best of all, no more stupid power struggles that ate away at the best of relationships. Life hadn't turned out the way he had planned, but then, no one's does. Although he had taken his lumps, he still found ways to enjoy his time. And, of course, some were far worse off. Still, he realized that he was ageing. There would come a time when he could no longer function in the classroom. This never occurred to him years ago, but it surfaced more frequently recently. He smiled. Maybe he would get lucky and die of a heart attack at his desk, and the kids could "carry him off on his shield." At worst, he would be forced to resign and put out to pasture. But in all likelihood, he would eventually decide to retire gracefully and slip into his dotage.

These thoughts were shelved, and he decided it was time to make dinner, turn on the television, and be entertained by worldly madness. Finally, after a simple supper and a dose of digital lunacy, he prepared his lessons. There was nothing earth-shattering in tomorrow's plans, but maybe a stroke of brilliance would enter his mind, and those glorious teachable moments would line up to be delivered. Not to worry, though, as his kids were wonderful; everyone found time to smile.

Such was his evening routine. Eventually, he repacked his briefcase for the morning, preparing to call it a night. This was the hardest part of the day. For once in bed, faint spasms of loneliness would haunt his night. The worst was the lack of sleep. He would stare at the ceiling for a time, hoping his dreams were not completely insane or disturbing, then finally doze off only to bolt awake after an hour or two, his mind racing with every possible worry he could think of. This pattern would repeat itself through the night, and the morning could only be salvaged with the strongest possible coffee. It was often like this.

All teachers have their favourites, and he had his. There were twenty-four students in his class, and for as good a group as they were, three stood out. Michael was the leader, the most conscientious of the bunch. He was a quiet yet gifted boy who thrived on challenges, both physical and academic. Tall and athletic, he grasped concepts easily and excelled in all areas of school. He seemed driven, and occasionally, the teacher would worry that he seemed to carry a burden and needed to let loose a little more, like Willy. Willy was the class clown. With a mop of flaming red hair, freckles, and quick wit, he could spark laughter from the class. He loved to engage in the most inane banter with the teacher to try to get an emotional response. It never worked. A simple stare was enough to let Willy know that his repertoire of knock-knock jokes was as much as he would get away with. So he was bright enough never to cross any lines, but the sparkle in his eye revealed an imp who would probably become a challenge once the hormones of adolescence took hold.

Emily was the third. In the teacher's eyes, Emily was an angel. A small girl with short brown hair and brown eyes, she flourished at school. She rivalled Michael academically, but more importantly, she loved to organize games at noon or initiate various causes to help others. Emily tended the class gerbil, Charlie. Charlie's cage was always clean, his feeder full, and water replenished. Every minute of her class day held meaning and purpose, and the pride she took in her work gave him such hope. The teacher never had children of his own, but he thought he would pray for such a child if he could.

What amazed him most was that Emily came from the worst of circumstances. Her family was impoverished as her single mother was the sole provider and worked two menial jobs. She had two older siblings who did their best to help by working odd jobs after school, but still, there was never enough. The teacher wasn't sure what became of the father but as Emily's mother was missing two teeth and rarely ever made eye contact during parent/ teacher interviews, he surmised it probably wasn't good. Although Emily wore second-hand clothes, she was always well-kempt and was as well-liked by the rest of his class as any of the others. Her nurturing instincts and kindness never wavered, and she let it be known early on that she was going to be a nurse. The teacher watched over her. He provided a variety of class snacks at noon to make sure her lunch was complete, and the school counsellor was always informed if she seemed ill or missed class to ensure the family cared for her properly. And, of course, Christmas needs were taken care of as he sent an anonymous package of treats and gifts for the family just before the holidays began.

His kids, as he called them, kept his soul intact. The teacher would observe the inhumane actions of others, the callousness toward those in need, the deceit used in most relationships and, of course, the neglect inflicted on the children who were brought into the world by people with no concept of parenthood. He had witnessed this almost his whole life, and his jaded persona was only equalled by his instincts to avoid anguish. Like a stray cat, he observed his environment, and his vigilance kept him safe.

And if this was all this life had to offer, he would be happy with it.

CHAPTER

2

Spring had been unseasonably warm and mild, and this Tuesday was the same. Jesse was on his way home after skipping class this afternoon. Behind the wheel of his ride, he was without a care in the world. He and his set had spent the better part of this afternoon parked at the beach, each leaning against his car, chuffing on joint after joint. And as young men do, they did their best to appear the coolest in speech and dress. Although their designer shades hid bloodshot eyes, the idiotic giggling revealed a drug-induced stupor that only got worse with each hit. They spent hour after hour like this, ignoring the passing of the day until finally, the boredom set in, and it was time to find entertainment elsewhere.

Jesse was a high school senior who avoided class as much as possible, believing there were far more important pastimes to engage in. As far as Jesse was concerned, he had the world by the tail. His wealthy parents had gifted him his car on his sixteenth birthday, and his generous allowance kept him in the trappings of "gangsta" fashion that allowed him to strut like a prize peacock. Of course, with all this came the image and attitude to go with it. Never mind that at home, it was "yes, Mommy and Daddy," out here, he was a badass. His parents had tried not to spoil him too much, deciding that a new import was adequate transportation and not too flashy. But Jesse always came, hat in hand, for more money and refurbished his wheels with all the high-performance extras to complete his package. The final touch was the sound system that could deliver his hip-hop to levels of ear bleed. Yes, young Jesse had it all.

Four miles from home, he rounded the corner that took him onto a street that passed his old elementary school. He had travelled this route a thousand times and knew he could drive it with his eyes closed. There was no other traffic as he passed the school, only a lone cyclist in the distance.

Emily had stayed late after class today. Her Easter weekend had been a good one. The family had been together with no one having to work, meaning they could enjoy each other's company. But school was always her favourite place. Today, Charlie's cage was dirty, and he needed attending. This was a joy for her. There were no other distractions, and he was the closest thing to a pet she'd ever had. Her teacher had needed to leave, but he said it was okay as the janitor was cleaning the hall outside. He would be there if she needed anything.

When Charlie's needs were taken care of, she sat petting him for a bit, then placed him gently back into his cage and watched him race along the spinning wheel, going nowhere. Finally, she picked up her backpack and left to get her bike from the rack outside the school.

"Jump Around" was thumping in the car's speakers when Jesse's cell phone chimed the arrival of a text. He picked up the phone from the passenger seat and stared at the screen. The hypnotic beat of the music blocked the outside world while the cannabis distorted time and space. Jesse sailed down the street, oblivious to all else but the light and text in front of his eyes. As he leaned toward the passenger seat to read, he didn't notice that his left hand holding the wheel was pulling slowly to the right.

In an instant, the impact sent the right side of the car lurching into the air. It came down, hit the curb, and continued forward until the back right wheel ran over what felt like a speed bump. Jesse bolted upright, pounding at pedals to stop, but his foot bounced off the brake and rammed the gas pedal to the floor. The car jolted forward with a horrible screeching sound that flared up from the pavement as trapped metal under his car grated on the pavement. The sound cut through the music, filling his ears until finally, the car came to a stop. He had no idea what had just happened, but his gut told him it wasn't good.

Jesse turned the stereo off, staring forward, dazed and confused. He opened the car door, got out, and slowly walked to the rear of his car. What he saw stopped him in his tracks, his mouth open and dry. He was right; it wasn't good. It was worse. The body of a child lay up against the curb. He looked up and around; there was a stillness in the air and no movement anywhere. The only sound was the throbbing in his head as his heart pounded. He shuffled toward the motionless figure. As he got closer, he saw long hair and a flowered shirt and realized he had hit a young girl. She lay face down, her left arm bent behind her back, the wrist broken, and her hand pointing to the back of her head. Her left leg was bent grotesquely at the knee in a V-shaped angle, with the top of the foot lying against the dirty pavement. He took one more step closer, noticing the blood pooling around her mouth and more blood soaking her light brown hair. She didn't move, and her brown eyes stared forward, empty and devoid of life.

Jesse had messed up big time, and he knew it. He began to whine like a tormented child. His arms moved up slightly from their sides with wrists limp, and a dark wetness began to form in the crotch of his baggy jeans. "I fucking killed a little kid!" he screamed. Turning, he stepped around to his right, not knowing what to do next. After a full circle, he stared at the lifeless body in front of him once again. She hadn't moved, and his panic intensified. The street remained empty of people and traffic, so Jesse bolted toward his car. He tripped after two steps, hitting the pavement before he could put his hand out properly. The coarse grit left over from the winter scraped a patch of skin from his chin and cheek, but he paid no attention to this or the bicycle handlebar that stuck out from under the passenger door. Getting to his feet, he put his arms out in front of him, stumbling forward until he caught the open car door. Jesse slid into the driver's seat, put the car in gear, and began to race off, closing his door at the same time.

With the bike trapped underneath, it screamed as the metal scraped the pavement once more. The noise made Jesse lose all control. He began to wail as loud as he could to drown out the demonic cry from under his car and his bowels emptied. Soon, the metal wore away, and the bike broke loose, crushed a final time before being spit out by the rear wheel to rest against the curb. Jesse drove as fast as he could, ignoring the smells from the car seat. He had to get home and make this go away.

At 5:30 p.m., the teacher made it home. It had been a useless afternoon. Afternoons like this were always meaningless when he had to attend mandated meetings. Administrators and other colleagues insisted on droning on as they loved to hear themselves speak, each one trying to outdo the other with their brilliant insights. But it was always the same boring garbage, recycled from a previous session. He had managed to stay sane by doodling on a paper pad using his pencil to fill in all the O's on the agenda sheet.

After parking his truck, he entered through the garage door. First, a glass of scotch on ice was in order. With his tie loosened, he sat at the kitchen table, gazing without focus at the oak grain. Other than the pain in the ass teacher pow-wow, the day had been uneventful, but then, that wasn't always such a bad thing. It wasn't his lot in life to be a movie star or famous athlete who could partake in all kinds of wonderful adventures at the drop of a hat. How different it must be for the rich and famous. He smiled. What was it Yeats had said? "And I being poor have only my dreams . . ." Well, it did no good to dwell on these. He needed to decompress, tend to his routines, and make the best of it.

The ice cubes now sat alone in the glass, and the next important decision was whether to refill when the phone rang. He turned his attention to the portable unit on the kitchen counter. Telemarketers always made a point of calling during the late afternoon. He debated just letting the phone ring. On the fourth ring, he decided to answer and got up, walked to the counter, and picked up the phone, pressing the Talk button at the same time.

"Hello?" he asked.

"Hi, it's me, Walt." Walter Simms was the school principal. As far as being a boss was concerned, Walt was mediocre at best but smart enough to leave his best staff alone and just stick to dealing with the usual problems that plagued all schools.

The teacher continued to stand but turned slightly to lean against the counter. "What's up?"

"I'm afraid I have some very bad news," Walt sighed.

The teacher was silent.

"Emily Carter was killed this afternoon in a street incident. According to the police, she was run over by a driver who fled the scene. There were no witnesses, but she was found by another motorist who called the police. She was dead when the ambulance arrived. Everyone is pretty shook up."

The teacher remained silent.

"Are you still there?"

"Yes."

"I realize this is quite a shock, and it's going to be really hard on you and your class. I'm going to contact the rest of the staff tonight and call a meeting in the morning. Are you going to be able to attend?"

"Yes." He ambled to his chair and sat down.

"Thanks. Listen, I'm not sure how tomorrow will be handled, but we're going to decide as a group on how to inform our kids and deal with the grief. So if you come up with any ideas that could help, please offer them up tomorrow."

The teacher sat staring but seeing nothing in the room. His mind's eye was fast-forwarding through a collage of images—some imagined, some real. In each, his students and classroom flashed by, blurry but recognizable. Only Emily's face was clear to him.

"Are you okay?" Walt asked.

He regained his focus. "Yes, I'll manage," he said. "I'll come in early and meet with you. We'll talk more then."

"Thanks again. If you need anything tonight, just call, okay?"

"Yes."

"Okay then, see you tomorrow."

He pressed the End button and put the phone on the table. This seemed impossible. A few hours ago, he made sure she was okay with Charlie and whatever else had to be done before leaving. It made no sense, like a horrible nightmare that belonged somewhere else. But it was real and he was awake, fully aware in the here and now. Still, the realization refused to sink in. He felt no sense of loss, just confusion. He replayed the events of the day over and over but stopped short of any imaginings of her death, as he knew it was vital to spare himself that. He tried to think of what needed to be done for tomorrow but couldn't move.

Hours went by. Any hunger was lost as he continued to sit. As darkness set in, the lights were left off, and his eyes adjusted until all colour was gone and only black and white images contrasted each other. The scotch glass was refilled four more times, but the ice stayed in the freezer. A cold numbness set in, and he grabbed his fingers just to feel something. Still, the images persisted until fatigue and intoxication took their toll. He didn't know what time it was when he finally stood up, placing the glass on the counter next to the phone. Slowly he started for the bedroom. There was no need for light or the extension of arms to ward off collisions.

He could navigate the required fifteen steps without any difficulty, and after sitting on the side of the bed for a minute or two, he fell back, lifted his legs onto the bed, and fell asleep fully clothed.

Sleep was fitful, and strange, disjointed dreams flowed throughout the night, but the scotch kept unconsciousness intact. The next morning, he awoke looking about his bedroom, confused at his dress until the reality of yesterday hit full force. His whole body ached, but he wasn't sure if it was from the scotch or the physical pangs of loss that were sure to creep over him.

With one arm against the wall, he staggered to the bathroom, undressed, and turned on the shower. The lukewarm water stimulated his instincts, and the routine of shaving, combing, and dressing set in. He stared in the mirror that hung above the sink with a tired pale face made worse with red eyes and dark swollen circles staring back. There would be no coffee or breakfast this morning. It was time to go to school.

The next three days played out like a sombre script. The school staff did what needed to be done to console one another and the students. Everyone tried to go about their routines. People passing the playground would only notice children carrying on as usual but up close, they would see faces cloaked in uncertainty. The finality of such a sudden death was beyond the grasp of the very young. In their world, everyone was supposed to be safe. Every mishap could always be fixed or get better. But Emily was not coming back. The teacher took this all in, and although he did his best to ease their angst, it was his own vacant emotional state that concerned him most. At the end of each day, he stared out the window near his desk and tried to feel something, anything. But nothing changed, and he simply stared at the vacant bicycle slots and the parents now lining up to take their children home.

Saturday was the funeral and the accumulated grief finally vented. The church was full, with many standing outside the main doors. He sat in the pew directly behind his class with their parents, watching. Except for the rustling and occasional coughs of those seated, the building was silent. Emily's mother sat with her eldest daughters across the aisle at the front. He watched her face in profile and saw that it was pale, with only the occasional blink revealing that she was still alive. The reddened swelling around her eyes and her pale lips gave the only hint of any colour. Life had inflicted another cruel blow, and like a dazed fighter, she sat without moving. The teacher would survey the church as much as possible, but his gaze would always come back to her. Finally, she began to rock slightly, her head lowered, her eyes closed tight. A soft moan came from her mouth. She began to shudder, then lifted her head to release the anguished sobs that could no longer be contained. The emotion spread, and one by one, mothers held their children tight and cried for this poor woman who was certain that life had forsaken her.

He heard the words of the minister and principal who gave the eulogy, but they held nothing for him. Only the grieving mother and his students kept his focus. He watched Michael, sitting like a soldier, staring straight ahead. Willy couldn't manage, burying his face in his mother's shoulder like many of the others and cried. In his mind, he pictured the Almighty looking down at this. God most certainly had his work cut out for this day and for many days to come. This shitty world has just gotten a whole lot worse.

Finally, mercifully, the funeral ended, and the church emptied. The teacher sat until everyone had left. He observed the Christian icons, hoping for some enlightenment, but none came. No surprise there. The world would continue like it had the week before and the week before that. With a furrowed brow and pursed lips, he got up and walked toward the doors, then into the daylight. He hadn't shed a tear.

The walk home was methodical. As always, he watched others drive or walk by. The clouds drifted across the sky, occasionally blocking out the sun. A breeze that touched his face blew a candy wrapper along the street, and the occasional bird flew from one tree to another. His senses took this all in and hammered at his soul, trying to stir something within, but it was pointless. His life held little now, and an empty future lay ahead. A sense of duty would compel him to work, but the days would be vacant and simply routine. The nights would unfold as they always had, carrying with them the tortured dreams with a haunting sleeplessness that waited at a distance like a vulture staring at a dying animal. These were the premonitions of a lost man as he put one foot in front of the other.

Eventually, he opened his front door, removed his oxfords, and hung up his jacket. Walking to the sink, he reached one hand for the same short glass used since the tragedy first left its mark. The other hand gripped the scotch and loosened the cap. With drink in hand, he stared out the nearest window, sipping the soothing spirits, bracing himself with his hand. The past week replayed itself in a loop until finally, he turned, searching for a distraction, any distraction.

And there it was. The teacher froze in his stance and stared straight ahead at the aged refrigerator door. Taped to it was a single sheet of plain white paper. On the left side was a simple childlike drawing of a tall thin man with a jack-in-the-box smile. The pencil crayons used gave him a brown jacket and blue tie. Beside him was a small girl with brown eyes and brown hair, smiling. Above the drawing, the same coloured pencil had written the following five words: You are my favourite teacher.

Now he began to tremble. The pressure in his lower chest started to build, and the trembling spread down his shoulders into his arms. His body began to sway while his eyelids clenched tight. His mouth contorted into the shape that revealed the agony that was about to erupt. His knees buckled, and the glass fell from his hands, breaking apart on the floor. He dropped to his haunches, tears streaming down his cheeks. His head fell back, and then it all came out. "Noooooooooooo!" he wailed. Huge hitching sobs mixed with cries of anguish filled the room. "No, no, no, no," he cried again. He fell forward with his head smacking against the floor.

He raised his arms up, and his clenched fists began to pound the hard surface. He repeatedly struck the ground until finally, two knuckles on his left hand gave way with an audible crack.

Exhausted and cradling his damaged fist, he fell on his side and lay still. For what seemed like hours, he lay there breathing softly. Dried mucus spread across his nose and cheeks. The throbbing pain from his head and hands became a comfort that signalled the end of the worst. Rising to his feet, he made his way to the bathroom to survey the damage. The mirror revealed a red forehead, and staring down, he saw the blue and swollen outer fingers of his left hand. He washed his face, then placed a dozen ice cubes in a plastic bag for his hand. He would see a doctor later, but now he just sat in the kitchen chair and gazed out the window. Oddly, a sense of relief and calm came over him, and as he sat, a plan began to form in his mind. Its roots came from a distant past long since pushed aside. But now it grew. Here was a path to survival. It meant connecting with an unhappy youth, but it felt like a sense of control was again possible.

Getting up, he walked to a hallway door and opened it. A series of wooden stairs led down to a bare, almost empty basement from the open entrance. He flipped the switch to his right, and several lightbulbs lit the stairs and the room at the bottom. He ambled down, the steps creaking under his weight. Each step was slow and cautious as the angle was steep and a railing had never been installed.

At the bottom, he looked around. The floor was cement with framing in place for three other rooms that were never built. The air smelled stale and slightly damp, but the entire area was clean and sterile to the point where even spiders refused to bother with webs or any other attempt to call this place home. All the other rooms were completely bare, with not even an old storage box lying about. For the most part, the larger room he stood in was empty except for a tall green metal cabinet in the corner with another small box sitting on top. There was no handle on the cabinet, just a lock set into the door. He looked at the cabinet, and the memories slowly surfaced, and one by one, they wove a tapestry of his youth. He continued to stare, and as he did, he saw a path to take himself away from the here and now. It might have seemed odd to someone else, but the more he contemplated the idea, the better he felt and the faintest hint of a smile formed at the corners of his mouth.

He never wept again.

CHAPTER

3

The young man pulled open the door to the employee entrance and walked into the sawmill. He passed the line of racked coats and placed his lunchbox in one of the pigeon holes along with the others who laboured here. He carefully inserted his earplugs, picked up his heavy leather gloves, and entered the production floor. The whine of numerous electric motors that ran the saws, hydraulic lifts, venting fans, and an assortment of other equipment filled the cavernous space with a drone that made normal conversation impossible. Without the earplugs, anyone working here would be stone deaf in months.

He took his place in the production line, waiting for the wood to come. His job was to stack the sawn lumber as it flowed past, carried by the black conveyor belts that ran endlessly during the eight-hour shift. It was mindless work, but the pay was good. Occasionally, he would look at the others who worked as he did, seeing the lack of hope and ambition in their eyes. He was the lucky one. Once the summer months were over, he would have enough money to go back to school and improve his lot in life. But not these others. They had squandered their lot on muscle cars, booze, and girlfriends who got pregnant too soon in life and now needed their support. For the most part, they were decent young men who had once carried the dreams of youth but were now resigned to coming home to their trailer or apartment at the end of the day, grabbing one beer after another, hoping the rest of the family did not make their lives any more miserable. As his time here was limited, he mostly kept to himself. In the lunchroom during his breaks, he occasionally joined in with the others' conversations if prompted, but he had very little in common with them, preferring to eat quietly and thumb through the outdated magazines and newspapers that littered the tables.

So he put in his time and counted down each day, looking forward to the last when he could pitch his gloves and earplugs as far as he could and say goodbye to the monotony, noise, and wood dust that filled his nostrils. For now, the hours were tolerable, and he would play games in his mind to help pass the time. There was only one real problem in this working life, and he could see it coming from the far end of the mill.

The yellow forklift approached that would carry each load of stacked lumber away for storage. On the machine was his problem: an ugly, red-haired, obese troll of a man, covered in a plaid shirt and frayed jeans held up by overworked suspenders as no belt existed that could wrap around such a slob. His name was Clyde, and as the nephew of the mill owner, he behaved as if the whole operation was his domain to do as he pleased. As he wasn't very bright, he was relegated to his forklift, although to hear him brag, he was destined for upper management just as soon as his asshole uncle gave him what he was sure he deserved. It never happened and never would.

Life in the mill would be fine as it was. But Clyde was a son of a bitch as well as stupid. He had the mean streak of a demented child and wasn't happy until he had made someone's life miserable, if only to assert his perverted notion of male dominance. Being the boss's relative, few dared to cross him lest they find themselves on the bread line looking for a new job. So the same way any predator picks out his target in a herd, Clyde decided that the young man would be his to torment.

It was easier for the young man on the production floor since moving the lumber prevented any malicious acts on Clyde's part. But once everyone was in the lunchroom, he would deride the young man with taunts of "schoolboy" combined with a barrage of vicious slurs regarding his manhood. Occasionally, one of the others would tell Clyde to "lighten up," but often, it only intensified the insults until he became bored and decided to regale the others with imagined and delusional stories of his sexual exploits. The young man often thought of using a piece of lumber to break Clyde's arm or knee. But as he was here only for the summer and needed the money, he simply stared at his magazines and ate his lunch as best he could.

Now Clyde parked near the young man's lumber stack, waiting to take it away. All the while, he watched with unblinking beady eyes that sunk into his round freckled face. His nose was underdeveloped such that his nostrils stood out like two black holes rimmed with pink flesh. He reminded the young man of a cartoon pig. But this was no comical character. His stares sent a clear message that as soon as was possible, he would bait and humiliate his quarry as best he could.

The rest of the shift passed without incident, and finally, it was time to call it another day. Before the young man left his station, he looked around, reminding himself that this was day twenty and tomorrow would be nineteen. Soon he could leave and never come back. The walk back to the lunchroom allowed him to remove his earplugs and gloves. A quick wash in the bathroom sink flushed the sweat and sawdust from his face and back of his neck. Feeling slightly refreshed, he looked forward to the drive home and the chance to enjoy a cold beer while making plans for his final year of college.

With his head down, he made his way to the lunchroom to pick up his lunch kit but as soon as he opened the door, he knew his day would not end well. The room was empty except for Clyde, sitting in the far corner with one dirty boot lying across a chair, the other resting on a lunch table. He didn't say a word, just sat there with a grotesque grin sunk in between his jowls.

He stopped once he saw Clyde. However, he didn't say a word as he looked at the malevolence in Clyde's dark beady eyes and knew something ugly was about to happen. The young man turned, walking slowly to the rack of cubby holes on the opposite wall, and as he did, a faint sulphurous smell began to build in his nose, growing stronger together with the hissing giggle that began to rise in Clyde's throat. The fat on Clyde's body started to jiggle, and his ugly eyes widened with anticipation.

The smell became foul and disgusting the closer he got, and his brow furrowed when he reached for his lunchbox that should have been almost empty. But when he lifted it, the weight told him it wasn't, and the putrid odour signalled him to prepare for the worst. And it was. Still without speaking, he set the box on a table, flipped the clasps on the side, and swung the lid over to the side. Human excrement lay on top of half the sandwich he had hoped to eat on the way home. A nauseous reflex built up in his gut, but it was soon overpowered by rage. He clenched his fists, standing motionless and staring straight ahead. He didn't speak. As Clyde broke into an uncontrolled moronic laugh, the young man closed his lunchbox and made for the parking lot. He refused to look at the cretin who had finally crossed the line of human decency. As the door swung open, he dropped his lunchbox into a plastic garbage receptacle and made his way to the parking lot.

He got to his car and reached for the door. As he did, he looked over his shoulder and saw Clyde standing at the mill entrance, still grinning.

"Hey, schoolboy!" he called. "What, no supper?"

The young man stared at Clyde without blinking, and under his breath, murmured, "Go ahead and laugh, you fat prick. You better hope that someday our paths never cross again." He opened the door and drove off.

The teacher stared at the gun cabinet in front of him. He knew his life had been built on the memories he kept in the dark recesses of his mind. There were many, and the ugly ones he treated as a curse. He reached for the keys in his pocket and selected the largest one, leaned over, inserting it into the cabinet lock. When the door opened, there they were, lined up in order, cleaned, and oiled, just as he remembered so many years ago. This was the old man's gun collection. It was the only thing of worth he had inherited from the miserable old bastard.

At eighteen, after receiving his high school diploma, he packed a duffle bag and left home for good with his clothes and four hundred and sixty-five dollars he had stashed away. It was a time of life that all young men look forward to, but most move on knowing there is some semblance of family help, should hard times take hold. In his case, there was no going back. He had found room and board with an elderly couple and soon landed a part-time job as a labourer. This made life much easier. It was now possible to attend college and not have to grovel for help. He had chosen his friends well, and they served as all the support he needed. By twenty-four, with a teaching degree in hand and a sense of freedom that only a prisoner could relate to, he began his adult life. At twenty-six, he returned home from work to find a police officer waiting for him with news that the old man had died and asking if he could attend to his father's remains and meagre estate.

Now, standing in front of the guns, he decided to hold them again, something he had not done since he packed them up after telling the mortician to dispose of the old man's ashes as he pleased. The weapons were laid out on the floor, one by one. Some would be useful, and the others simply surplus. Two were shotguns, and he picked up his favourite, the old twenty-gauge that had been his hunting partner so many years ago. It felt good in his hands, and he shouldered it easily, the stock tight to his cheek. The other was a twelve-gauge that was of the kind found in any sporting goods store. His shotgun sat on the floor next to the twelve-gauge and the other three to the side by themselves. A nine-millimetre handgun and an assault rifle stood apart from the rest. It was interesting as they had no use as hunting weapons, but he remembered the old man becoming obsessed with society's future collapse and how it would be every man for himself. Their sole purpose was as antipersonnel weapons. In turn, he held them, checked the action of each, and realized they were as familiar and easy to bear as anything from his youth.

Finally, he reached for the hunting rifle. To the untrained eye, it appeared ordinary, but he knew better. The barrel was longer and heavier than normal, with a twelve-power scope designed for distance shooting. A military-style bipod was mounted near the end of the stock to steady the aim, and the trigger had been modified so that the slightest pressure would fire the rifle. It was of a calibre smaller than most but accurate beyond belief. The old man had once bragged that this gem of a weapon "could drive nails at two hundred yards." It was indeed a heavy firearm and one that could only be used from a resting position. But as he opened and closed the breach, the smooth action made the blood in his veins rush with a sense of excitement from long ago.

CHAPTER

4

The teacher had been driving for more than two hours now. The last fifty kilometers had taken him deep into the coniferous forests that spread across mountain after mountain. The road was gravel and in need of maintenance as the scattered potholes made the going slow. But these areas had been mainly abandoned since much of the available timber was gone. The air was crisp and clear. With the windows down, his senses were flooded once again with the fresh scents of pine and fir. More than once, he stopped the truck, sitting with his eyes closed, breathing deeply and feeling the sun on his face. Although it had been decades since he last set foot here, he had no problem navigating the network of secondary roads that would take him to one particular harvested expanse. Two firearms were leaning into the seat beside him with a case of assorted ammunition on the floor. The other items that he would need rested beside him. It was June now, and the days were warm and long, even this high in the mountains. The school year was coming to an end, and with it, extra free time. But today was test day—his test.

One last turn took him into the old cut-block. He slowed to a stop and turned the motor off. Getting out and standing on the packed ground, he stood motionless, watching and listening. The air was still, without a sound except for the odd chirp of unseen birds, some close and others in the distance. The old logging block had done its best to regrow a new stand, and the young trees that had a foothold here were now almost twenty feet high. He would not be able to sight across this treed area, but the spur road he was on suited his needs perfectly. It stretched in a clear straight line ahead of the truck for slightly longer than a quarter-mile, coming to a dead-end at a small open landing that had been used by the bunked trucks to load the fresh timber and haul it to the mills.

What would it be like after all this time? Could he still fire a weapon and not flinch at the explosion of each cartridge? Would the sting of the recoil make him hesitate? He remembered the adage of riding a bike and smiled. The urgency of this task was consuming; like an itch, it needed to be relieved.

Reaching across the driver's seat, he grabbed the twelve-gauge shotgun and a box of shells. He chambered one shell and then loaded five more into the magazine. He picked up a large plastic bleach bottle, walked up the road ten yards, placed it on a large granite rock off to the side, and walked back. He clicked the safety to the left, aimed at the bottle, and fired. The crack of the igniting powder forced his eyes shut, and the assault on his ears blocked out all other sound. The ringing was a pounding echo, but after three or four breaths, it softened. He lowered the gun to see the bottle, which had been blown six feet back off the rock, peppered with black holes from the birdshot. Sliding the pump back, the spent shell was ejected, and a new one chambered. He shouldered the gun once more, then walked forward, repeatedly firing until the magazine was empty. But after each step, he became steadier, not closing his eyes and noticing only a small blur in his vision after each shot that came from the vibration against his cheek. The bottle was shredded and without form as plastic remnants lay scattered in a circle.

He lowered himself to the ground, sitting on the scattered dandelions that formed a carpet up the middle of the spur road between the ruts. He felt as if he had run a marathon; the strength in every muscle pulsed in rhythm with his pounding heart. It was good. This was a catharsis like no other. There was no anguish, no sense of loss or doom, only the sensations of the sun and the ground and the silence. The birds had stopped calling out, and still, there was no breeze to move leaves or branches. But as he sat back and looked up to his right, he noticed a large raven perched in a mangled old fir tree that had survived the chainsaws. It looked at him, moving only to preen several feathers, then continued staring. It was oblivious to the blasts from the gun and only seemed curious at the strange form hunched on the ground.

Now it was time to continue the test. The teacher smiled at the bird, then walked back to the truck, placed the shotgun on the seat, and reached for the heavy rifle. He walked to the front of the truck, extended the bipod, and then placed the rifle in a firing position in the center of the road. Next to it, seven cartridges were placed side by side in the weeds to the rifle's right. There were two large square pieces of white cardboard on the seat of the truck. Each one had a thin cross drawn in the center with a black felt pen. Picking these up, he began to pace up the road, softly counting each step. He bent down at one hundred yards and placed the first target to the left side of the road, then sandwiched it upright between two small rocks. He continued for another hundred yards, doing the same, only on the right side. Returning to the rifle, he lay prone and chambered the first round. Sighting through the scope, it was difficult at first to find the left target as the magnification reduced the field of view, but soon, there it was. Carefully, he rested his index finger on the trigger, bringing the crosshairs to bear at the center of the two lines. He took two relaxed breaths. On the third, he exhaled slowly and softly squeezed. The crack of the rifle was sharp and piercing, but there was no flinch in his muscles. The heavy rifle cushioned the blur as his right eye stayed true to the scope and never left the cross. He smiled. There was a small hole just above the center of his aim.

He had forgotten that this rifle would shoot high at this distance. Chambering another round, he made the correction and fired a second round, this time striking dead center. Much better. A third shot was fired. Looking again, he hesitated in disbelief. There was no third mark on the cardboard. He raised his head and stared to the side, thinking this was not possible. Again, he looked carefully through the scope and, after several seconds, smiled for a second time. The second hole was now slightly larger. "You old bastard, you were good for something after all," he said softly. One could indeed drive nails with this rifle. Its accuracy more than made up for any loss of hitting power.

Reloading, he aimed at the distant target to the right and fired three more shots. At this distance, the gun would fire true without any correction, but it was too far to be sure without walking to the target. So he did. And there they were: three small black holes, all touching each other where the black ink lines crossed. This day was getting better all the time. He turned and began the walk back, but not before taking a quick skip step like a little kid, kicking a rock to the side of the road. He reached the truck carrying the targets and shredded plastic bottle and gave a quick glance up and to his left. The raven hadn't moved; it just sat silent and continued to watch.

"Now you're the kind of company I like," he said to the bird. "You're interested, you pay attention, and you're not a pain in the ass. Well done." The raven cocked his head to the left ever so slightly, staring down.

There was still one more target on the truck seat. Reaching for it, he noticed an open bag of balloons on the dash together with a felt pen and masking tape. These were leftovers from a class party of some kind and normally weren't given a second thought. But the idea that came now set one final test in motion. He pulled one orange balloon from the bag and gently began to inflate it. When it reached the size of a large apple, he stopped, tying off the end. There was still one cartridge by the rifle, and a true test of marksmanship was sitting in the palm of his hand. Grabbing the tape, he turned to walk but hesitated. Reaching back onto the dash, he took the pen and removed the cap. Ever so slowly, he drew one eye on the balloon, then another, and finally, a big toothy grin below. It now resembled an ugly dwarfish Halloween pumpkin but would serve its purpose very well.

The walk from the rifle along the road would be the last one today. He needed to be methodical now and consider all the variables. The shot would be three hundred yards and take the steadiest of nerves, but it could be done with no breeze. At that distance, the bullet would drop five inches. It would be very difficult to compensate even with the best of scopes. At two hundred yards, he began pacing the final stretch. When the final step was reached, he turned and walked to a stunted pine tree off to the side. He then taped the tied end of the balloon to a bare branch at eye level. He laughed softly. No, it wasn't "Wilson," but the balloon would help him put William Tell to shame if he succeeded.

Picking up his targets along the way, he reached the rifle, dropped the cardboard, lowered himself into position, and chambered the final round. All he could see without the scope was the faintest orange dot. He lowered his head and peered through the eyepiece. After a few adjustments, there it was, grinning like a troll and mocking him as best it could. With his left hand under the stock, he nudged the rifle ever so slightly until his best guess placed the crosshairs five inches above the ugly teeth. One last breath, and he pulled the trigger as the air left his mouth. The rifle gave a final ear-splitting bark, and in less than a heartbeat, the balloon was gone.

It was done. He rolled onto his back and stared at the sky. The epiphany washed over his body like a warm embrace. The realization that he had carried this skill his whole life made all else insignificant. He lay there without blinking. The raven gave a loud caw, flapped its wings, and took to the air. It circled him in a lazy flight, continuing its hoarse cries, and as he watched its tribute, he felt it was something more. This was an invocation impossible to ignore. His skill was awakened, and with that skill came a new purpose.

After a final minute, the raven turned south and flew off. The test was complete. He got to his feet, brushed the loose grass and gravel from his clothes, and picked up the rifle and spent cartridges. A soft breeze now came across him, and he stood one final time on the road with an air of confidence that was his reward. Placing the rifle and cartridges in the cab, he started the engine and drove along the spur to the landing, where he turned the truck around. It was time for the next step. It was time to go home.

CHAPTER

5

He sat at his kitchen table in a denim jacket and blue jeans, but the scotch in the glass in front of him was not an anesthetic this time. It signified a job well done. Even still, he was nowhere near better. His anger continued to fester. He did what he could. Four times he had called the police, hoping that an arrest was imminent. But the answer was always the same. "Sorry, sir. Nothing new has turned up." They expect that the "big break" would somehow appear on someone's desk? No distraction helped.

His nights were still a terror. There was no respite from the incoherent nightmares of the worst from his past. Images of a dead Emily came and went like a carousel in his mind. He feared a creeping madness might take hold—one that could destroy him completely.

But there was his plan. Insane as it seemed, it could keep him from complete self- destruction. With the first piece in place, he decided to continue, knowing this was not a path of redemption. There was no need for that. This would land a blow for the "good guys," and vengeance was as good a start as any.

Something ugly and evil was going to have to die. It was the only thing that made any sense now. Playing by the rules, trying to make the world a little better didn't always work out. And when your best efforts are rewarded with grief of the worst kind, well, then it was time to raise the stakes and play at a different level. But "something" obviously meant "someone." And he was a teacher for Christ's sake, and teachers didn't do that. At best, they gave stern warnings or wrote strongly worded letters. But killing someone? Another flashback stirred his memory to a dark day before he left home.

He had been sitting in his backyard, target shooting with an air rifle. While reloading, he saw an iridescent flash of green go past and stop at the farthest corner of the yard. It was a hummingbird hovering near the neighbour's trellis that supported a growth of flowered columbine. It would dart from flower to flower, stopping only for a few seconds at each to feed.

Now that would be a shot; pretty much impossible, he thought. But being young and impulsive, he would try. He finished loading the rifle and brought the sights to bear, tracking the tiny bird as it moved. He pulled the trigger slowly, and the rifle fired, almost silently. But the sound of the lead pellet striking the feathers was unmistakable. The bird dropped, disappearing into the grass. He lowered the rifle to his lap and sat blinking with his mouth half-open. Only then did it dawn on him what he had just done.

Placing the rifle on the lawn, he walked slowly toward the trellis with eyes scanning the grass at his feet. Each footstep met with hesitation, hoping to forestall the inevitable. Then at the base of the trellis, there it was. The bird lay on its back in a bed of uncut grass. Its wings were splayed to each side of its white underbelly in the form of a cross, a shape not lost on him. The feathers at the upper left of the breast were parted in a circle and stained red. Its head was turned and lowered to one side with a drop of blood hanging from the open bill. A small, black, lifeless eye stared at him as he felt his throat and chest tighten.

He knelt on one knee to pick up the limp form. It was still warm to the touch, and he hoped it would show some small sign of life, but he knew better. This was a mistake, a very bad one. Some mistakes could be taken back, but not this one. He had sinned and killed out of vanity and stupidity. Others might consider such an error in judgement trivial at best. But not him; not someone who had endured the torment of domestic cruelty. The gravity of his actions sank deep into his being, overwhelming him.

He placed the dead bird back where it had fallen, then got up, turned around, and walked to the back of the house. A shovel was leaning against the cracked stucco siding. He carried it back, dug a small hole, and buried the hummingbird. It was then that he decided his hunting days were over, and he would never kill one of God's innocent creatures again.

So here he was, seriously determined to commit a crime of the highest order. His mind raced back and forth between a desire for vengeance and the inherent need for rational thought. But his decision was final. It would awaken a new persona, one that was strong and self-assured. Strength and confidence are wonderful things. They drive fear and uncertainty back into the recesses of the mind, safely locked away. He walked taller now, with every action driven by purpose. Really, he had nothing more to lose. There was no family to worry about, and any possible headlines would become yesterday's news very quickly. Why stumble through the time he had left, living a life of regret and shame, knowing he could have done more, regardless of what others might think. Nothing innocent would be harmed—only vermin. And vermin came in all shapes and sizes, like wasps or mosquitoes, and especially the worst that humanity had to offer.

Now he needed to complete the plan. This would take some time, but it was also the easiest part. There was no reason to rush. The summer months were free from any obligations, and just the thought of success was enough to temper impatience. There was a second, even more important advantage. He was as clean as a whistle; he had no criminal record, not even so much as a parking ticket. He had no outstanding debts, unpaid taxes, or incidents of any kind that might warrant any investigation. He was intelligent, methodical, and could pick the time and place of his choosing. This was a personal vendetta, but if something in the planning failed or self-doubt became overpowering at the last minute, it would be easy to pick another time. He was in control.

A target would have to be selected. The possibilities seemed endless, but this could not be random. If he couldn't get to Emily's killer, then he would find a suitable alternate. He needed to be sure his choice was worthy and accessible to ensure a high probability of success. Best of all, a personal connection to the target would make the result so much better. The internet would be the best place to start. It would provide search options for names which, in turn, would give locations, and most importantly, the best routes in and out. But he was tired now, and tomorrow, he would be back at school.

His evening routine was followed in the usual way. After supper, he tried to watch television, but it was too difficult to focus on much of anything. So he treated himself to a long hot shower and made his way to bed. Maybe tonight would be better.

This was a good time of year to be a teacher. The year was wrapping up, while the strain of the year's tragedy lessened with each day. With the warm weather, a good portion of the class day was spent outside. At the end of the week, the school organized a track and field day with the usual events and a special barbeque funded by the community to help bring everything back to normal. But for today, the teacher decided a field trip was in order. The class was off to commune with nature.

A wildlife sanctuary had been established near a local lake. At the south edge of the lake was a shallow swampy area that had been designated as an ecological reserve, as it was not useful for anything else. An environmental group had petitioned to have the area preserved for the sake of migrating birds and all the other marsh life that went with it. With its final approval, a host of politicians jumped on the opportunity to claim they were instrumental in saving this pristine wilderness. Of course, after the approval, the local paper was full of photos of political hacks of every variety, smiling and shaking hands in front of a pond of swimming ducks. But they managed to fund a walkway with a viewing platform that led into the wetlands. So the teacher, leading his small army of eco-warriors, got off the bus, carrying backpacks, dipping nets, plastic tubs, an assortment of plastic microscopes and lenses, and headed to the platform.

The day was spent chasing tiny specimens of all shapes and sizes. His kids emptied their catch into the plastic pails filled with swamp water, then viewed them under the various lenses to a chorus of "oohs" and "ahhs." It was amazing to watch how they stayed focused for an entire day, never losing interest in the marvels they found. The teacher ensured they were gentle, and each little water bug was released to live another day. As usual, Michael led the way, deftly netting one prize after another.

"Hey, Mr. E," Michael called. "Check this out!" And he ran to the teacher to show him his catch. "What is it?"

Mr. E, the teacher thought. He loved that name; familiarity and respect all wrapped up in a single letter. "I'm not sure, Mike," he said, looking inside the plastic cup full of water and a squirming insect. "But go tell Willy that I'll pay him five bucks if he puts it in his mouth." With this, he laughed and watched Michael make for Willy in a straight line.

On the other hand, Willy was spending most of the day clowning around on the platform. Jumping from place to place, he entertained everyone with his bug imitations.

"Hey, Bug Boy," Michael called out as he walked to Willy. "Mr. E is gonna give you five bucks if you put this tiny little guy in your mouth." Most of the class gathered around the pair, trying to get a glimpse of the terrified creature.

"Ewwwww! Not a chance!" Willy said, recoiling. "That thing has eyes like my sister. Yuk! It's gonna take a lot more than five measly bucks for me to eat that thing." And with that, he pranced off, continuing his shenanigans until he tripped over one of the girls kneeling on the platform and wound up in the pond.

These were easy days that allowed the teacher to relax with his kids and let them learn independently. Within his thoughts, he could not help but question his mission. But neither could he push away each new idea or detail that would bring him closer. From time to time, he ignored the mayhem behind him and stared out over the water, planning each step, vetting each possible choice. But one stood out. One deserved to be held accountable for his transgressions. This one would be shown the error of his ways, with extreme prejudice. Finally, he nodded to himself and turned to his class. It was time to load the bus.

He had his target.

CHAPTER

6

The top of the hill was dry and secluded, covered only with sparse grass and a few scattered pines. The teacher was sitting here, leaning against a large grey piece of granite, which stuck out of the ground by itself like a tombstone. The cross-town trip had taken him almost an hour as it had the previous three days. It was five o'clock in the afternoon, and as he sat, he scanned the end of the cul-de-sac two hundred yards below with a pair of binoculars. His focus was a plain, neglected house at the end of the street. It was a faded brown colour, the paint on the siding pale and peeling. The roof shingles were covered with moss, and a gravel driveway led to a carport to the building's left. The front yard was covered with a patchy dry lawn and assorted weeds that hadn't been watered since the last rain. Over the past days, there had been no indication that more than one person lived there. But if anyone unexpected answered the door, he had any number of excuses that could get him out of trouble.

He had been watching the house for almost an hour now. If his patience paid off, the truck should be arriving within minutes, just like the days before. But this was a scouting trip; simple, systematic reconnaissance that would verify location and timing. *Yes, the internet is a wonderful thing,* he thought. It was easy to track down almost anyone, and the satellite imagery provided the route in and out.

Dressed as nondescript as always, he had ridden the bus to the western edges of the city. Traversing a series of side streets through a light industrial area, he eventually made his way along several residential streets and finally, through a small city park that bordered the hill where he sat. The park was reasonably well maintained, with a narrow asphalt path through various ornamental and natural trees. It had a small open area of lawn, not much bigger than an acre, in the middle where a few individuals let their dogs run or mothers sat on blankets, watching their small children chase brightly coloured balls from one end to the other. More importantly, the park bordered the street with the plain brown house. As this was the poorer part of town, the park was empty most of the time.

Giving his eyes a rest, he picked up a small stick lying to his right and while scratching aimless patterns in the ground, he pondered his progress. He vaguely remembered a line from a song: something about a movie character contemplating a crime. But, he didn't envision himself as a character in a Bogart movie, although he wasn't making plans to build a go-cart either.

Long days and nights were spent on each detail. The difficult part had been getting the twelve-gauge ready. As proficient as he was, he was no gunsmith. He managed to remove a good portion of the end of the barrel with the hacksaw, but it had taken several hours of filing and the use of emery cloth to remove the sharp edges. At least this had given it an appearance he could live with. The stock was walnut and somewhat easier to shorten, to the point where only the pistol grip remained. The whole length of the shotgun was now only twenty-six inches. It could easily be concealed in a black equipment bag that most athletes used regularly. To complete his needs, he had purchased a dark blue tracksuit with black running shoes. Finally, he managed to find black denim pants, a T-shirt, jacket, and driving gloves. All of this was arranged one day at a time over the summer.

Next Friday, fate would end a life, possibly his own. Friday was the best day. Summer was coming to an end soon, with the daylight hours getting shorter. It would be almost dark by seven-thirty, and most residents would be settling in for the evening. With very little foot or vehicle traffic on the streets, he could use the cover of darkness to make his way back. This would be difficult. He decided it would be stupid to return the way he came, so he would need to head east. This would take him to the industrial area that bordered a small creek flowing near the edges of the downtown area. He had never been here before and only had the satellite imagery to plan a route. But the creek was overgrown for the most part, with only commercial lots or storage yards along its route. He would use the creek to cover his tracks. The depth of the water would be minimal, giving him a chance to distance himself while hidden. By following the flow of the water south, he could make it to a jogging path and stay hidden until the early morning hours. With luck, Saturday morning would simply reveal an eager jogger off on a morning run.

It was the sound of an engine that broke his thoughts. Picking up his binoculars, he turned to his left, scanning the street below. He recognized the sound made by the broken muffler and watched as an old white pickup with a dented passenger door made its way toward the brown house. He looked at his watch showing five-sixteen, almost the same time as the previous days. The truck slowed and pulled into the carport with the squealing brakes signalling a stop. With a clunk, the driver's door opened and out came a figure carrying what looked like a bag of groceries and a case of beer. "There you are," the teacher whispered softly, watching the figure round the front of the truck and disappear to the side entrance.

He placed the binoculars in his backpack, got up, and dusted off the back of his jeans. It was time to make his way leisurely back through the park to the bus stop. The next time he would come this way would be on Friday.

He was awake at eight the next morning. It was sunny, with just a slight hint of the cooler days that were on their way. He showered, shaved and, after combing his hair, stood and looked without blinking. His face reminded him of one that he would have on any typical teaching day. But this day would be different. Strangely, he felt no anxiety or hesitation. Considering his intentions, he thought this odd but knew as he hadn't pulled the trigger yet, there was still plenty of time for both. After putting on his socks and tracksuit, he ate a simple breakfast of toast and coffee while gazing out his kitchen window. He continued to look outside and made a point of observing every detail he could: the shape of the leaves in the tree by the driveway, the colour of the houses that he could see, even the little bits of trash that had blown down the street during the night. Everything was important, as nothing would be the same after today. He rinsed his cup and plate and made his way to the other bedroom.

It was all there, neatly arranged on the bed from the night before. The black athletic bag was open with a three-inch slit cut at one end. Beside it was the modified shotgun. The magazine had been loaded with five rounds of buckshot with another in the chamber. Next to the shotgun was a plastic bottle filled with water, a roll of black tape, a small folding knife, a clipboard, and a peanut butter and jam sandwich. Neatly folded below the bag were black jeans, a jacket, a T-shirt, gloves, and a garbage bag. He carefully placed these in the bag to form a bed along its length. Finally, he placed the shotgun on the clothing with the other items. He smiled at how organized everything looked, then used the two looping nylon handles to close the bag and clipped the shoulder strap into place.

At ten o'clock, he put on his running shoes, picked up the bag, put on a pair of dark sunglasses and made his way to the door. He carried no wallet or identification and, after locking the door, he slipped the key into a space between the step and the ground. It would now be a twenty-five-minute walk to the bus stop. He made his way down the street, looking like any other weekend jogger setting off for the gym.

At two o'clock, he stood on the hill and looked around, then sat down against the rock and opened his bag. The bus ride had been uneventful, with only a couple of other riders staring out the windows. The streets leading to the park were almost empty, except for two young boys headed in the direction of town who paid no attention to him.

He reached into his bag to pull out the sandwich and the plastic bottle of water. This would be his only meal until he arrived home if he managed to get that far. It didn't take long to eat, but he chewed as methodically as always and finished off his meal with half of the water, pouring the rest on the ground. Reaching into the bag once more, he grabbed for the knife and tape, placing them on the ground to his right. He carved five small holes in the bottom of the plastic bottle with the knife, each about a quarter-inch in diameter. Finally, he pulled out the shotgun and fit the top of the bottle over the end of the barrel. The fit was snug as he knew it would be, and using the tape, he secured the bottle to the barrel. The silencer was in place. He put the shotgun back in the bag and pushed the bottom of the bottle just outside the slit at the end of the bag. Now he would wait for dark.

The room was small and plain. The once white walls had now yellowed and were bare except for one picture. A bag of kitchen garbage lay on its side not far from the sink. The countertop was cluttered with unwashed dishes, scattered utensils, and empty beer cans. With three of its six lightbulbs burnt out, an old light fixture hung above a table and cast a dull glow around the room.

Clyde sat in one of four chairs at the table, finishing the remains of a TV dinner. Once done, he reached for his third beer while staring at the picture on the wall. It was a framed picture of a dark-haired woman with her arms around two small children; it was a photo of his wife and kids who had packed up and left one spring day three years ago.

"Dumb bitch," he muttered to himself. What the hell did he care if she buggered off. It wasn't his problem if she couldn't live the way she was supposed to. No, she always had to piss him off and provoke him and never listen to reason. Then she had to go and call the cops—two times for Christ's sake. But he was a clever one; hitting would leave bruises. It was much smarter to twist arms and fingers or just grab hair and shake hard. That would bring her to her senses. But still, she managed to lock herself in the bathroom and call the bloody police. It took threats of much worse to keep her from pressing charges. He knew it wouldn't come to that because, after all, he wasn't a bully. No, he was the smart one. If only people did what they were told, things would be so much easier. But the crazy woman left anyway and stole everything from the bank account to boot. Boy, if he ever found her, she'd be sorry. *But, screw it,* he thought. *They were all just a pain in the ass.*

He looked at the stove clock and saw it was almost seven; it was time for some fun. Finishing his last beer, Clyde slid the chair back to a small wooden table resting against the near wall. An old computer tower hummed next to a blank monitor on top of the table. After a few keystrokes, the screen lit up. *Yes,* he thought, *Sweet Sally, here I come!* It was a minute into his search when the doorbell rang, just once.

"Shit!" he cursed. "The side of the house? Who the hell is at the side of the house? Must be that asshole from next door." He pushed his chair back and got up, walked past the bag of garbage, then turned left, thumping and cursing down the hall to the door.

It was on the last few steps at the base of the hill when his heart started to beat faster. Dressed in black with the shoulder strap holding the bag on his right hip, the teacher reached in

41

and pulled out the clipboard, cradling it with his left arm to his chest. To anyone else, he looked like someone canvassing the neighbourhood for charity, except that the gloved hand holding the grip of the shotgun, with his index finger on the trigger guard, was hidden. He clicked the safety off, making his way down the street, scanning to the sides. It was dark now, and the area was clear; only the dull light making its way through some of the curtains gave any indication that the surrounding houses were inhabited.

He felt his pulse racing now, each breath exaggerated as he walked faster. Reaching the gravel driveway, he looked one last time down the street to make sure it was still empty. He rounded the driver's side of the pickup and stopped at the wooden door. "Okay, let's get this party started," he whispered. Without hesitation, he pushed the doorbell, then took one step back and waited. Standing motionless, he heard a muffled voice coming toward the door. His finger moved onto the trigger. The tarnished brass-coloured doorknob turned to his left, and the door opened.

There stood Clyde, his right hand holding the knob inside. Dressed in oversized sweatpants and a stained T-shirt, he was easily recognizable. Even with most of his hair gone, he still had the face of a pig, with a belly to match. With eyebrows furrowed and a puzzled stare, he stood, looking over the strange man standing at his door.

"Who are you, and what the hell do you want?"

The teacher said nothing, just smiled, and leaned to his right to look down the hallway. It was empty. As hard as he could, he kicked the door completely open with his right foot, knocking it out of Clyde's hand, then pulled the trigger. The muffled blast was louder than he expected, but the plastic bottle had done its job. The buckshot caught Clyde full force in the lower pelvis and threw him back onto the hallway floor as if in slow motion. The teacher stepped inside and closed the door behind him.

Clyde lay on the floor, staring at the ceiling, his left hand on his bloody crotch. "Ugh," he moaned, then lifted his head up. The teacher dropped the clipboard, reached into the bag with his left hand, ejected the spent cartridge, and chambered another. He stepped forward to Clyde's left and looked down.

"What's the matter, you fat fuck?" he said. "Don't you remember the schoolboy? I know a pecker full of buckshot hurts a lot worse than a pile of shit. But at least you won't have to eat it." He lifted the grip, and the plastic bottle pointed down at Clyde's chest. Clyde raised his right hand and held it out.

"Nooo!" he moaned again. "Wai . . ."

The second blast was louder, but with the door closed, there was no need to worry. Clyde's lumpy torso was torn open, his hand and head fell back to the floor, his face rolling to the side. Both of his eyes were open and motionless and blood oozed from his mouth. The teacher picked up the clipboard and put it back in the bag. Then he turned, opened the door, and stepped outside.

Now, time was everything. He had to get clear of these houses and make it to the creek. With minimal light, he jogged through the backyard to a wooden fence. It was easy enough to climb over, but once he started running again, he tripped on a kid's toy, falling to his knees. Stifling a curse, he knew he had to slow down. This was like hunting again; walk, stop, look, and listen. *Be patient,* he thought. Making his way, he used the cover of parked cars, houses, hedges, and whatever he could crouch behind. Soon he came to a tall, chain-link fence topped with barbed wire that enclosed a paved storage site. This was good. He had made it to the industrial area, and the creek couldn't be far. Staying to the rear of the fenced properties, it was easy to avoid the lighted streets.

The creek was lined with scrubby maple, alder, and thistles that had always been there. There was never any attempt to make this part of town visually pleasing. Those who did make it this far found it often strewn with discarded tires, mangled shopping carts, or other garbage. Holding onto a stem, he walked easily into the water. This cover would hide him well, but it would also cover his scent if a dog were used in a search. The water was cold but bearable and shallow enough that it barely covered the ankles at this time of year. There was almost no ambient light here, so he had to be cautious. A sprain or cut could cause big problems.

Not much more than ten minutes passed when he stopped moving altogether. There were voices ahead and to the left. He took seven more deliberate steps, then stopped again, noticing a tall security light illuminating a fenced lot. Two older men looking dishevelled and grubby sat leaning against the fence. Beside them stood a shopping cart filled with stuffed garbage bags with several others tied to the sides. They were no more than twenty feet from the creek foliage, passing a bottle between them and mumbling incoherently. He crouched low and began his slow slog again.

"I gotta piss!" grunted one of the two and got up, swaying on his feet. He staggered toward the creek bank, grabbing onto a crooked maple to steady himself. The teacher froze again, no more than ten feet from the vagrant, lowering his face to keep his pale skin hidden. He could hear the man mumbling while relieving himself. It was over soon enough. When the teacher lifted his face again, the two sat splayed against the fence, each tugging at the bottle.

Fifteen minutes later, he saw the one last thing he needed. Behind a tall, grey cinder block building was a large disorganized pile of broken wooden pallets. He pulled himself up out of the creek and opened his bag. Quickly, he changed into his tracksuit once more, then wrapped the unloaded shotgun in the dark plastic garbage bag and taped it shut. After moving ten of the pallets to the side, he hid the shotgun in between the slats of the lowest pallet and piled more around the ones he had moved. "Almost there," he whispered, then wrapped his dark clothes into a bundle and stepped into the creek. He looked at his watch. The luminescent dial showed ten forty-five. So far so good. Continuing downstream a little farther, he found a broken piece of cement slab that was

44

once part of a sidewalk. He lifted one edge out of the water, laid the bundle of clothing, spent shells, and remaining cartridges on the bottom of the creek bed, and lowered the slab on top.

Shortly after midnight, he was sitting within sight of the bridge that allowed the jogging path and bus route to cross the creek. Safely hidden, he pushed his arms, as if wearing a jacket, through the looping handles of the closed bag which drew his shoulders near, so it rested like a pack on his back. With his legs pulled against his chest, he wrapped his arms around his knees and waited and watched.

At five-seventeen, the sky was light enough to see easily in both directions on the route home. Stiff and cold, he got up and walked slowly out to the center of the path. Good, no people. He began a slow jog, stopping only to catch his breath, and was amazed at how out of shape he was. *The Flabby Assassin!* he thought to himself, laughing out loud. But he continued running when the increasing traffic went by and then resting again when he could.

He walked through his door at eight thirty-five, peeled off the bag, tracksuit, wet socks, and sneakers, and stood there naked, except for his underwear. With blistered feet, he made his way to bed, crawled under the covers, and was asleep at once. It was done and now came the waiting.

CHAPTER

7

Simon Ross sat at an oak dining table covered with hand-written memos, opened and unopened correspondence, dog-eared instruction manuals, magazines, and dated novels. The adjacent living room was filled with the same clutter, with no bare space on any coffee table, couch, or chair. Stacks of newspapers and telephone books leaned against the wall nearest him. If anyone were to look in the other rooms in his house, they would see much of the same.

Simon was ill but never acknowledged it. It was not hoarding to him as he knew each item's importance; it would be foolish to throw any of it out. He would sit by himself most days, reviewing his finances, reading various newspapers, or emailing like-minded individuals he had come across online. Evenings were spent with the TV on while he read; he rarely ventured from his home, doing so only if his needs required it.

He was a tall, middle-aged individual with a slim athletic build. Nothing ever seemed to bother him much, and it was either this lack of stress or simple genetics that maintained a head of hair that had yet to turn grey. He appeared youthful for his age. Years ago, he had received a significant inheritance that allowed him to bide his time in any way he wanted. He'd had numerous female relationships in his younger days, and several were quite serious, but he never married. Whenever he felt pressured to commit further, he'd get cold feet and would end it as amicably as he could. Those days were, except for several female friends, gone now. His only live-in companion was a belligerent stray cat he had taken in and doted on, even as it scratched his dusty furniture to ribbons. Today, he sat, like most other days, and made a hand-written analysis of various mutual funds that would ensure comfortable days ahead. And, as odd as he was, he was the teacher's best friend.

They had known each other since elementary school and had been through much together, sharing the adventures of youth. But more importantly, they had helped each other survive the ordeals of adolescence and adulthood. They trusted each other without question or reproach.

A week had passed since the killing, and the first days of the new school year went smoothly for the teacher. None of the authorities had approached him or made contact in any way. To make his days even better, he felt no guilt or remorse. If anything, he was noticeably upbeat and often smiled sincerely. With a new group of students, he could start fresh. Michael or Willy would still drop by his classroom, and he was always willing to discuss how they were doing while offering any encouragement he could.

His actions had been a catharsis of the highest order. If retribution were always this therapeutic, then it was at the top of his list. But he knew he was not in the clear yet, and would probably never be. That was fine. If the events caught up to him, he would solve the problem simply and quickly. He now kept the nine-millimetre handgun as close as he could. The term "final solution" was often used by others in a different reference. But if cornered, the nine-millimetre would be his final solution.

However, today was Saturday. As the day was pleasant and warm, he decided to venture out, pick up a few provisions, and later go for a run. He felt inspired to improve his level of fitness. Losing weight would be a good start. As always, he would be methodical, with reasonable goals. This would be good for the soul as well. Just as important, he needed to reaffirm his actions. He decided to take a calculated risk and put a friendship to the test.

Shortly after lunch, around 12:30 p.m., he drove to the south end of town, parked, then walked toward the screen door of a modest two-bedroom bungalow that Simon had purchased years ago. It needed some external maintenance, but such cosmetic things never concerned Simon as there was no one around to motivate him. And, of course, reading was much easier.

Opening the screen door, the teacher knocked several times and waited. In less than a minute, Simon opened the main door.

Simon smiled, took a step back, and said, "Hey, c'mon in."

"Good to see you," the teacher replied. "It's been a while. How have you been? Is that ugly cat still carving up your couch and everything else?" He walked past Simon, making his way quickly up a short set of steps to the main floor where the kitchen fridge housed a supply of beer that was kept for an occasion such as this.

"Now, now, now, be nice," called Simon as he closed the door. "Kitty is easily offended. If you two are ever going to be friends, you need to try harder." He had never properly named the cat.

The teacher came out of the kitchen, grabbed the newspapers off a tattered side chair, tossed them on the floor, sat down, and opened his beer. "There's no point. Your beast is as antisocial as you are. You're made for each other, so I won't get in the way." He bent down and smiled at the large orange feline sleeping in a sunny spot on the floor.

"Anyway, I've been fine as usual," said Simon. He sat down on a couch opposite the teacher, staring intently at his guest. After a pause, he continued. "You seem different today. I'm not quite sure how, but you scurried up the stairs two at a time without using the railing." Simon was always the observant one. "You don't look as bummed out as usual . . . You win the lottery?"

"I wish," chuckled the teacher. "I've been pretty busy lately. You read the paper at all?"

"Which one?" asked Simon.

"Anything local, with anything of significance."

"Sure. But the only excitement was the random killing of some guy on the other side of town. Apparently, when he didn't show up for work for two days, someone found him shot up in his house. I guess the police are at a loss as to a motive. His estranged wife was questioned, but it never went further as she lives a couple of hundred miles away. So why might it be important?" At that, he leaned over and picked up a small blue ball off the coffee table and threw it at the cat. The cat opened his eyes, yawned and stretched, then went back to sleep.

"Simon, I need to tell you something."

Simon looked up and stared at him with a puzzled expression. "What?" he said.

"It was me," said the teacher.

"It was you, what?" countered Simon.

"I shot the asshole."

"You did what?"

"I shot him."

"You shot him?"

"Yup. I blew his nuts off with a shotgun and then finished him off."

"Seriously? You're not kidding?"

"Yup."

A long silence hung over the room with each looking at the other, Simon trying to process what he had just heard. Finally the teacher spoke. "Are you going to be okay?"

"Yeah, but what the fuck did you do that for?"

"He was an asshole," replied the teacher. "Don't you remember when we were working our way through university? I was always pissed off because this mean-spirited son of a bitch was always on my case, trying to make my life miserable. Well, near the end of that job, I made a promise to myself to fix his sorry ass if I ever got the chance. Emily's death was the breaking point. If I couldn't reach her killer, some other ugly, useless prick was going to have to die. So I pushed the envelope a little and hunted Clyde down instead."

"Boy!" exclaimed Simon. "When you hold a grudge, you don't mess around."

"Yes," said the teacher. "And I feel a whole lot better."

Simon sat looking serious. "Why are you telling me this?"

"I don't know, Simon. But my actions came very easily to me, which is scary but also very therapeutic if that makes any sense. So I guess I just needed to tell someone. I'm sorry I involved you, but I trust you. I always have," replied the teacher.

"Good point," said Simon. "If it were anyone else, I wouldn't be this calm. But I've known you a long time, and you're not crazy or impulsive. He obviously had it coming." He laughed. "Imagine . . . a shotgun-packing grade school teacher killer." He laughed again, then composed himself and asked. "But aren't you worried about getting caught?"

"Not really," said the teacher. "I mean, I might get lucky, and nothing comes my way. But the cops aren't stupid, and they may figure out what happened and target me. In any event, I've covered off that possibility."

"Meaning what?" asked Simon.

"I have no intention of going to prison," the teacher continued. "Could you imagine someone my age, and a teacher to boot, going to prison? I wouldn't last a month. But if it came down to it, I wouldn't go nuts and barricade myself in a house and shoot it out. I wouldn't harm an innocent person. The police would just be doing their job. So the best solution would be to eat a bullet."

"Shoot yourself?"

"Yup. It would be quick and relatively painless if done right." He sipped his beer again, staring reflectively at the floor. "I'm getting older, Simon. Even though I feel unbelievable relief, like I've lanced the biggest boil, life is getting boring, and there is not much more to lose." The significance of this conversation sunk in, and Simon stared blankly at his cat. No one spoke. Then Simon looked up.

"You always were the pragmatic one," said Simon. "Just a sec; I think I need a beer myself." He got up, retrieved a cold beer from the fridge, and sat down again. "So I need to ask you, was this a one-time event? Or do you have someone else on your death radar?"

After a long, silent pause, the teacher took a slow drink, emptying the can and placing it on the floor beside the chair. "I'm not sure. Nobody comes to mind right now. But it's so tiresome to see the lowlifes of the world make things shitty for everyone else and get away with it."

"I understand," said Simon. "I can't imagine doing anything like that myself. But then again, it seems anybody is capable of anything these days. Are you sleeping at night?"

"Better than I ever have," replied the teacher. "I dream like a normal person, I guess; no nightmares or waking up in a cold sweat. So I'll just carry on like I always have." With that, he stood up. "I better go. But thanks for listening. It's what you're really good at."

"Hey, no problem, but what's the rush?"

"Just some ordinary stuff I have to get done on my day off. Run a few errands and then get a little fresh air," replied the teacher. It was best to leave now. He could tell Simon wanted to push for more, but there wasn't a whole lot he had to offer. It would have been an insult to them both to let this devolve into idle chit-chat.

"Okay," said Simon. "But make sure you give me the heads up if I ever piss you off."

The teacher laughed again. "See ya later, Simon." Then he walked back down the stairs and out the door.

Two more weeks passed, with each day continuing easily, without conflict or stress. The weather was soft and soothing, with the Indian summer providing an even warmth, and the teacher enjoyed his walks home each day more than ever. Although he continuously mulled over his actions as he walked, none of his thoughts haunted him in the slightest. In fact, it was quite the opposite. He marvelled at the precision of his "hit." The planning and timing were perfect. Two days ago, he managed to return to the bridge late one evening. After parking close by, he retrieved his shotgun with ease, carrying it nonchalantly in a backpack to his vehicle. Now, with his head up, he walked with an air of self-confidence and made a point to smile at those he passed. Still dressed in his conservative attire, he considered buying some new clothing with brighter colours, but caution dictated that he not draw any unwanted attention his way.

For him, teaching was different now. His new class dynamics were similar to last year's, but there had been a trade-off. He refused to make an emotional investment in this group. The cost was too high. Having to endure another death like Emily's would be too much to take. It would be safer now. It was easy enough to relate to each of these kids and try to enhance their lives. But every attempt was made to change the classroom. A quiet, young man named Tyler was assigned to care for Charlie, the gerbil. However, the walls had been stripped of all reminders of last year. New posters were in place, and the best students' work usually kept up from previous years was now filed away in a cupboard. Maintaining this professional distance would make it much easier to carry on. And, of course, there was always the nagging concern that he would be found out. But the worry was minimal. The contingency plan was in place, and he knew it could be carried out without hesitation.

There was more balance in his life now. Going home at the end of the day was no longer a chore. If anything, it was something to look forward to. His fitness routine was paying off dividends. He could run without having to stop and bend over to catch his breath. Evening meals were put together with much more forethought, and his weight loss was significant. The traditional evening pour of scotch was now limited to weekends only. It was nice to get compliments from his staff. Of course, they all thought he had gone for extensive counselling or a European vacation during the summer to get rid of his grief. But little did they know.

He often thought about what Simon said the last time they spoke. Was there anyone else on his death radar? No, he had done what he needed to do. But could he do it again? Definitely. It wouldn't take much to spur him into action if needed. It was so much better to enjoy life without having to worry about the actions of others. But, if for any reason he lost significant sleep again because someone within reach was not worthy of living, he would make another plan. Even though his firearms were cleaned once more and locked away, the nine-millimetre was always a close companion, and another visit to the shooting range in the forest would be a trip worth taking if only to stay sharp.

The previous week, Michael came into the teacher's classroom after school while he sat marking papers and eating a sandwich.

"What's up, Mike?" he asked.

"Nothing much," said Michael. "I just wanted to talk to you about all that's happened. I mean, first, Emily gets killed, and the driver gets away. Then there's all this talk about some guy getting shot on the other side of town, and the killer gets away again."

The teacher put down his pen and rubbed his eyes. "Yes," he said. "It is kind of strange for a place like this, where it seems like things like that seldom happen. And then again, sometimes unfortunate events happen in bunches."

"What I don't understand," Michael continued, "is why people do things like that. Are they just born that way, or does something happen to them later that changes them?"

"Recently, a friend of mine mentioned that at the right time, under the right circumstances, any one person is capable of anything—good or bad. But I don't think that people are born killers, or if they are, there aren't many of them. Most times, a series of events line up where somebody just loses all control. And after it happens, it's too late to take it back. Are you worried about all that's happened?"

"Not really. It just seems weird, that's all."

"Well, don't sweat it. I don't see anything like that in your future. In a few years, you will start making plans for your life that you will have control over. You'll have dreams about life on your own and a career. And you'll get bigger and stronger and chase girls."

Michael's eyes widened, and he began to blush.

"But then again," said the teacher, "I think the girls are going to start chasing you real soon."

Michael lowered his head and chuckled, his cheeks glowing redder.

"Oh, yes! I see them looking at you in the hallway," the teacher said with a smile. "You're going to need to be able to run real fast. But don't you worry about anything else, young man. You are going to be just fine."

"Thanks, Mr. E," said Michael. "See ya later."

He turned and walked out of the room. The teacher sat there and watched him leave. He had just done what he always did, nurture and protect. But the question he had to ask himself was, which one was he? Was he a natural-born killer, or had he evolved into one? He stared at the papers on the desk in front of him without focusing. It didn't take long for the conclusion to come to him. He was both. Like a sword, he had been fashioned from a hidden potential by the events of his adult life. It saddened him. He valued this ability to help his kids make their way in the world. Yet, life had set him on a course to a breaking point of possible self-destruction. Had he not done what he did, he was sure another dark path would have eventually consumed him.

This day was over. He stacked the assignments before him, then placed them in his briefcase. Putting on his jacket, he looked around the classroom and made a mental note of every detail he could. Just like the day he killed Clyde, he knew this could all be gone in a heartbeat, and for a while, memories would be all he had.

During the first week of October, he had gone on a date of sorts. Constance Anderson, the school counsellor, needed an escort for a reception given one evening for a local artist's display. Several years younger than him and on the post-marriage treadmill, she was attractive in a matronly manner. Always dressed professionally, with her long auburn hair tied back and minimal makeup, Constance was the steadying influence on staff. She involved herself whenever and wherever needed and, after Emily's tragic death, had stepped to the forefront to soothe frayed emotions.

The teacher was the only suitable bachelor she knew. She was moved by his concern for Emily and all his students. While he sat at his desk one lunch hour near the end of the week, she casually walked into his classroom and approached him.

"Could you do me a favour?" she asked.

He looked up and noticed her blushing slightly, pushing her hair behind her ear with her right hand. "Soitenly!" he replied with a smile. "What can I do for my favourite counsellor?"

"I need a date for tomorrow night. An artist friend of mine is having a showing with a reception at a local gallery. And I've gone solo to far too many functions of late and thought it would be nice to have some intelligent and handsome company."

"Absolutely," he said, smiling. "Just let me know when and where. I will pick you up in my boring, dirty truck and whisk you off to the ball."

The arrangements were made, and later the next evening, he arrived dressed in his best sweater, shirt, and tie. Constance met him at her door. Wearing a black satin dress, with her hair over her shoulders and sporting a little more makeup, she now looked beautiful. It caused him to hesitate. After trying his best not to look her up and down, he offered his arm and turned to walk her to his vehicle.

"You look amazing," he said. "Is this the same woman who wears glasses while packing a cup of coffee down the hall every morning? I should have washed my truck."

"C'mon, silly," she answered. "You've got a job to do tonight."

The evening went better than he expected. It was a small informal setting with drinks and snacks. The twenty or so guests were an eclectic mix of professionals and members of the local art scene. He managed to mix well, contributing to the various conversations with ease and a smile. But, he was drawn to Constance. He couldn't keep his eyes off her, and she reciprocated with flirtatious smiles. The sexy, low-cut dress she was wearing clung to her slim athletic body. Had she done this for him? *Just great,* he thought. *The possibility of being a normal human being comes my way, and what am I to do?* But, he knew the answer. There was no way. Being a homicidal criminal wasn't conducive to a normal life. He had crossed the line, and there was no going back. It was impossible to become involved in such a relationship again. The potential for collateral damage was too great of a risk. No, if his instincts proved right, he would play his role tonight, and that would be it.

At ten that evening, the event ended, and she suggested they go for a drink. It was a pleasant way to end the evening. She made a point of sitting beside him, and the waiter brought them two glasses of red wine. They discussed their jobs and, eventually, their lives. As he knew she would, Constance asked why he had remained single and whether he would ever consider a relationship again. He was gentle yet as honest as possible in answering. Being alone was easier, he explained. No matter how good the relationship, the pitfalls and resulting grief were not worth it. She deserved better than a loner. But he thanked her for a great evening and offered to help with any other favours she might need. She laughed, then like she would do to a small boy, mussed up his hair and said it was time to go.

The idle chit-chat on the way to her house made the drive easier. When he stopped to drop her off, she thanked him again. He took her hand, gently kissed it, and said, "See ya Monday." She opened her door and, after getting out, lowered her head and smiled once more. The evening was over.

That had been a Friday night. The next morning, after a two-mile run, shower, and breakfast, the teacher wandered the aisles of a large supermarket. As he casually pushed his shopping cart, he went over the events of the previous evening. Did he regret what he said last night? Most certainly, but what choice did he have? He needed to put himself "out there" now if only to quell any rumours that he might be a weird recluse. But to consider anything more was flirting with disaster.

With his cart almost half-full with various fruits, vegetables, and other groceries, he rounded a corner to make his way to a till, but three steps later, froze mid-stride. His hands tightened on the cart handle, and his eyes opened wider. He cautiously turned to the right and took three more steps to get a better look. At the deli counter, there stood an old man, holding a shopping basket and waiting for his purchase. *I don't believe it,* thought the teacher. *Could it be him? I thought he would have been dead by now.* He pushed on further, trying not to stare, but he had to be sure.

He walked another twenty feet, then slowly reversed his direction. Now he could see the face of the hunched figure clearly. "Well, well, well, Teddy," he said softly in an inaudible whisper. "You have been delivered to me."

CHAPTER

8

The ride was more challenging than he thought it would be. Even though his physical state had improved with his significant weight loss and enhanced endurance, he hadn't ridden a bike in years, and it was arduous. But it suited his task perfectly. He had been scouting various classified ads and had the good fortune of finding this ten-speed at a garage sale one afternoon. It was purchased easily with cash, leaving no paper trail. The owner had even thrown in a helmet that fit a little loose but would do the job. He had thought about buying the riding attire he saw others wear but decided that spandex was a bit much for his middle-aged physique. So he simply put on his tracksuit once more and prepared himself for this day.

However, this day would be different once again, even if the intended outcome was the same. His backpack would contain his usual bottle of water together with the loaded pistol. But there would also be another pair of thin black driving gloves and a thirty-two-ounce ball-peen hammer. To complete his needs, he had disguised himself today. Riding in the open would expose him to a gauntlet of traffic and security cameras, any one of which could take him down. He started with a fake black beard and moustache, which clung tightly to his face. This was a difficult adjustment as he was always clean-shaven, and the itch was something he could do without. But the false nose that had covered his own was a stroke of brilliance. As Halloween approached, all kinds of costume accessories were available in numerous stores. After a short search, he found exactly what he was looking for. It was wider than his nose with a slight hump along the bridge and completely changed his facial features. The colour was a close enough match to his own skin, and the skin adhesive that came with it made for a quick and easy fit. A pair of dark sunglasses were slid into place. He was ready to go.

After seeing Teddy in the supermarket that day, he quickly paid for his groceries, then sat in his truck waiting. It wasn't long until the old man came out and made his way to a small black sedan. The teacher watched him place two small bags in the back, get in the driver's seat, then slowly and carefully pull out of the parking lot.

It was easy enough to follow him at a safe distance. The car made its way through town, heading north toward an area of small hobby farms and scattered rows of homes built on large lots lining this route. Several orchards in the area grew apples and plums that had since been harvested for the season, and the land sloped gently, traversed by old paved roads with the usual patchwork of filled-in potholes and ragged asphalt edges. It was for this reason that recreational cyclists were a regular sight here. Vehicle traffic was minimal, making these routes ideal for road bikes.

He stayed a good two hundred yards behind Ted but kept him in sight, waiting to see if he was heading home. Eventually, the car made a slow right turn into a long driveway that ended at an open garage attached to a larger beige house, a spacious-looking rancher that appeared to be sided with cedar planks. The car pulled into the open space next to a white sedan. The teacher didn't slow at all. He simply made a note of the location and kept driving. The road meandered north for some distance before veering to the northwest, where it joined the highway out of town. At this point, the teacher turned right, and over a distance of eight kilometers, he wound up driving east and then south back to the town. He would travel this route five more times to complete his reconnaissance; twice by driving and three by bike.

Ted Saunders was also a teacher, or at least he had been. In his case, the term "teacher" never applied. To the students, he was known as Teddy the Terrible, a vain, arrogant, violent man who ruled his classes by fear. He was taller back then, with military, brush-cut hair, and always dressed in athletic clothes. Simon and the teacher had the unfortunate circumstance of being assigned to two of his classes. The physical education class was intended as a ten- and eleven-year-old boys' athletic group setting, but boot camp would have been a better term.

Ted also taught an English class, but that too would have been a stretch. It was in that Grade 6 year that many young boys would learn what a sadist was. Although he was slightly more civil in this class, it was only because there were girls present. The teacher had no obvious memory of the girls being harmed. No, Ted would bide his time until his urges got the best of him, then find a reason to vent these impulses on a hapless lad without hesitation. If they were lucky, it would be over quickly, with a mean slur or a cuff to the back of the head. But often, it was worse. And, after each incident, you could see the right corner of his mouth twist up in an ugly smile. It was a mystery why only the boys were subjected to this terror. In groups, they would often offer up their own theories, then voice their wishes that he would die in a car accident or suffer some other terminal misfortune.

But the teacher was smart. He had gauged Ted early on, and living in a violent household had provided the skills that he put to good use in school. Whenever Ted was near, he would keep any movement to a minimum, simply blending in with his head down. If asked a question, he would answer quickly without hesitation, using a tone that was flat and devoid of emotion. He taught these skills to Simon as well. It was the other unfortunate ones he felt sorry for because often they learned too late. He was sure the verbal and physical abuse would leave a lifetime of scars. But those were the bad old days. Today, a teacher like Ted would be terminated in a heartbeat. Not then. Teachers weren't questioned, and incidents were rarely reported. Even if they were, parents often dismissed the accusations as a wild or exaggerated story. For most, that Grade 6 year couldn't end fast enough.

The last he heard, Teddy the Terrible had finally crossed the line, and his obsession had gotten the best of him. In his gym class, a native boy was not as attentive as he should have been during basketball drills. While Ted gave instructions, the boy began tossing his ball into the air, paying no attention to Ted, and on the third toss, fumbled it. The bouncing echo of the ball on the floor set Ted off in the worst way. Before the boy could pick it up, Ted sprinted to retrieve it, then threw it directly at the young man's face. The boy's nose didn't break, but the amount of blood was too much to ignore. Ted wasn't fired. As was the custom, he was simply transferred to another district and placed on probation.

But everyone saw what happened, and no one forgot.

The teacher's previous travels in this area had been well worth the effort. The cluttered regions in town made a gradual transition to dispersed small businesses, and eventually, to the semi-rural area he had followed Ted through. Although the roads were reasonably straight, they rose and fell slightly with the odd hill or gulley along the way. The beige house was the second of six others as he approached from the south. The north side of the lot had a dense row of pyramid cedars at least eight feet tall, providing privacy from the adjacent neighbours. The south side of the lot was bordered by a slat picket fence, no more than four feet tall. It would provide almost no visual protection, but he would take what he could get.

He noticed other details immediately. The apple orchard across from the houses had a fenced-in water pumping station that the municipality had built. This and the fact that the trees still had their leaves would provide cover if he needed to observe the house or disappear from the road. On his second trip, he intentionally wandered into this orchard with his bike. Using his binoculars, he focused on the garage and memorized the model of the white car and its plate number. The garage built onto Ted's house stood out about eight feet farther than the main building's front entrance and offered one significant edge: it was always open during the day and closed at night.

This would be a crime of opportunity. He assumed the white sedan next to Ted's car was his wife's or whoever lived with him. If the white car was gone on the planned day, he would deal with Ted as quickly as he could and ride away as though he was just another cyclist. Hopefully, the fall weather would be cold enough to keep the neighbours inside. If the opportunity was not there, no problem. Indeed, circumstances had made him impatient but not stupid, so he would not let blind emotion ruin this. His intelligence had always served him well. He could wait if he had to. With a little luck or divine intervention, it would only be a matter of time until Ted was an ugly memory at best.

The air was colder this morning. The sun provided some warmth, but as soon as the scattered clouds blocked it out, the teacher could almost see his breath. He rode at a steady pace, keeping his head down whenever he could. This was how many other riders carried themselves on a bike, especially if the going was harder. He decided it was best to play the part.

Several times along the way, he thought that maybe it was foolish to risk this attempt. After all, Ted probably didn't have a whole lot longer to live. However, this was quickly brushed from his mind. Even though he knew the risks would be far greater this time, if he waited until the winter had passed and the old man died a gentle, peaceful death, he'd regret it for the rest of his life. Ted could still enjoy his days. He had never been held accountable for all the misery he had caused. He still had the opportunity to enjoy family occasions, be entertained by a movie, or savour a warm day. Undoubtedly, this was available to him without the slightest worry or haunting of past deeds. No, this needed to be set right, and the sooner, the better.

The teacher passed the small business area that bordered the edge of town. It wouldn't be far now. He pedalled slower. It was important not to be winded, and the slow ride provided extra time to go over the plan once more. A group of riders coming from the opposite direction passed him on the other side of the road but didn't bother to look his way. It didn't surprise him; they were obviously in their "zone." But, it also reaffirmed what he always knew—that he was never noticed. Maybe it was a hidden talent—his face, mannerisms, choice of clothing, or the way he moved. Whatever it was, it gave him an advantage he wasn't going to squander.

The last dip in the road was now in sight. Beyond it was the row of houses on the right. He lowered his head again and pedalled slightly harder to make the oncoming grade easier. When he looked up again, a white car crested the rise and came toward him. He kept his pace. Sure it was a white car, but it could be any white car. He refused to let his thoughts race ahead. In all likelihood, he would need to pass by just like he had three times before. But if this was the day, he would lower his head slightly, avoid eye contact with the driver, and try his best to catch the make and plate number as it passed. With his eyes down once more, he pedalled close to the edge of the pavement and listened.

Now, he thought. He lifted his head slightly again as the sedan began to pass. He only saw the plate's first three letters, but that was enough; the plate was a match.

It was now time to move. He rode faster and made the top of the rise quickly. Only two hundred yards to go. Down went his head for the last time as he counted his breaths. After the tenth one, he glanced up and to the right, and there it was. He smiled as he coasted to the driveway. The neighbour's yard was empty, the garage door was open as usual, and there was only one car inside.

The great room inside the large beige house was next to the garage. An inner door and a long wall separated the two. The entire floor was carpeted in a thick pile except for the small areas near the garage and front entrances. The walls were mostly white, painted over the drywall, except for the farthest one opposite the garage entrance. This had been covered with stained cedar. Various framed photos and two paintings hung neatly in place. To the right of this feature wall, an open entrance led to the kitchen. A big, standing, oak bookcase leaned against the next wall to the right. It was filled with hardcover novels, several reference books, and a section of stacked photo albums. The room was dimly lit with three standing lamps. In the center were two loveseats set at right angles to each other, the first with its back to a large picture window looking out onto the lawn and adjacent road. The drapes had been drawn to within three feet of each other. The second faced the feature wall. A round oak coffee table was placed in front of and between the two seats. To the right of this second love seat, a brass reading light stood five feet tall with the light and focusing shade bent over and down. It was shining on an antique Victorian chair, fashionably upholstered in burgundy velvet, with a maple back and arms highlighted by the light.

Ted Saunders sat in the chair. He wore slippers, black slacks, a plaid shirt, and a brown cardigan sweater. He was motionless, his eyes directed to the book held slightly in front of him. He turned the page, and, as he did, he heard the handle to the garage door click open, with the door squeaking on its hinges as it opened.

"You're home early," he said, still looking at the pages in front of him. "I thought your bridge tournament went all day."

The teacher had carefully leaned his bike against the protruding garage wall nearest the front entrance. Walking slowly into the garage, he stopped in front of the car to the black sedan's right. With his sunglasses still on, he opened the top of the backpack, put the black gloves on, and set the hammer in place in the pack with its black, gripped handle pointed up.

He saw no indication on his previous trips that anyone else, other than the two car owners, lived in the house. But if he was wrong, or the plan went south, he had an excuse ready. After all, a lone cyclist with a weak bladder could always ask to use the bathroom when in need. This was a stretch, of course, but it was all he had, and he would take this chance.

Holding the open pack in his left hand, he placed his right on the garage door. His heart began to pound harder. Once again, he could hear the pulse in his ears. Turning the handle to the left, he pushed the door open and stood in the entrance. In front of him was a large room. Slightly to the right of center was a brightly lit lamp with a chair facing away from him. A figure he immediately recognized sat in the chair, reading a book. *It must be a good one,* thought the teacher. Ted hadn't looked back or lifted his head at all.

"Jesus, Alice! Have you gone deaf? You're supposed to be playing cards," he called.

The teacher said nothing. Staring straight ahead, he reached into the pack and pulled out the hammer. He was six steps away from Ted and, after the second one, raised the hammer into position. After the fourth, Ted set the book in his lap and turned his head to the right.

"I'll ask you . . ." he began but never finished his sentence. The hammer came down on the top of his left shoulder, shattering the outer edge of his collar bone and the humerus in his left arm with a loud crack. The force of the blow sent him over, and he fell on the floor, first on his side, then rolling on his back. His book lay splayed on the floor. The teacher stepped around the chair and pushed it back with his leg. Ted lay stunned on the floor. His mouth was open, and his eyes widened, darting in all directions. The teacher knew time was critical, and he should finish the old man off quickly and leave, but he couldn't. Not yet. He needed to confront this man. He lowered himself onto one knee, bent over, and stared at Ted's face.

"Hello, Teddy," he said.

The old man turned his head slightly to the right and blinked, trying to focus. "Who . . . What . . ." he said, barely able to get the words out, wheezing as he spoke.

"I'm a dark angel," said the teacher. "I'm your dark angel, Teddy. It's time to pay for your sins. We all have to pay for our sins, don't we, Teddy?" he said smiling.

A look of confusion spread across Ted's face, and his eyes began to dart from left to right again.

"Don't you remember, Teddy? All those years ago, all those children you hurt. No? Here, let me help you remember." He lifted the hammer and pushed the head into the front of Ted's broken shoulder.

Ted's face tightened into a grimace. "Nooooo," he cried. "Stop, stop, stop!"

The teacher dropped the hammer to his side. "Don't you remember the day Alan Shultz forgot to do his reading homework? You threw his book onto the floor and told him to pick it up. When the poor kid bent over to lift it, you kicked him across the front of the classroom. Not very nice, Teddy. And don't forget Tommy Mills. When you saw him staring out the window during class, you pulled him by the hair from one window to the next, shaking his head at each one, telling him he could look out windows after school. Now that was mean.

"But the worst always happened in gym class. Didn't it, Teddy? Like the time Brian Kowalski finished last in the distance run. He was fat and slow, but that didn't matter, did it? You made us all take off a running shoe and form a line. Brian had to run the gauntlet on his hands and knees between our legs while you told us to make sure he knew what a running shoe sole felt like. I don't know how you got away with that one. He had welts over his back for two weeks. There were many others we could talk about, but I don't have all day."

Ted's eyes stopped moving, and he stared at the ceiling. "They needed it! They deserved it!" he said louder now. "Ugly, horrible boys!"

The teacher's brow furrowed. "But you have to tell me, Teddy," he said. "Why always the boys?"

Teddy turned his head again and looked at him. "Because they're boys!" he said louder. "Horrible, little bastard boys who just wanted to screw my daughter! They were just like the rest, all the same."

"Your daughter?"

"She was my daughter! My girl! Nobody else's! Mine!"

"Jesus," the teacher said softly. "You're worse than I could have imagined." Still on one knee, the teacher straightened his back and stared across the room. He felt calm, like this was any other routine task. "It's time to say goodbye now, Teddy."

He looked back down again, making eye contact and putting his hand firmly on Ted's right shoulder. The broken one wouldn't be a problem. He placed his other gloved hand on the old man's face, covered his mouth, and pressed firmly against the sides of his nostrils. Immediately, Ted began to squirm and tried to moan. His left arm twitched at his side, useless. Two minutes later, all movement stopped, and his dead eyes stared at the ceiling again. The teacher took off his right glove and gently felt under Ted's jaw for a pulse. There was none.

Quickly, he picked up the hammer and put it in the pack with his gloves. The entrance was still open, and he made his way out, closing the door behind him. Stopping at the garage entrance, he looked to both sides. All was clear. Seconds later, his pack was shouldered, and he turned his bike left onto the road.

He didn't notice the raven flying in silent meandering circles above the house.

The teacher crossed to the right side with his head down, pedalling in a slow, deliberate manner, as he would during any lengthy ride. There was no panic or urgency. The farther he rode, the calmer he became. After several minutes, there was still no vehicle traffic, but off in the distance, two cyclists were riding toward him. They approached and, like him, rode with their usual determination, oblivious to the lone rider passing by.

By the time he was halfway home, he had slowed to a leisurely clip. The occasional car now passed him, and every time one did, he avoided all eye contact and kept his pace. This was his second killing. Like before, he replayed the experience in his mind. Once again, he was calm, without worry or remorse. When Ted's body was found, it would take some time to figure out what exactly happened. There was no blood, and only a medical examination could determine how he died.

Ten minutes later, he opened his door and pushed the bike through, leaning it on the kickstand. He dropped the pack onto the floor of his bedroom and took off his clothes, then went to the kitchen and poured himself a glass of scotch. He sipped his drink as he made his way to the bathroom, and standing in front of the bathroom mirror, he began to pull off the fake beard and nose. It was time for a shower.

CHAPTER

9

So what would they say? If he kept this up, it was only a matter of time before his luck ran out. Then, the eventual discussions of his actions would be fodder for the public and media alike. Radio and television hosts would put an army of shrinks, police specialists, and other mouthpieces with something to say in front of a microphone. They would editorialize from every angle. Was he a psychopath, a sociopath, or a serial killer? Coffee shops would buzz with discussions about how a respected teacher went cuckoo and started killing.

Yes, he was now a killer. There was no doubt about that. Simple murder had progressed to the next level. There was no point in trying to analyze his actions. No one would understand. But it was quite simple. He just fucking hated the worst of humanity. Any virtues in the world were far too often overwhelmed by the inherent darkness in people, allowed to grow in every corner of society like a noxious mould that ripened with age. It was evident everywhere. The resources spent on the military, police, courts, and the numerous agencies patched together to pick up the pieces were all the proof anyone needed. Day after day, those who preyed on others could continue. He supposed that those who knew him best, and maybe a few others, would be able to understand his actions. But in the grand scheme of things, their numbers were insignificant and didn't count.

So what would he do next? He didn't know. It was probably best to try to exist within the norms of society. Of course, he would have to live with the persistent thought that, at any time, it could all come to an end with some bright police officer who would piece together his actions. But this did not bother him in the slightest. He would carry on as he always had and enjoy his days for as long as possible. Would he kill again? Not now; it was time to stop. He repeatedly reflected on his past. There were no more inner demons to exorcise.

It was well into November now. On this Saturday morning, he had run a total of six kilometres, making sure the route was as arduous as possible. Hills were a favourite choice. Even though on some, he needed to slow to almost a walk, he kept up the best pace he could, never stopping. The days were even cooler now, and it was a great time to run. It hadn't snowed yet, and the days were sunny. The trees around him were enhanced with fall colours. The air on his face felt wonderful; breathing in gave him vitality and clarity.

When he reached his home, he began his routine of peeling off his clothes and getting ready for a shower when the phone rang. He threw his damp T-shirt onto the bedroom floor, then combed his hair back and away from his face with his fingers. The phone was on the kitchen table.

"Hello?"

"Was that you?"

"Jesus, Simon!" he exclaimed. "Most normal people offer a salutation of some kind after being greeted."

"So, was that you?" continued Simon.

"I need to shower, then I'll come over," he said and hung up. "That idiot needs to get out more," he said out loud with a tone of exasperation.

The shower was long and hot, and, as was his latest custom, he turned off the "hot" tap for the last thirty seconds. The ice-cold water made him gasp, but the sensation after he finished was well worth it. He quickly combed his wet hair and put on a pair of faded jeans, a grey T-shirt, grey hoodie, and loafers after towelling off. He looked in the mirror once more, thinking that a shave might be in order, but decided against it. Picking up his keys, he walked out the door. It was time to go see Simon.

As always, Simon met him at the door, then stepped to the side to welcome him.

"C'mon in."

"Thanks," replied the teacher and hustled up the stairs two at a time, making his way to the kitchen fridge for a beer.

"So, was that you?" said Simon for the third time today.

The teacher opened the cold can and walked into the living room. The sun shone through the open blinds, lighting up the dust that always hung in the air. The cat was spread out on the floor next to a mangled area rug used to sharpen his claws. The teacher found the same chair he sat in the last time he was here. Nothing had changed. The newspaper and other literary detritus he had pitched onto the floor were as he had left them. He sat down.

"For the umpteenth time, Simon, you need to hire a cleaning lady," he said. "If you don't trip and break your neck on that thrashed rug, you're going to die of an asthma attack from this bloody dust! And yes, it was me."

"I thought as much," said Simon. "The local rag has been lit up with articles on 'our latest murder.' I was going to call a couple of days ago but thought it best to wait. There seemed to be a lot of uncertainty about Teddy's death. But I thought that if he was intentionally snuffed, there could possibly be hundreds, if not thousands, of suspects who would have loved to rub out that asshole."

There had been several conversations in the staffroom at work about the death of Ted Saunders. But, as the teacher did not subscribe to any newspapers, the second-hand information he listened to was vague at best.

"At first, they just mentioned his 'sudden passing,'" continued Simon. He walked over to his favourite spot on the couch and sat down. "Then, they described his death as 'suspicious,' saying that a complete medical examination had been ordered by the coroner. Finally, this morning, I read that the authorities had 'conclusive evidence that his death was, in fact, a homicide.'"

Simon looked at the teacher. His eyes grew large and bright, and his smile was big and wide. "So, how'd you do it?" he said with anticipation. "Did you shoot him?"

The teacher took a long slow drink of his beer. "Simon, how could a gunshot be considered 'uncertain' or 'in need of a medical examination?'" he said. "No, I softened him up with a hammer first. Then I smothered him with my hand. But in between, I made sure we had a short conversation about what he did to us. I had to jog his memory a little about the pain he caused. You remember what he did to Shultz, and Mills, and Kowalski?"

"Yeah, I remember," said Simon. He looked down at the floor, a blank expression on his face. "Those were terrible days for sure. The hurt and fear were bad enough. But the humiliation so many of those guys had to live with afterward was the worst part. Poor Shultz, he was a sensitive kid, the artsy type. I don't think he could make eye contact with anyone for at least a week after. And kids being kids, the others gave him a bad time about it, too.

"I'm glad you clued me in early to what made that sadistic son of a bitch click. I've put it behind me for the most part. But occasionally, over the years, I've wondered what I would have done if that had happened to me. I would like to think I would have gone to his house late at night with a can of gasoline and matches, poured it on one side of that cedar house, and hoped for the best. But then, maybe I would have just walked up behind him in the hall after recess one day with a baseball bat and clubbed him as hard as I could. We were almost eleven then, and even an eleven-year-old kid could leave a pretty good mark on his melon with a wooden bat.

"And maybe that's what somebody should have done early on. Then all that bullshit could have been brought to a head, and somebody would have done something about it. It might have saved a lot of others a mountain of grief.

"Well," finished Simon in a soft voice. "I'm glad he's gone. And, you just covered that ugly face with your hand and smothered him?"

"Yup. He couldn't really fight back. I busted up his left side pretty good with that hammer. So all he could do was just kick his legs out a little bit. It didn't last long. My initial plan was to use the hammer to cave in his skull. But, that would have been too quick and messy."

"Good. I hope he suffered in the end. I hope all that ugliness flashed in front of his eyes before the lights went out."

Simon got up and stepped toward his cat, and sat down on the floor next to it. The cat opened his eyes and stretched while Simon stroked his orange fur and patted his head. "I never thought much about our school days until this came up," he said. "Things got a lot better once we got past that crap, especially high school."

The teacher nodded.

"We had a lot more freedom," Simon continued. "There were school dances and weekend parties. We chased girls and bragged about who would get laid first.

"But, I think the best part was going into the bush. Remember when we would pile on my dirt bike with a couple of fly rods and a pack of beer and spend the day fishing in the river? We never gave a shit about anything; we had so many dreams and the world by the ass. But it's gone now. Everything is too complicated, and we can't go back."

Again, they both sat in silence, staring at the cat. Simon got up and moved back to his spot on the couch. "So what now?" he asked "You think you'll get away with it?"

"Didn't you ask me that the last time?"

"Yeah, but you have to know your actions are going to bring a lot of heat into this area. Killing some useless bum could happen anywhere. But this last one in such a short period has kind of put people on edge."

"I know, Simon. I was a little impatient with Ted."

"Ha!" laughed Simon. "Spoken like a true teacher."

"But under the circumstances, I did the best I could. I know the police won't give up either. But I'm done. I did what I set out to do, and now it's time to cool my jets, which brings up a good point. I need to stay away from you for a while. I can't run the risk that you might be implicated in any way. If any suspicion falls on me, they'll look at all my contacts, trying to find an accomplice. You don't need that."

"I wouldn't worry about it," said Simon. "There's no evidence tying anything to me. Then again, I could always plead insanity." They both laughed out loud. After a minute, they sat in silence, staring at the cat, who was oblivious to everything except the grooming of his fur.

"You're a good friend, Simon. Maybe both of us deserved to be dealt a better hand in life. But, we did the best we could. I'm going to carry on like I always do and see if I can wait out the storm. It would be nice for the kids' sake to avoid a scandal and not destroy their faith in someone they trusted. Then again, today's headlines become yesterday's news real fast. And kids are resilient.

"So I better go. Like I said, I'm going to keep a low profile. But if you need something, call me, okay?"

"Okay," said Simon. "If my stupid neighbour keeps playing his stereo too loud, you'll be the first person I call."

The teacher laughed again as he put his beer can down and walked to the stairs. "See ya, Simon." He hurried toward the door and left.

The teacher parked in a lane under a tall oak tree, one of many lining this drive through the cemetery. Their broad red and yellow leaves had now almost all fallen and been removed from the grounds. The few that remained hung still, lifeless in the morning chill, the pointed edges curling inward as they dried out. Even though he knew better, the trees seemed old and dead, their gnarled branches ugly and misshapen.

It was a cold, late November day. The sky was overcast, thickened by dark grey ridges. But he still wore his sunglasses as he turned the ignition off, opened the door, and stood beside his truck. He was wearing a dull green barn coat, faded jeans and brown hiking shoes. The air held a sense of imminent snowfall. He looked around to see if anyone else was here today. There was no one. Reaching back into the truck, he picked up a bouquet of flowers from the passenger seat and closed the door.

He hadn't attended the burial. Emily's family had requested that they be the only ones there. *It was just as well,* he thought. *The grief that day had been hard enough to endure.* But he knew approximately where her grave was; the walk would be short. He carried the bouquet in one hand and crossed the lane, making his way onto the lawn opposite the truck. The grass was stiff with frost, holding the imprint of each step as he walked. Stopping briefly at the first grave he came to, he began a slow search. Reading the headstones, he kept a respectful distance from each, not wanting to step on the ground directly above the buried caskets.

At the third and last row of this area, he saw her headstone, the second one in from the lane. It was made of grey granite, with her name carved into the rock near the middle—Emily Carter, no middle name. A small potted plant had been placed to the right of the headstone. It had survived the early frosts, maintaining an upright, green shape. *Probably from her mother,* he thought.

He avoided looking at the dates below her name and stepped gently forward, bending down to place the flowers at the base of the stone. *They are nice,* he thought. The florist had done well, although he could only guess as to what kind they were. They were mostly fall colours, with the odd bright red and yellow to contrast the rest. He stood up and stepped back.

"I'm sorry, Emily," he said. "I'm sorry I didn't send you home with the others. That was my fault; Charlie could have waited another day. And I apologize for my offensive actions of late. I know they won't bring you back or punish whoever was responsible for taking your life.

"But I was just so angry. The world needed you, and you deserved so much better. You overcame the worst and were doing so well. Some might call it determination, but that doesn't work for me. It was just the way you were, full of hope and always eager to make the best of everything.

"After you died, the helpless feeling I had just overwhelmed me. So again, please forgive me. I'm still teaching, even though it's different now. I'm trying to help the kids at school and move on. But I won't ever be content until whoever did this terrible thing to you is caught and punished, okay? So I'm going to leave now, but I just wanted to let you know how I feel and that we all miss you, Emily."

He adjusted his sunglasses, straightened his jacket, and he was about to leave when he heard a familiar sound, up high and to his left. The teacher turned and looked up. A row of conifers lined the other side of the burial plots. In the tallest one, a raven sat and cawed. The sound came through clear and loud in the cold air. The teacher stood still. The raven stretched its wings wide, then, with a quick flap, became airborne. It flew directly above him, circling and cawing repeatedly.

Rational thought told him this was just a coincidence, but his gut told him it was more. Just what exactly "more" was, he couldn't describe. It was a haunting feeling, devoid of any fear or uncertainty. If anything, it strengthened his resolve and resilience. So he smiled at the bird and waved, then watched it break off to the south and fly away. He followed his footprints in the frost and walked back to the truck.

CHAPTER

10

The detective leaned back in the black padded office chair with his tan wingtip shoes on the old desk in front of him. He was in the spare room just down the hall from the main office where most police officers sat when they weren't on patrol. The office walls were mostly white, but they obviously hadn't been painted in years, and a yellow hue clung to them. They were bare except for the odd scuff mark or indent in the drywall. A green filing cabinet was the only other piece of furniture in this small room. On the desk was an open laptop, plugged into the nearest receptacle next to the desk phone if he needed it. The computer screen was bare, except for the glowing image of a forest lake and several small icons in the upper left corner.

He wore grey pants, a light blue shirt with a black tie, and a navy blue blazer that hid the sidearm at his right hip. His jet-black hair was combed straight back with a smooth sheen highlighted by the lights above. His dark eyes scanned the room. They were acute to every detail but revealed little if any emotion. As he sat, he glanced at the silver Seiko watch on his left wrist. He had been sent here from the "big city" to help solve two recent murders. In themselves, these killings weren't out of the ordinary. But, they had occurred only months apart in this smaller city where such things were rare. As well, they were not your usual crimes of passion, which were often solved within days. These were well planned as the lack of evidence and witnesses suggested. The local police force had gone through their usual investigative procedures, but as they had a raft of lesser crimes to deal with, they were overwhelmed and needed help.

Two minutes later, a young constable appeared at his open door.

"Sir, here are the files you asked for," he said. "The photos and statements are in each, as well as the results of the lab work."

"Thank you, constable," the detective replied. "If I need anything else, I'll come up front. Is there any hot coffee available?"

"Yes, sir. A fresh pot is ready to go."

"Thanks. I'll follow you there."

That was the best part of these smaller detachments. The officers had the advantage of being familiar with the heartbeat of almost any criminal element here. And there was always someone who took the time to bring in the occasional morning donuts and keep the coffee hot and ready. After filling the ceramic mug labelled "guest," he returned to his office, sat down, took another sip, and opened the top file.

He scanned the pages: divorced white male, forty-nine years old, lived alone and worked as a forklift driver at a local lumber mill. He had no criminal record, but there had been several incidents of suspected domestic abuse. No charges were ever pressed, and his ex-wife now lived three hundred miles away with no contact whatsoever—no phone calls, no mail, no child visitation, nothing. The photos showed his body lying in a hall, the close-ups revealing two shotgun blasts, one to the pelvic area and one to the chest. *That would pretty much do it,* he thought.

Now came the interesting part. The killer used buckshot, which is primarily used in law enforcement or for bear defence. It had no practical hunting application in this area. There were no shell casings left behind and no fresh or unusual fingerprints at the scene. None of the neighbours reported seeing or hearing a strange vehicle that night. The only evidence left behind were five small pieces of clear plastic that had been torn from the bottom of a water bottle. They had traces of burnt gunpowder. *He used a homemade silencer,* he thought. This was well planned. But what was the motive? Nothing had been taken; the victim lived from hand to mouth financially and, except for the fact he had a big mouth at work, there was nothing in his past to warrant this kind of crime. He put the file aside and reached for the other one.

Ted Saunders: eighty-four-year-old retired teacher living on the outskirts of town with his elderly wife, no criminal record. One daughter living alone, residing forty miles away, single, never married. The photos showed him on his back next to an upholstered chair, an open hardcover novel by his left side. No obvious signs of a struggle, but the medical exam revealed severe bruising on the top of the left shoulder with a shattered clavicle and humerus. This was caused by a blunt object of some kind; none was ever found at the scene. The cause of death was asphyxiation. There was no attempt at robbery. Interviewed neighbours had witnessed nothing unusual; no loud noises, no strange vehicle, nothing.

This was nuts. As far as the local police were concerned, these two murders were completely unrelated. Neither victim knew or had any dealings with the other. They came from completely different backgrounds, and the age difference was significant. Yet each killing had been meticulously planned and carried out. And that was the part that bothered him. This was going to take some time.

After parking in the driveway, the detective walked past a For Sale sign on his way to the main entrance of the house. He knocked three times on the door and waited. Almost at once, the door was opened by a slender elderly woman. He judged her to be in her late seventies or early eighties. She was neatly kempt with short grey hair, wire-rimmed glasses, and a floral print dress. *Madam Librarian,* he thought.

"You're the detective I spoke to earlier on the phone?" she asked.

"Yes, Mrs. Saunders, may I come in?"

She nodded and stepped to the side, welcoming him inside with a motion of her left hand. He walked past her into the large living room area, scanning the room as he went.

"Thank you," he said. "This shouldn't take too long. I just need to ask you a few questions about your husband's death." The words always struck him as such a stupid cliché that was heard repeatedly on most TV crime dramas.

"I understand," she replied. "Would you like a cup of coffee?"

"Yes, please. Would you mind if I had a look around the room as this is where the incident took place, I believe?"

"That would be fine." She turned, walking through the entrance to the kitchen and out of sight.

He thought this odd. It had only been two weeks since her husband's murder, but she showed no obvious signs of grief. Her age or a continued state of shock might explain this, but he sensed no great loss on her part. Stepping slowly through the room, he made a mental note of everything he could. The bookcase displayed a variety of literary works—nothing out of the ordinary for a teacher. The walls held several prints of various artists, none of which might be considered contemporary. In fact, the whole room seemed dour and dreary. He noticed the feature wall and walked toward the portraits.

There were three, each showing a family of three members at different stages in their lives. They were arranged in obvious chronological order, with the earliest to the left, where he saw a bright, smiling family with Ted standing in the middle, his arms around his wife on his left and what he surmised to be his daughter on the right. Ted and his wife appeared to be in their mid-thirties, with the daughter possibly nine or ten. The second picture in the middle showed the same family arranged in the same standing order. He estimated that this photo had been taken approximately five or six years later. Ted was still showing a wide toothy smile. Alice was smiling too, but it appeared strained or staged. The most striking difference was their daughter. There were no teeth visible in her smile as her lips were tightly pressed together. Only the corners of her mouth were slightly turned up, and her eyes seemed darker, with her brow furrowed.

It was the third one—a graduation picture—that struck home. All three stood in the same order, with Ted still smiling in a suit and tie and his wife to his left in a formal dress, her smile forced. She reminded him of Joan Crawford in *Whatever Happened to Baby Jane?* But most noticeable again was the daughter. Dressed in a blue graduation gown, she clutched her diploma to her chest and appeared stiff and uncomfortable. She wasn't smiling. Once again, her lips were closed, tightly forming a straight line across her face. There was no joy here.

"Here you are, please have a seat. I think it best that we sit in the far loveseat nearest the window." Her voice had startled him. The last picture he saw had held his gaze. It was evident that something was seriously wrong with this family.

She placed the tray of one cup of coffee, cream, and sugar perfectly in the middle of the wooden coffee table. Then she sat furthest to the right on the cushioned seat, her back straight with her legs together, crossed at the ankles. Then she pointed at the floor in front of the reading chair.

"That's where I found him," she said. Her voice was calm, as was the expression on her face. She showed no emotion at all.

Still standing, the detective reached into his jacket pocket and pulled out a small notepad and pen. Flipping the cover over, he held his pen at the ready. "You found him later in the day after you had come home from playing cards?"

"Yes, around five-thirty. I had brought some groceries in with me for supper. I knew right away something was wrong with him, but I thought it was a heart attack or stroke. So I immediately called 911. I had no idea it was a murder."

Her words, "It was a murder," not, "he was murdered," struck him as odd. Once again, he searched her eyes for any sign of angst or grief. Nothing. "So, Mrs. Saunders," he continued. "The obvious question is, can you think of anyone who might hold such a grudge against your husband that they would do something like this to him?"

She held a blank stare without focusing. "No, no one."

"Is the young lady your daughter in that picture?" he asked, pointing to the photo.

"Yes."

"Was she here at all during, before, or after?"

"No. After I called her and explained what had happened, we got together to collect his ashes at the funeral home. There was no service. You should know that we never had much contact with her since she left home years ago."

"May I ask why?"

"Sometimes families grow apart." She looked at the floor and offered nothing else.

"Does she live near here?"

"No."

This is like talking to a robot, he thought. Regardless, he believed her answers were true, even though she only stated what was necessary. In this case, he thought it best not to push, not now anyway. "Could you give me her name and contact number?" he asked.

He offered her the notepad and pen. She took them carefully, placing the notepad on the coffee table, and began to write. He reached for the coffee and took three obligatory sips. After writing, she stood up and returned the items.

He placed the coffee cup on the tray. "Thank you, Mrs. Saunders. I think that will be all for now," he said. "But if I may,

I would like to ask you one last question. I noticed your house is for sale. May I ask why?"

"When Debra, that's our daughter, left home, I wanted to move. But Ted wouldn't hear of it. So we stayed."

"Okay, thank you."

He walked toward the door, and she followed, two steps behind. After opening it, he stepped outside and turned to face her. "Goodbye, Mrs. Saunders. I'll be in touch."

"Goodbye, detective," she said and closed the door.

He got into his car and sat, motionless. If there were any secrets to unlock, it was at this end first. In all probability, these cases weren't related, but he didn't believe in coincidences. He needed to talk to the daughter.

Two days later, he sat in his office, his feet on the desk like before, with the open Saunders file on his lap and a cup of coffee in hand. Forensics had picked up nothing unusual at the scene, and this time, there was no blood present or a firearm used. Whoever did this was methodical. He was reaching for the other file when his desk phone rang.

"Yes?"

"Sir, Miss Saunders is here to see you," the receptionist answered.

"Please send her in. Thanks."

He put his coffee down as he stood up to wait. Shortly, the receptionist appeared at the door and then stood aside as a young woman walked to face him.

"Please come in, Miss Saunders." He motioned toward the plastic utility chair placed opposite his.

She sat down, placing her purse on her lap, holding it with both hands. She appeared to be in her mid-forties, possibly older. Her blonde hair was greying slightly and was cut very short, almost boyish. With her blue eyes, he considered her attractive. Yet she wore nothing to enhance her looks, no makeup at all. Her black overcoat remained buttoned up, and with grey slacks and Mary Jane shoes, she looked every bit the essence of plain.

"First, Miss Saunders, please let me express my condolences for your loss." He watched her face closely, looking for any sign of grief.

"Thank you, detective." Her eyes remained dry. Her expression showed no emotion, and, like her mother, she hadn't asked to be called by her first name.

"Miss Saunders, we are coming up empty as to who might have killed your father. Can you help us at all in that regard?"

"No, I'm sorry."

"I understand you live about forty miles from here in a small satellite community. And you're employed as a receptionist in a dentist's office?"

"Yes, that's right."

"Your mother implied that you are somewhat estranged from your immediate family with almost no contact. May I ask why?"

She hesitated, staring at the floor, then made direct eye contact and, without blinking, replied, "My father abused me."

He sat, speechless. He had expected as much, but when she offered it up, he was still caught off guard.

"It started shortly after my twelfth birthday and continued on and off for three more years."

"I see. I'm sorry. Did you try to tell anyone?"

"Not at first because I didn't understand what was happening or why my father was doing it. Then later, I went to my mother and told her. At first, she refused to believe it, but then I threatened to go to the police."

"And what was her response?"

"When I wasn't home, she confronted him. She told me this later but kept the details to herself. That's when it stopped. She asked that I keep it to myself as it would cause a scandal, he would lose his job, and we would wind up poor with no friends. Those were her words. So I did."

"And that was the end of it?"

"Pretty much. Occasionally, he would try to hug me, but I would pull away. Then after I graduated, I moved away, got a day job, and with my mother's financial help, took evening courses to get the job I have now."

"I understand you never married," said the detective. "Any long-term relationships?"

She looked down at her hands, still clutching the purse. Her knuckles were white.

"No, I've developed haphephobia. Do you know what that it?"

"The fear of touch or being touched?"

"Yes. I've had it for many years and have been in therapy with little success. But I've managed to live a reasonably happy life with friends I socialize with."

"And, you've never confided with anyone about your past?"

"Not about that," she said once more, looking down again.

"So there is really no one that you are associated with who would do this?"

"No, my circle of friends is small, and I've worked very hard to put those years behind me."

"I understand," he said. "I'm sorry for dredging it up, but it helps me know more about your father. That's all I need for now, but if I need to speak with you again, would that be okay?"

"Sure, that would be fine."

He stood up, motioning once more toward the door. "I'll see you out," he said. "Please take care, Miss Saunders."

After she left, he sat down in his office again, and a picture began to form in his mind. An abusive man can make a lot of enemies. An abusive teacher can make even more, especially from years ago.

He needed to think. The detective left his office and went back to his hotel room for the night. All paintings, vases, room service binders, or any other possible distractions were stowed from sight. He prepared to meditate. A single reading lamp mounted in the wall was the sole source of illumination. The light focussed on a small brass bell placed on the surface of an oak desk. It was the only object there.

He sat on a simple padded chair facing the dull shine from the engraved surface of the bell. The fingertips of his hands were gently pressed together in front of his face, below his eyes. Although he had the appearance of a clairvoyant, the detective had no intention of conjuring anything mystical. It was simply important to be able to focus with a clear mind.

Most would look at these killings and find no evidence to indicate they were related. He would agree. But his instincts had always served him well. This time, his intuitions forced him to look deeper. If there was a connection, it was necessary to consider the possibility that a serial killer was honing his craft. If such an individual were on the loose, they would fit a distinct profile. The homicides took place in the same township with different locations. There was a sufficient "cooling off period" after the first kill; any potential blood lust was under control to a degree. But this was where any semblance of continuity fell apart. What was the motive? There was no indication of financial gain. As far as he could tell, there was nothing visionary in the attacks—no symbols, messages, or other evidence to indicate a psychosis was in play. In fact, there was a complete lack of any hedonistic incitement at all—nothing sexual, no indication of torture, or any taunting of the authorities. No, this was personal. But why risk so much for two miserable individuals who had already paid the price for their actions?

These victims could not have been more different. Yet, their backgrounds could hold the connection that would be the key. At some point in time, they had crossed paths with this man. It was most certainly a man, as only a male would typically inflict this degree of violence, and the victims had slighted the murderer beyond redemption.

He breathed deeply before standing up to stretch. *This would take time and patience,* he thought. He had plenty of both.

CHAPTER

11

The teacher stood beside his desk, placing the day's marking in a file folder, then into his briefcase. It was snowing outside, and the windows were lined with frost. He noticed how dark it was now at the end of each working day. This was not his favourite time of year. The darkness kept everyone housebound with only the thought of the Christmas break and the season's celebrations bringing any real joy. Even worse, it was almost impossible to run or cycle this time of year, and he had come to depend on the pain and pleasure of both. Now he would have to find some sort of suitable replacement until spring came again. He didn't worry about Christmas itself. There would be several social occasions that he could attend and mingle with friends. He would spend Christmas Eve and Day alone, making the best of it like he always had. Those days were for family, and he had none. He refused to intrude on others, even though they would often invite him to dinner. A couple of times, he and Simon had met for Christmas dinner, but they both agreed that it was a pathetic attempt at best, so they had decided to abandon the idea.

With his briefcase in hand, he reached for his coat and car snowbrush and headed for the classroom door. He was stopped short as Constance poked her head through the opening and smiled.

"Hey, you!" she said.

"Hey there," he replied.

She took a step in through the doorway. She was smartly dressed in a blue business suit, looking every bit the corporate executive. With her long hair and strategically applied makeup, she was as attractive as ever. "I've got a question for you," she continued. "The staff Christmas party is coming up, and I was hoping you would be there so that I could chase you around the dance floor."

"Ah, the wench grows bold!" he said with a chuckle.

"Smartass. You know you are one tough nut to crack. You hide behind your professional exterior and never let anyone close. What deep dark secrets have you got buried away?"

The comment hit full force. What could he say? *Well, since I've iced two very ugly individuals over the past two months, you might not really want to look my way,* he thought. His sardonic wit always came up first. But, he had been pinned into a corner and needed to get himself out as gently as possible.

"You know I've been like this since you first met me. I guess it comes with living alone for some time now. But looking at you dressed like that can break apart any tough cookie." Whoops! Encouragement. He knew it as soon as he said it.

"Well, far be it from me to rock your world too much. But, you should really show up and let loose a little."

He breathed out a soft sigh of relief. She had saved him. "Absolutely," he answered. "It'll be fun."

"Okay, I'll hold you to it." She smiled, turned, and walked out.

He paused for a moment, then reached into his briefcase and lifted the flap of a hidden sleeve and unzipped it. Reaching in, he felt the metal of the handgun, gripping it firmly. "Keep it close," he told himself. "You cannot take anyone else down with you." It was a sobering reminder. He removed his hand and grabbed the briefcase and snowbrush. It was time to go home.

On the night of the party, he arrived shortly after eight. Wearing a new jacket, shirt, and dress pants, he walked through the doors of the rented hall and stopped to survey the scene.

There were tables and chairs placed in a circle around a small dance floor with a disco ball that someone had scrounged from a garage somewhere, hanging from the ceiling. In a corner just outside the tables was a bar. He had arrived fifty minutes late—fashionably late—hoping he would not stand out as a single wallflower. He observed the different groups methodically, looking for Constance, but she was nowhere in sight. *Odd,* he thought, considering she had gone to the trouble to make sure he came. He made a casual walk around the tables, smiling, waving to various colleagues as he went. He reached the bar at the same time as Walt Simmons, who approached him.

"Hey, Walt, where's Constance tonight?" he asked. "I thought she would have been here by now."

Walt signalled the bartender for a drink. "You probably haven't heard," he said. "Her nephew died last night of an apparent drug overdose."

"He what?"

"Yeah, I guess he was at a party last night with a group of other high school kids, and someone was passing out something nasty. Several of them succumbed. That's pretty much all I know. I don't know how badly hurt the others are, but Constance found out in the early hours of this morning. She's pretty badly shook up."

"I didn't know she had a nephew here."

"He's not a local boy. He lives north of here in Manchester Creek. It was her sister's son, and they were pretty close; only seventeen years old."

The bartender handed Walt a drink. "What can I get for you, sir?" he asked.

The teacher put his hand on the bar and nodded toward Walt. "Whatever you poured him will be fine, thanks," he replied. He looked down at the floor.

"Well, that's more shitty news we have to deal with," he said. "I should probably call her soon."

"Good idea," Walt said and then put his hand on the teacher's shoulder. "Sorry to put a crimp in your evening."

"It's okay, thanks."

Walt picked up his drink, turned toward the tables, and walked away. The teacher reached for his and held it in his hands with both elbows on the bar. He stared at the ice cubes floating in the glass. *It never stops,* he thought. It was just one more pile of garbage. He paid no attention to the lights reflecting off the facets of the circling ball. The music was just noise thumping in his ears. He pictured Constance at home, trying to come to terms with her grief. She didn't need this. And, there was no point in staying here. He lifted his glass, poured the drink down his throat in one swallow, and put the glass down on the bar while turning for the door. He walked with his head down, avoiding eye contact. Next, he was sitting in his truck with the motor running, still parked.

As he sat huddled toward the steering wheel, waiting for the air to warm, a new thought crept into his mind. Was he a curse, a person who carried an ugly malevolence with him that would pick and choose which innocent being to inflict with pain? Did it use this to force him to act, like a mean kid prodding a vicious dog with a stick? For as much as he didn't want to believe it was possible, he couldn't discount it either. Most people had all kinds of choices in life. Events could be altered or futures manipulated. But not for him. Every possible diversion was blocked off, every occurrence sticking in his throat, impossible to avoid or ignore. He slammed his hand on the steering wheel, then put his truck in gear.

The detective sat in a padded chair facing the large wooden desk in front of him. The office surrounding him was spacious, and habit forced him to look at the furnishings. The walls were mostly bare except for one painting of a seascape to his left. On the wall across the desk from him was an assortment of framed university degrees. *Very ornate,* he thought. A tall stalked plant of some kind stood in the corner to his right. Its large flat leaves drooped to the sides. He tried to think of what type of wood the desk was made from, but the diversion did him no good. So he pulled a pen from his pocket and continued to sit, pulling the cap off and on. He hated waiting but now had no choice. This would be a meeting that might finally shed some light on this investigation.

The sound of footsteps coming down the hall alerted him. A tall woman entered through the open door and sat in the plush black chair below the framed accomplishments. She was middle-aged, although it would be difficult to guess exactly, and wore circular dark-rimmed glasses. Dressed in a fashionable green skirt and matching jacket, she obviously held some rank in this building. He found himself sitting across the desk from Susan Richards, the director of personnel for the local school district. She held a manila folder in her hand. She leaned forward and opened it on her desk.

"Thank you for your patience, detective," she said. "It took a little bit of time, but we found the employment file for Ted Saunders." She said this in a professional voice, expressing no sadness or regret at his death.

"Thank you," he said. "Could you tell me how many years he worked in your school district?"

She surveyed the file and flipped the first page over. "Sixteen years," she said without looking up. "Then, in 1979, he was transferred to a nearby district."

"Transferred? May I ask why?"

"His file lists the use of excessive force during a disciplinary incident involving an eleven-year-old male student."

"Could you be more specific, please?"

"During a physical education class, Mr. Saunders threw a basketball at an inattentive student, striking him in the face."

"Was the boy injured?"

"Yes, a bleeding nose and split upper lip."

The detective grimaced. "Sounds excessive to me, too. Were there any other complaints regarding incidents of suspected abuse in his file?"

"There are three other specific complaints documented here. Two involving excessive shaking of students and one of hair being pulled. His principal at the time wrote a letter of reprimand, which I have a copy of here."

"May I read it, please?"

She handed the letter over, and he read it carefully, then returned it.

"Ms. Richards, do you think it's possible that other incidents of this nature were not reported?"

"Judging from his file, I think it's quite possible," she said. "Please understand that parents were very hesitant to lodge complaints during this time for two reasons. Teachers were held in high regard, so questioning their actions usually never happened. Corporal punishment was still on the books. Also, parents and students were often afraid of possible repercussions of such actions."

"Yes, I remember," said the detective. "Ms. Richards, due to the nature of Ted Saunders's death and the complexity of our investigation, could I ask you for two things?"

"I'll do my best, detective."

"First, could I get a copy of the file in front of you?"

"Not a problem."

"Second, could I get the class lists of students Saunders taught while in your school district?"

"That will take a little bit of time. All our older school records were copied onto microfiche and then later converted to digital files. It will take about a day to spring the personnel to retrieve what you're looking for, but we'll get it for you. And, you'll need document management software to search through it."

"Thank you very much, Ms. Richards. Your help is greatly appreciated." He stood up and offered his hand, which she shook with a firm yet pleasant grip.

"You are very welcome. If we can be of further assistance, let us know."

"I will." He smiled, then walked through the office door.

Four hours later, he was at his desk again. He had gone through the entire file, and after listening to the daughter the other day, a none too pretty image of Ted Saunders had emerged. He got up and walked into the main office. A young officer sat at his desk, busy with his paperwork. The detective walked over.

"I understand you headed up the initial investigation into the shotgun slaying?"

The officer looked up. "Yes, sir, that's right."

"I've got another job for you. I need you to go to the employer of this Clyde character and get a list of anyone he worked with at that mill. Concentrate on the individuals that were part of his shift."

"Yes, sir."

"Then comes the fun part." The detective smiled. The young officer sat upright, a look of concern on his face. "I'm getting the class lists of all the students Saunders taught while working here. I want you to cross-reference the names on your list with the ones from the school district and look for similarities."

The officer's eyes got wider. "Sir, that's going to take a fair bit of time."

"Yes, it will," said the detective. "But this is the part they never told you about at the academy. All that TV crap you see on *Hawaii Five-O* and *Magnum P.I.* is all a pile of bullshit. It takes a lot of grunt work to do the job right. Don't worry, I'll make sure you get some help."

"Yes, sir. Thank you, sir."

The detective nodded and headed for the coffee pot.

CHAPTER

12

She answered the phone on the fourth ring.

"Hello?"

"Hi. How are you doing?"

"I thought you might call." Constance recognized his voice. "I'm okay, I guess, just have a bad case of the blues. Did you go to the party?"

"In and out pretty fast," the teacher replied. "Walt told me what happened. That put a damper on my evening. I really didn't feel like making small talk with the others, so I sucked back my cocktail and hit the road."

She forced a chuckle. "Same old, same old with you."

"What can I say? But, never mind me. Can you explain what happened, or is it still too raw?"

She sat down at a table and placed both elbows flat. Her fingers rested on her forehead, holding back her dark hair. "My nephew, seventeen years old, winds up at a house party. Then someone shows up with what was supposed to be ecstasy and starts passing it around. It wasn't long before people started dropping like flies. So, someone called 911. They managed to revive everyone except my nephew. He was pronounced dead at the hospital. The police suspect that whatever it was, it was laced with fentanyl."

"Manchester Creek isn't a big town. How do they get a hold of this stuff?"

"I spoke with the police after. They explained that the drug trade uses local biker wannabes. They make the rounds for the larger gangs, spreading this garbage from town to town."

"It never ends," he sighed. "So what are you going to do next? Do you have someone to help you through this?"

"Yes, I'm leaving tomorrow to see my sister and spend the holidays with her. Great Christmas, huh?"

"I'm glad you'll be with family. And I'm sorry for your loss. Anyway, I just wanted to check in, make sure you were okay."

"Thanks, I'm going to start packing now. But, I appreciate the call, and I'll see you back at school, okay?"

"You bet. Take care." He hung up, put the phone down, and sat quietly without moving, his mind conjuring up the images of grief-stricken parents lined up at a hospital. Reaching down to his right, he picked up his briefcase from the floor. *Maybe this Christmas will be more eventful than usual,* he thought.

It was two in the morning. A dull glow came from the open laptop resting on the kitchen table. The teacher sat staring at the images and text that scrolled past his vision. He had been at this for five hours now. The search engine gave him site after site, and as he fought through the repetition, he managed to glean new information at each stop. Eventually, a clearer picture of the drug networks began to emerge. Just like any corporate entity, this underworld employed a strict hierarchy in command and distribution.

The dirty work was done at a street level, where drugs and money were exchanged daily. Middlemen then acted as go-betweens, retrieving the cash and resupplying the dealers. They then sent the money further up the food chain, where it was collected, then laundered. Eventually, the clean money was invested in legitimate businesses. The bosses were very well insulated. The best the police could do for now was intercept activity on the streets. They had been trying to break into the higher echelons, but informants willing to break ranks were impossible to find. The sentences given out for convictions weren't severe enough for anyone to risk retribution.

Nothing new here, he thought. Then he stopped at a press release. It showed a photo of the back of a man being led into a building by two police officers, one on each side. His head was hunched forward with long, brown, straight hair that reached just below the collar of his black leather jacket. What stood out was the emblem in the middle of the man's jacket. It was a depiction of a garish, troll-like head with fangs and horns. In bold letters above the image was the word Demons. The teacher read the article below the picture.

Police lead Alex Russel into the courthouse for sentencing on drug-related charges. Mr. Russel was convicted last month after being charged with possession of narcotics with intent to traffic. Mr. Russel is a member of a bike gang known as the Demons, an alleged, low-level criminal group involved in drug activities. Police have stated that this group is one of several believed to be working the drug trade inland and under the direction of coastal operatives.

The teacher examined the picture again. He wasn't sure if the emblem was threatening or comical. Obviously, whoever had put the image together was not a gifted artist and had stolen one too many ideas from the comic books he read. Still, they had established themselves as a menace. He tried to continue his search, but fatigue forced his head onto his arm already on the table.

It was the cemetery. How he got there, he didn't know. The sky was completely dark, devoid of any stars. But a yellowish full moon lit up the shallow layer of snow on the ground. The surrounding trees were completely bare, with no leaves or needles, and appeared as black silhouettes, menacing the graves they stood over. He wore no jacket, only nondescript pants and a shirt of some kind. His feet were bare, yet he didn't feel the cold. There were no headstones this time, only short white crosses spaced evenly in rows.

In the distance, he noticed a hunched figure kneeling over a dark shape. He walked forward slowly, the snow barely reaching the level of his toes. As he approached the figure, he realized it was a child on her knees, leaning over a body lying beneath her, its legs straight and together, arms by its side. One of the crosses stood near its head. A sense of dread came over him. He wanted to turn and walk back, but he couldn't. His methodic steps continued. Finally, he stopped short of the kneeling figure. It was a girl. Her face was hidden, but he recognized the brown hair, cut short just below her ears, even with her collar. The white shirt she wore was patterned with red flowers. He had seen it many times. She was crying softly. The body on the ground was a young man dressed in a black shirt and pants. The skin on his face was pale, and his lifeless eyes stared at the moon. His uncombed dark hair lay back over the top of his head, splayed in the snow.

The fear he felt began to ease, yet he refused to walk any further.

"Emily?" he said, his voice barely more than a whisper.

She didn't lift her head, just continued to sob with her hands placed on the young man's arm.

A breeze began to blow across his face, and he looked to both sides, but nothing moved. He lowered his eyes to her once more. "Emily?" he said again, slightly louder this time. It was then the raven came gliding in and landed softly on her shoulder. It held its wings high, shaking them gently before folding them at its sides. Its black feathers were aligned perfectly, reflecting the moonlight like a halo around them both. The raven turned its head to the right, one yellow eye looking at him with purpose. Emily lifted her head away from the young man and her eyes met his, her face as radiant as the last time he saw her. She smiled as she always did, her brown eyes looking at him with childlike affection. Any uncertainty and angst he had left disappeared.

"For me," she said. Then she lowered her head and stroked the young man's forehead and hair softly. She paused, then looked up at him once more. "For us."

The teacher awoke sitting upright, still in his seat, his arm numb at his side. His breathing was slow and measured, as was his heartbeat. It was a dream that most would have recognized as a nightmare, but the teacher would only replay it over in his mind, etching it firmly in his memory. It was still dark out; only the ambient streetlight came in through his windows. He had no idea what time it was, but there was no point in trying to go back to sleep now. He got up and went to the bathroom sink to wash his face.

The inside of the bar was dark, with only the lights above a stage providing any illumination to the four corners. The stage was in the center of this establishment, with a mosaic of abused wooden tables spread off to the sides. Metal framed café chairs, a throwback to the seventies, were scattered between the tables, no one having bothered to arrange them properly from the previous night. The coverings of most were ripped or split, revealing stained foam cushioning beneath the cloth. The walls were a dark wood of some kind, the only decoration being two neon-lit Budweiser signs hanging at opposite ends of the room. To one side, a wooden counter stood out from the wall with an unshaven grey-haired bartender standing behind, arranging glasses next to three decorated taps positioned above a stainless-steel sink. The smell of stale beer permeated the air throughout.

It was two o'clock in the afternoon, and besides the bartender, only three other people occupied the place. An older blonde stripper hung on to the chrome pole in the center of the stage, pivoting in a circle to the sound of the Rolling Stones's "Honky Tonk Woman." Her pendulous breasts hung low as the years had begun to show. But she was a professional, taking great pains to present herself as best she could, her thick black lashes set in front of blue eyelids and bright red lipstick highlighting her smile. With a green sequined G-string and black high heels, she let go of the pole and strutted over to a male patron sitting by himself next to the stage. She bent down, presenting her ample buttocks to the old man looking up at her. An oversized, frayed tweed jacket hung from his bony shoulders, his long white hair combed back over his ears. He, too, hadn't shaved in days. He clutched his empty glass, and although his limit for the day was spent, he still managed to place a five-dollar bill into the strap over her hip.

In the farthest corner sat the third person. He had chosen his seat strategically, his back to the wall, with the shadows making recognition difficult at a distance. He was a large man, pear-shaped to the waist, barely managing to fit in his chair. His head was clean-shaven with the green image of marijuana leaves tattooed into the skin in the back of his skull, their stems hidden in the skin folds above his neck. A black goatee surrounded his mouth that was set in a scowl. His right leg was propped on the opposite knee, displaying a brown leather boot adorned with a chain stirrup. A stained grey T-shirt and torn blue jeans with a studded black belt completed his attire. The table he sat at was bare, but the chair next to him was draped with a black leather jacket highlighted with a patch bearing the image of a troll.

He was Alvin Wagstaff, a name he hated with a passion and kept hidden as much as possible. To the members of his gang, he was known as Bear, and the mention of any other name sent him into a rage. Not that he intended to engage physically with anyone. No, Alvin had grown up the only child of a single mother. As a plump kid, he endured the indignities of cruel classmates who often ran circles around him, yelling, "Porky Pig." But eventually, the fates smiled on young Alvin. A growth spurt had him entering high school six feet tall, and even though he was still overweight, he found out quickly that size was a big equalizer. With a blank expression, to which he later added a hateful frown when needed, those around him decided he was best left alone. Friendship eluded him as well, but that was fine. As long as the torment stopped, he didn't have to engage in any of the after-school physical challenges that adolescent young men often used to establish themselves. At sixteen, Alvin decided he had had enough of school and moved north to live with an aunt who found him a job delivering building supplies.

He was happy to be an unknown in a new town, and it wasn't long before he found others like himself, marginalized loners craving an image of respect. Soon, drunken banter led them to acquire motorcycles together with the biker lifestyle that went with it. Alvin had finally found himself. Being the largest of the group, it followed that it would be his gang, and the Demons were born.

The music ended. The blonde stripper covered herself with a robe and walked off the stage. At the far left of the room, the door opened, and two jacketed members walked through, stopping to allow their eyes to adjust to the dim light. Alvin raised his hand, and they made their way over to his table, signalling the bartender as they walked by. Both wore long hair and goatees as well, one brown, the other a dirty blonde colour.

"Yo, Bear," said the blonde one. "What's up?"

"Max . . . Joey," he replied, acknowledging both of them with a nod. "Sit down, and I'll tell you."

They sat opposite him, Max to the left and Jesse to the right, scratching the brown stubble on his chin. Neither spoke but waited like obedient dogs on their master. Then the bartender came over and placed a pint of beer in front of each. "When they're empty, we'll take a reload," said Alvin, staring at the older man with no sign of gratitude.

"We need to meet here from now on," he continued, "or someplace like it. The heat has been snooping around since that stupid kid croaked in Manchester Creek. So from now on, no operational calls, and that includes cell phones. No conversations in public either. Who knows, they might be able to pick up what you say from a block away. When we talk business, it will be at a different spot, each time inside, so they can't bug a table or some other stupid shit."

"So how long do we have to put up with this crap?" said Max. "It's like being in some kind of electronic lockup."

"It's just when we need to talk business, dickhead! You can use your phone, or video game, or whatever the hell you want. Just don't screw up when it comes to our trade. *Capiche?*" He decided it was necessary to occasionally raise his voice to the "dogs" to keep them in line.

Max slid down in his chair, his eyes lowered. "Jesus, I was just askin'. You don't have to get so pissed off."

Joey just sat slouched, clutching his beer in both hands like a baby bottle. He remained silent.

Alvin leaned toward Max. "Listen, our contacts on the coast are getting nervous. If they feel the pressure, then we feel the pressure. So we gotta keep a low profile for a while. Don't panic. When we get the word, we can fire up the dealing again."

Max looked up again. "Fuck 'em. We should just go out on our own. We could find our own supplier and keep all the cash ourselves."

"And we could find ourselves hanging from a tree with our throats cut. These are not people you can screw over and get away with it. Our territory is their territory. And they don't like mistakes. It was bad enough that Russel got sent away, the fuckup. But we still have the three of us and the other three. Where are they anyway?"

Joey spoke. "Bobby and Frank are working. Murphy had to take his old lady to the doctor." He lowered his head and continued drinking.

"Okay, you two pass the word along. No phones! Remember that, okay? When I hear more, I'll let you know. Besides, it'll be spring and time for the big jamboree in a couple of months. Then you guys can cut loose, maybe even get lucky and get your ends wet. C'mon. Let's shoot some pool."

The teacher sat on the concrete floor of his basement. The door to the gun cabinet was open, boxes of ammunition were stacked neatly off to his right. In his hands was the assault rifle. The cement was cold and uncomfortable, but he didn't mind. This was how he often sat as a child, cross-legged on the floor, field stripping each weapon the old man handed him, then cleaning each for inspection. He may have seemed childlike in this posture to someone else observing these actions now, but there was sound logic in this method. Every part could be removed and placed in sequential order in front of him for reassembly. The ammunition was easily accessible, the empty magazines at the ready.

It had not been an easy couple of months following the Christmas break. The students and staff appeared to wander the halls in a funk. Maybe it was the time of year, but the looks on their faces hinted at a joyless existence. No one argued this point, most putting it down to the post-Christmas blues, suggesting things would get better in the spring. It was hardest to see Constance. Her daily appearance lacked the flair of a few months earlier. When they happened upon each other, her smiles were forced, and one- or two-word greetings were all she had to offer. Then again, he thought that maybe his observations were exaggerated. Could it all be just an excuse? Was he looking for an opportunity to plan the operation that brought him to sit alone, choosing his weapons, sorting and counting cartridges? The recurring dream that brought him here was still fresh and vivid in his memory. It served to motivate him, banishing the boredom and monotony of the winter days. In truth, he relished the idea of hunting down another vestige of human trash. He had reached the point where others' transgressions, no matter how distant, could easily light the fuse that would send him into action.

He pulled the trigger guard down, releasing the firing mechanism, and placed it first in line. The breach and barrel came off easily. Finally, the firing pin and wooden stock were placed in order. He reached into the open cabinet, pulling out a black synthetic stock with the feature he wanted. The rear portion behind the pistol grip could pivot on a locking pin, allowing the whole piece to fold neatly, transforming the rifle into the compact weapon he wanted. He reached for two thirty-round magazines. Their long, curved shape would add to the menacing appearance of the firearm. However, such appearances were secondary in nature and belied their brilliant design. Both could hold thirty military cartridges, but he would put only twenty-six in each. This would reduce the strain on the spring in the magazine that lifted the bullets into place. Again, he marvelled at how well his memory served him as his hands worked smoothly and without hesitation. If nothing else, brutality in itself could also be a teacher—one that would never allow anyone to forget.

This had been a practice run. After reassembling the rifle and emptying the magazines, he locked it all away and returned upstairs. In the middle of the living room, a new, larger backpack was lying on the couch. On the floor beside it was a complete outfit, one that was functional yet nondescript. A green, army surplus field jacket centred these clothes. Its rumpled, faded look with numerous pockets wouldn't draw attention and could hide any number of accessories. He had considered cargo pants, but he'd rather look like a hobo instead of a grunt. Jeans were a better choice. Hiking boots and a brimmed bush hat completed the ensemble. Off to the side were his pair of binoculars, a safety kit, and a compact, one-man, self-inflating life raft. Later, he would add matches, a space blanket, and a prepaid cell phone.

The teacher sat at his kitchen table, scotch in hand, looking carefully at an unfolded road map. He now considered his kitchen the war room, often laughing at the thought. It was only logical that if one were going to plan any number of ambushes, it would be easiest where one was the most comfortable. He smiled and looked up. Maybe the letters HQ should be hung above the kitchen door. But it was best not to get too cocky and just focus on the task at hand. He looked down at the map again.

It was amazing how arrogant people could lay the groundwork for their own demise. In his web search, he had discovered the scheduling of a major biker event. The organizing gang had called it the Sin City Jamboree. It was designed to be a three-day booze-fueled festival near the border. Of course, the page advertising this was festooned with numerous black skulls, snakes, iron crosses—the usual images found in any tattoo parlour—and lewd photographs of past events. More importantly, this site had given the location and the best rides to get there. These highway routes were deemed the shortest, most scenic, or fastest ways to travel to the site.

The teacher knew it was impossible to wage this level of war against the whole organization by himself. But he could put a dent in their business dealings by hitting where he could. One of the suggested routes travelled along a quiet highway he and Simon had used to go fishing as teenagers. The highway followed their favourite river, with a secluded camping area the forest service put in as a rest stop. The jamboree organizers suggested this would be a good halfway stop for riders coming from the north. With luck, the Demons would come from there. Yes, he would focus on the riders wearing the idiotic patch. If others got in the way, then collateral damage was a distinct possibility.

The event was now two weeks away, coinciding with the beginning of spring break. He held his glass high, then drained the last of the scotch and melted ice. Oh, lucky man.

CHAPTER

13

The side of the highway was dry and dusty, the remnants of winter sanding taking flight whenever a vehicle passed by. It was a typical spring day. Scattered clouds passed overhead, keeping the temperature pleasant. A breeze came and went, warm and sweet, carrying the scent of the sunflowers that grew on the hillside above the pavement. Other than the odd passing car, there was no one else here, just one lone man, dressed like a drifter with his pack at his feet and an extended thumb, hoping for a ride.

The teacher had started this trek just as the sun was rising. It had taken three hours to reach this part of the highway, walking with his head down, the floppy brim of his hat covering the upper part of his face. Sunglasses would have helped, but he didn't want to appear as anything but a simple backpacker travelling the country. Instead, he wore dark-rimmed glasses, the unused part of his Halloween disguise. It was twelve klicks to the junction of the old highway that followed the river, and the campsite was slightly less than thirty kilometres past that. With luck, he could make his destination before dark.

It was Thursday, two days before the beginning of the jamboree. Phoning in sick was the only way to have these days available before the weekend and the beginning of spring break. The thought of this "theft of time" was somewhat disconcerting, but he needed to be in place before the riders came. He staked his success on the premise that they would travel on Friday and spend the night at the campsite. Of course, he could be wrong, and this would all be an exercise in futility. But, his gut told him otherwise. The first chance to mount their wheels and blast down any highway to a party after being snowbound would be impossible to resist.

At ten-thirty, an older red and white pickup passed him and slowed to a stop on the gravel shoulder. The burnt-out brake light, a rusted tailgate, and wheel wells suggested it had seen better days. The teacher picked up his pack, ran up to the passenger door, and opened it. A portly middle-aged man with overalls, a dirty John Deere ball cap, and a handlebar moustache smiled at him.

"Thanks for stopping. I could sure use a lift," he said.

"Not a problem at all," replied the man. His hands on the steering wheel were large, tanned brown, and heavily wrinkled. They reminded the teacher of ginger root. "Where you headed?"

"I'm going south, then into the hills not far from here. It was a long winter, so I thought I'd take some time to wander the outdoors and breathe some clean air. If you could get me to the junction where the old highway splits off, that would be great."

"Up along the river?"

"Yup. I'll spend tonight at the old campsite past the junction."

"Well, my good man, this is your lucky day. My ranch is fifty miles south of the junction. It'll be easy to get you where you're goin'. Throw your bag in the back and hop in."

The teacher picked up his pack, placed it in the truck box next to a wooden crate, and hopped onto the vinyl seat. The door closed with a metallic clunk that he hadn't heard in years. The cab had the smell of old straw, while the oily grime that clogged the man's fingernails had darkened most of the dash and bench seat. Scattered nuts and bolts were wedged between the dash and windshield. A screwdriver and wrench rested on the seat between them. The man grabbed the manual shifter, found low gear, then gently eased out onto the pavement.

The teacher decided that some pleasant, disarming small talk would help maintain his persona of innocence.

"What's in the box?" he asked.

"My new irrigation pump," replied the driver. "Mostly, I range my cattle, but I have some cultivated land where I grow what winter feed I can. The rest I buy to keep them going during the snowfall. How about you? You rich or somethin' and don't have to work?"

"Ha! Wouldn't that be nice?" he said. "No, I got laid off after twenty-five years with the same company. I got a little severance money to keep me going for a while. But staying in my house all winter to save cash brought on some cabin fever. So this will be a cheap way to get out for a while and clear my thoughts; maybe dream up a new battle plan to earn a living."

The driver shook his head. "Ain't that the way it is these days? No sense of loyalty. You bust a gut for some company, then when you get older, they throw you out with a smile and a handshake. Not me. I worked my whole life on farms. After I inherited my stake from my parents, I saved until I could buy the forty acres next to me. Yup, I'm my own boss, don't have to kiss nobody's backside. And, someday, when I croak, they can plant me there too. You got a wife and kids?"

"No kids, been divorced for quite a while now. But it does make this whole job loss thing a little easier. I just have to look after myself."

They reached the junction in short order and started down the narrow old highway. It was only two lanes of worn pavement with a faded yellow line that meandered down the middle. After passing a few small farms to get to this point, there was only forest and pavement from here on. The trees were old pines, their black, scaly bark bearing the marks of old scars and frost cracks.

The crowns bore the sagging broom-shaped branches that were a sign of the mistletoe infection that often plagued these decadent stands. Beneath the trees, the pine grass grew in a lush carpet with buffalo berry shrubs scattered wherever the light managed to reach the forest floor. Off to his right in the distance, he could catch glimpses of the river that followed this stretch southeast. Soon it disappeared, lost among the gnarly pines.

They drove in silence while he stared out the side window, noticing that the farther they went, the more the terrain sloped down toward the river. The highway had been stabilized by larger boulders and rocks to keep it from sliding. The mountains became a little steeper, and in the distance, he could see the hills where, years ago, Simon would ride his dirt bike for hours while he fished the river. He knew this area well. The memories of those carefree days brought a warmth to him that made him feel whole.

"So what'll you do when you get back?"

The voice startled him from his daydream, and he faced the highway once more.

"I'm not sure," he replied. "To start, I guess I'll take whatever I can get, then maybe try and find something secure." He thought it best to be evasive and hoped the driver wouldn't ask about a specific occupation that would force him to lie. "But I don't want to leave where I live. Been there a long time. It's my home."

The driver grabbed the peak of his ball cap and lifted it to reveal a mostly bald pate with straggling remnants of hair pasted into place. He scratched the top of his head, then set the cap firmly back into place. The teacher felt good driving with him. Here was someone who only wanted to exist without strife or grief. He had worked hard, and the honesty that emanated from him was a welcome comfort. He asked for no help yet gave it without question. The values he carried were simple but strong and fortified him in times of hardship. The teacher envied this man. His was a life worth fighting for.

Ten minutes later, the teacher could see they were approaching a dirt road to the left. It lay at right angles to the highway and disappeared quickly into the woods. On the far side of the entrance was a square, wooden sign mounted on two four-inch posts. It read: Slade River Recreation Site. The driver geared down, easing the old truck to the side of the highway.

"Well, here you are, friend."

"Thank you so much," replied the teacher. "You're a good man, better than most I've come across lately. I wish you well." He extended his right hand that the man shook with a firm, respectful grip. He opened the door and hopped onto the gravel, reaching back to grab his pack.

The driver looked at him. "You know, I can tell you're a pretty good guy yourself. Just keep pluggin' away, and the world will turn."

"Thanks. You take care," he said and then closed the door, savouring the ancient clunk one last time. The driver reached for the shifter and eased out onto the pavement again. The teacher waved, then stood, watching the old vehicle make its way south. He shifted his pack higher onto his shoulders and walked toward the dirt road. Stopping on the yellow line in the middle, he surveyed the route south. It lay in a straight line for about three hundred yards and then began a turn to the left. He knew instinctively this would be his spot.

As he made his way along the rutted road into the bush, he looked carefully to both sides. The pine grass stood about a foot high; the rest of the undergrowth was sparse and scattered. There was almost no deadfall to either side. It had probably been cut up as firewood at the campsite. He walked off to the left along the last stretch to the open area. The ground was soft, almost entirely lacking in twigs or other wood remnants. There was little chance that a footstep would crack a fallen branch and give away his position.

He reached the opening in the forest. It was circular, two hundred feet wide at best. Any vegetation had been beaten down by tents or vehicles, with only stubby or flat weeds remaining. In the center was a ring of small boulders making up a fire pit. Charcoal and half-burned remnants of wood lay cold in the center, mixed in with broken bottles and wrinkled scraps of tin foil. A half-dozen short lengths of a pine log, used as seats, lay scattered nearby. Set about twenty feet into the trees at the far edge was a pit toilet, its door battered and left ajar.

He estimated the entire length of the road to this point at slightly more than a hundred yards. The thought of spending the night here crossed his mind but was quickly dismissed. Even though it might be somewhat more comfortable, there was a chance that someone might decide to use this area. It was best to set up his ambush and bivouac near the river. If anyone were to arrive, it would be easy to recon the site to size up an adversary.

He went back onto the edge of the pavement, walking to the turn in the highway. The white boulders to the side were large, most exceeding three feet across. Mixed in were an assortment of smaller rocks with large invasive weeds sprouting wherever they could. He reached his spot. From here, it was a straight line to the turnoff with a slow series of lazy turns past him to the south. His line of sight in both directions was excellent, with almost a half-mile visibility to each side. Now came the most important need; a place to shoot. It didn't take long to find. High up on the gentle bank, a large potato-shaped boulder was stuck in the gravel, its narrow end pointing up. Next to it, a smaller rock, half its size, butted against it. With a mostly flat top, it would provide the bench he needed. He smiled. Yes, indeed, the universe was unfolding as it should.

He stepped down the bank, crouching where the two stones met. This was perfect. He could easily track an oncoming target from left to right, and even if he was spotted, a rider would be moving far too fast to avoid a bullet. Still, something was wrong, something he could not pinpoint. It wasn't observable as everything so far fell into place as planned. This was more like a premonition, a feeling of impending danger. He went over the plan again; everything seemed fine. *Simple, nervous apprehension,* he thought. This was going to involve a lot of movement, something he hadn't encountered so far. Bullets would fly, one after the other, and they would not stop until he was satisfied the task was complete. He closed his eyes and shook his head. "Let's go to the water," he said to himself. "It won't be far."

He stopped at the edge of the riverbank, letting his eyelids relax once more. It was the smell that sent him back in time, the mix of fresh running water, the aroma of the forest. A soft breeze carried this to him, along with the sound of rippling water and distant birds calling. It was as if he had never left. He sat down on the moss, watching the riffles make their own pictures on the surface. The water flowed steadily but not fast. At the edges, it was clear, showing the worn river rock at the bottom. A little farther out, it became a mix of blue and green, deeper and hiding the trout that had challenged him those many years ago.

The pack slid off his shoulders, and he leaned back, resting on the nylon, gazing at the clouds through the tree canopy. The premonition was still with him. Maybe it was a warning. Here he was, after so many years, savouring this small slice of heaven. Yet, he fully intended to spill a lot of blood on the pavement nearby. Was this an act of desecration? Was it simple guilt that would not let this hint of peril go away? He could just leave. But, without a doubt, the powers that sent him here would invade his sleep until the job was done.

He shook his head once more and squeezed his eyelids shut until they wrinkled. "Okay, enough of this bullshit," he said to himself. "No more 'what ifs,' or 'maybes,' or 'buts.'" It was time to prepare. He unbuckled the rain flap of the pack and slacked off the release cord that had closed the opening. The black gloves sat on top. He put these on, then reached in farther, pulling out the folded raft. After fixing the CO_2 canister, he yanked out its pin and listened to the gas rush into the yellow, rubberized tubing. Within a minute, it was fully inflated and placed against a tree near the water's edge. The three-piece paddle was assembled, then placed in the raft. This would be his escape. The old trapper's cabin would be on the other side of the river, no more than five or six miles downstream. It was where Simon used to drop him off to fish before racing back into the woods far up the mountain. The raft was only big enough for him to flop into with his pack, but it would take him to safety without expending much energy. Once at the cabin, he would lay low for a while until it was safe to walk out back to the highway and make his way home again.

He walked halfway back to the highway and stopped to look for a place to spend the night. A moss-covered flat spot next to a large pine caught his eye. This was as good a site as any, he decided, and placed the pack against the tree, opening it once more. Reaching in, he pulled out the components of the assault rifle in order and pieced them together. His binoculars and two curved black magazines were the last to come out, taped together to make a reload quick and easy. The magazines themselves were already stacked with cartridges. It would just be a matter of releasing the empty one, then turning the pair over to load the second if needed. But if his marksmanship held, one would be enough.

With the loaded rifle resting against the pack, he kicked out a section of moss three feet from his tree for a fire pit. He filled his canteen at the river and began a search for enough dry wood to build a small fire for the night. With everything in place, he pulled two protein bars from his pocket before sitting down to wait and listen.

The rest of that day and night passed as if the world was deserted. Only one vehicle, probably a car, had driven by just before dark. Once the darkness settled in, an eerie stillness enveloped him. But, it was more of a comfort than a concern. Without any ambient light, the stars lit up the night until the moon made its way overhead. He was wrapped in his space blanket, with the small fire burning and the call of a nearby owl to break the silence. He stared at his little fire, replaying the events since Emily's death over and over. There was no remorse, only a critique of his methods and procedures he could have done better. Honing one's craft required such an analysis. Eventually, fatigue got the better of him, and he slumped over onto the grass and moss and slept a dreamless sleep.

The morning chill woke him. The sky was clear and bright, with only the occasional cloud visible between the treetops. He was stiff from the lumpy ground, stirring slowly to gain sensation in his extremities. After walking a short distance to relieve himself, he filled his canteen at the river, then sat down by the cold remnants of the fire to eat two more protein bars with some dried beef he had packed to supplement his meagre rations. Surprisingly, his hunger was minimal, but not his sense of anticipation. Today would either set the stage or fail him.

It was time to get into place. After filling his pockets with half of his remaining provisions, he set the pack in the raft. With the binoculars in hand and the rifle slung over his shoulder, he made his way to the large boulder. If they came and entered the campsite, identification would be easy. But, what if they rode past? An attempt could be made, but first he would have to quickly verify the targets as they rode by, making the chances of success sloppy at best. It was critical to stick to his plan. Time and patience would guide his actions once more.

The morning hours passed while the sun began a steady descent to the western hills. Once again, only one vehicle, a pickup with a fishing boat in the box, drove by. Still, he waited, getting up and moving about only to ease the muscle soreness and cramps. It would be twilight by six o'clock, and they would need to arrive before that or risk missing the entrance in the dark. He removed the magazine from the rifle, checking the action again.

Everything was oiled properly, the slide and ejection port were clean. He became nervous, fidgeting almost uncontrollably, his right leg bouncing up and down. A tension began to build in his chest, and a hint of self-doubt crept over him. Was it all just wishful thinking? Maybe he was just a pathetic wannabe soldier who had watched too many lone wolf movies. He settled himself once more to wait.

Another hour and a half passed. He kicked the ground in frustration and stood up with a small stone in his hand, throwing it at a tree in disgust. "Just a big bloody waste of time," he said aloud. "Stupid fucking Rambo screw-up!" He sat down once more to decide what to do. Then he heard it in the distance, faint but clear.

The series of rumbles were unmistakable. They varied in pitch and rhythm. *Good,* he thought, *there's more than one.* He slung his rifle over his shoulder once more, and holding the binoculars, made his way through the trees next to the highway. Once he found a hidden vantage point, he crouched low, scanning the highway to the north. The rumble grew louder. Soon there was some movement in the distance. A group of three riders were approaching. As they came within a quarter-mile of the campground entrance, they began to slow down, their engines revving and backfiring with the shifting of gears. He refocused the binoculars, concentrating on their clothing. They wore no distinguishing leathers, and the bikes they rode were in keeping with an outlaw image, but there were no distinctive patches on their backs.

Still, he watched. They stopped short of the sign. This area was obviously new to them. The sleeping bags strapped to the handlebars and full saddlebags told him they were spending the night. He watched them slowly make the left turn onto the gravel road and then disappear, one by one, into the trees. He smiled. Even though they were not the group he wanted, his hunch was a good one. If one group of riders chose this site, others probably would too. Once again, he sat down to wait.

It was almost five o'clock; the sun was just touching the edge of the western horizon. The air was still and the forest silent. He scanned for any sign of life, but there was none. The tension was palpable. It was as if any living thing that called this place home had gone to find refuge, like the townsfolk who waited for the gunfight to be over. He held the binoculars in both hands, staring at the ground in front of him, listening.

There it was again; more engine noise approaching as before. He crouched into position. The binoculars were beginning to struggle in the dimming light, but soon he saw them. There were more this time; the rumble of the chopper engines reverberated off the sides of the mountain. It was like thunder, and if it was meant to be a calling card, intimidation was the message sent. They came closer. He counted six, and each one was dressed in black leather. They came in formation, two groups of three with a lead for each trio. He lowered the binoculars to clear his vision. There could be no room for error here; target confirmation was critical. Once more, he lifted the binoculars to his eyes. The gang slowed, gearing down and braking to a stop in front of the entrance, their bikes also loaded with bedrolls and packs.

The lead rider looked from side to side while the others revved their engines erratically, waiting for a signal. The one in front was likely the boss. He was a large man, and his beanie-like helmet sat on the top of his shaved head, near the back. A black goatee surrounded his mouth that held no expression. Black sunglasses rested on the bridge of his nose, and a betting man would wager that he rarely took these off. He turned his head to the left and nodded. Then, one by one, they engaged their transmissions, following him into the forest.

The teacher honed the binoculars and watched. As they turned onto the dirt road, he noticed that the backs of their jackets were crested with a red figure and bright red lettering above. Demons. He moved along the edge of the road until he was directly opposite the entrance. The sun would set within the hour. When it was completely dark, he would move again.

The dial on his watch signalled eight o'clock. A few clouds moved across the darkened sky, blotting out the stars as they passed. The waning moon was in the east. He looked around to see how well his eyes had adjusted to the lack of daylight. He could see in monochrome with the lighter forest cover set in contrast against the black trees. With care, any wood debris could be sidestepped.

The binoculars would be of no help. Placing them high on a rock would make them easy to find later. He pulled back the bolt on the rifle, then let it release, chambering the first round. After pressing the release behind the pistol grip, the back of the stock swung into place. Everything was ready. He crossed the highway, making his way into the forest to the left of the access road. Just as he had done as a boy, he took no more than six or seven steps at a time, always looking to the ground before placing his foot down to stop and listen, his eyes glancing from side to side. It was the sound of laughter and voices that came to him first. A glow in the distance told him where they were.

Crouching low, he made his way to within a hundred feet of the clearing and stopped, lowering himself to one knee. They were all gathered around a large campfire, most of them sitting on pine rounds that had been cut before as crude chairs. Two sat cross-legged on the ground, while two more had moved their choppers near the glow of the fire and sat perched on leather seats. Each of them held a beer can in one hand. A bottle of hard liquor was passed around, riders swallowing in gulps respectively as others looked on. From behind a large pine, he continued to watch without moving. If he waited until they were drunk, he could quickly make his way into the clearing to take them down. But this could be messy. He would have to kill all nine and three of those he knew nothing about. They could just as easily be innocent working stiffs, headed off to a bigger party in the morning. Then again, his rifle could jam, and even in a drunken state, it might be possible to bolt for the forest cover. Or worse, they might turn on him and beat him to death. No, he had seen all he needed to. He got up from his crouch again and slowly began his walk back to the highway.

After no more than a dozen steps, a loud voice came from the fire pit. Turning back to look, he saw the Demon leader stand, still wearing his sunglasses, his jet-black goatee parting as he opened his mouth again.

"Listen to me, you ugly bastards," the leader called out. "We're the Demons, right?"

"Fuckin' A!" they replied in unison, their arms outstretched, beer in hand.

"And don't fucking forget it!" he said, staring at the fire. Then he grabbed the glass bottle from a hand next to him and, with his head tilted back, drained the last of the amber liquor and threw the empty bottle into the rocks surrounding the fire. It smashed, sending pieces of glass in all directions. Then he sat once more and reached for another beer.

The teacher turned and continued his walk. Tomorrow was going to be one hell of a day.

CHAPTER

14

The sun had crested the eastern ridge two hours ago. There were no clouds in the sky this morning and no breeze as well. The eerie stillness that had pervaded the forest yesterday was still present. The teacher stared at the smouldering remains of his small fire. It was built next to the rock that was to be his shooting platform. He had not slept soundly, but that was not unexpected. It had been cold, even with the fire. The only support to lean against during the night was the tall boulder that hid him. Everything that wasn't needed now was stowed in his pack. The last of his protein bars and jerky had run out before daylight. It was just him and the assault rifle in his lap. His green jacket was dirty now, having spent so much time up against rocks and trees. The bush hat sat low on his head, resting just above his eyebrows. A black kerchief was tied loosely around his neck, with a loose triangle of material resting at the top of his chest.

He felt no fear; in fact, he felt nothing at all. It had all the hallmarks of just another day at the office. If anything, it was boredom. Even the sense of peril that crept through him a day earlier was now lost somewhere. But he didn't care. This would be over quickly. If the Demons were the first to ride out by themselves, great. If the other three stragglers emerged first, he would let them pass. Should they all come out together, no problem; he would take down the ugly black ones and, amid the confusion, the others would probably beat a hasty escape while he headed for the river. But there was always that unforeseen glitch, that hidden variable that could jump into any scenario, laying waste to the best of plans. *Piss on it,* he thought. *Whatever happens, happens.* He had all the advantages, the element of surprise, and the firepower to go with it.

The first engine rumbled to life at nine-thirty. Now the excitement began to build throughout him, and with it, a surge in strength. More engines now, a rumble announcing the storm to come. He rose, then lowered himself to his right knee, his body pressed against the flat rock. His left foot was set firmly into the ground. He pulled the kerchief up from the top of his chest and set it on the bridge of his nose, hiding his face. Clicking the safety off, he set his left arm on top of the flat surface and rested the rifle on his upturned palm.

The engines grew louder; they were on their way. He lowered his cheek onto the stock and, looking through the sights, centred his aim on the campground entrance. It took only a moment for the first rider to clear the forest road, turning left. He was followed by two others, but none were dressed in black. The teacher smiled. The engine noise became deafening as the three accelerated closer. To prepare, he tracked each rider as they approached and lightly touched the trigger twice.

"Don't forget Zombie Rule Number Two, the double tap," he said to himself, smiling again. "What a great movie."

One by one, they rode past like roaring ducks at a carnival shoot, paying him no attention. He was well hidden, but he knew their ability to focus with an alcohol-induced morning stupor would be limited. He watched them pass, making a note of the noise. The din of open exhaust pipes would muffle the sound of gunfire. He refocused on the entrance again. Two bullets to the torso would be enough; at the very least, the riders would lose control, and maybe a broken neck from a crashed chopper could finish the job. The excitement in his body rose to the next level. He could feel the blood rush in his ears. The second wave of thunder ignited in the forest, much louder than the first. He breathed deeper now, calming himself. Seconds later, the first black jacket turned onto the highway, followed closely by a second and then a third. Soon all six began to accelerate. He focused his aim on the zipper of the first jacket. Taking one more deep breath, he exhaled slowly and pulled the trigger.

The first bullet hit the lead rider in the sternum, the second, slightly higher and to the right, and he remained motionless for a second, but his head slumped on his chest. The motorcycle continued in a straight line for a short distance, then veered to the left. Two more slugs hit the next black jacket, piercing both lungs. The blond-haired rider grabbed his chest, causing the bike to fall to the right in a slide, sending sparks up from the pavement. Alvin was third in the line. He leaned his head to the right to improve his line of sight, trying to make sense of what had happened. The bullet caught him in the upper left chest, and the next one broke his collarbone.

"Shit!" cursed the teacher. The leaning rider had thrown off his aim, but he knew the chopper would go down. He tightened his left hand on the fore-end of the stock to maintain his focus and continued to fire. He watched the fourth rider jerk backwards as the next two hit just below his neck. Sensing something was wrong, the fifth twisted the throttle wide open, and for a second, his bike lurched forward. But he died in his seat while his ride left the highway in flight and crashed into the trees to the pavement's right. The gas tank split open, and within seconds, a fireball burst up along the length of a tall pine, turning it into a candle. The last also tried to make a run for it but went down on the centerline as the final two bullets tore out his throat.

In less than a minute, it was over. The teacher lowered his kerchief and took a deep breath. The ringing in his ears blocked out everything else. He stood up and looked to the right and then the left. It was clear in both directions. With calm, deliberate steps, he made his way onto the pavement, the rifle in both hands, the barrel pointing to the lower left. Motorcycles lay splayed on both sides of the highway, their black-skinned riders sprawled in heaps close by. As if taking a stroll, he came closer. If any showed signs of life, he would end it. He owed them that much. The only audible noise came from the pine tree's burning crown and the still idling engine of the sixth chopper. He passed the first four; nothing moved. Glancing over the bank, he saw the fifth lying on his stomach, fifteen feet from the burning wreckage, his face buried in the grass. The last bike lay on its side, not forty feet from him, its rear wheel turning pointlessly while the engine chugged on. He walked toward it, leaned over, and turned off the key. The engine sputtered its last. Taking three steps back, he looked down at the open, lifeless eyes of its owner. "You are now forgiven," he said softly. "Whatever transgressions you committed are cleansed." He stepped back further, still looking at the dead rider.

He heard the shot and felt the bullet hit at the same time. It spun him to the right and sent him on his back.

"What the hell?" he said out loud with a hitched breath. "Christ! I've been shot!"

He stared incredulously at the sky, his eyes darting back and forth to each side. How could he have been so stupid, so sloppy? A dull ache radiated from the upper left side of his back. He struggled to move, but his left arm was useless; every attempt to move sent waves of pain through his left side.

"Shit!" he cursed. "Not here, not now! Not on some shitty chunk of pavement."

A splattering thud hit near his right ear as a second shot split the silence. *I gotta move!* he thought. He bent his left knee and pushed with his foot, rolling slightly to the right. He turned his head as best he could to look in the direction of the gunfire. A hundred feet away, a large black figure was struggling to get up. It got as far as its knees and stared at the teacher. The figure's black leather jacket was open, and blood had soaked the once white T-shirt beneath. The right side of its face had been removed by the coarse pavement, and only a mangled bleeding pulp remained. The scalp above its missing eyebrow was torn open, streaming more blood and covering its useless eye, and its right hand held a black pistol. It was obviously human, but the lack of a defined face gave the appearance of a macabre being from a cheap horror flick—a Demon indeed. What was left of a black goatee parted, and its bloody mouth opened.

"Othahfuckah!" the rider moaned loudly and raised his pistol. His arm and pistol wavered as he struggled to aim with his remaining good eye. The pistol fired for the third time, but the bullet went wild again. The rider bent over, and using his left hand as a brace, planted his foot. With a screaming howl, he gained an upright stance, lurching in the teacher's direction. The teacher watched as the mangled hulk stumbled toward him, determined to keep erect and walking.

The teacher lowered himself to the pavement, ignoring the pain he felt and breathing heavily. Then he held the pistol grip as tightly as he could and pulled the butt of the stock into his armpit. Another bullet hit harmlessly near his head. Rolling to his right again, the teacher saw the maimed rider close to within forty feet. The rifle magazine was still more than half-full. Pulling the butt tighter into his armpit, he lifted the rifle up, swinging it in the direction of the rider—the black hulk. Again, he squeezed the trigger. Round after round spit out of the end of the barrel, but nothing hit. He stopped, and using the remaining strength in his arm to steady the weapon, he fired again. The rider's pant leg tore open, and blood began oozing down his thigh. The teacher fired again and again until the magazine emptied. Like a sewing machine, five bullets stitched their way diagonally up the rider's bloody torso, and he stopped, the pistol falling from his hand. A final red bubble emerged from his torn lips, and the dying rider collapsed face down on the centerline. The teacher lay back down again, looking at the sky, completely spent. His breathing came in short staggered breaths as the pain in his back began to build again. "I'm done; I'm finished," he said, gasping.

For several long minutes, the teacher lay there without moving, the rifle at his side. This was the worst; dying like a wounded animal struck down on a lost highway. The treetops lost their definition and began to blur. He felt weak, his mouth was dry, and except for the agony in his shoulder, he felt dead. As his eyes began to close, a black shadow swooped over him. He blinked hard in disbelief. But it was real; the rush of air as it passed left an audible signature. It came over him again, like a blur only a few feet above his face. He tried to focus, but it moved too fast. Soon, he saw it again, clearer now and high above him.

The raven began to circle now, cawing loudly with urgency. It was crucial to try once more, even if it was going to be the last. He pushed with his left foot again as hard as he could and rolled himself onto his stomach. The pain was excruciating. Bracing with his good hand, he got to his knees.

"Don't faint," he grunted, then propped himself with the rifle and made it to his feet. All the while, the raven refused to be silent.

"Thanks," he said, blinking hard again to stand steady. Looking up, he saw the large black bird turn hard and fly low over the trees toward the river.

"If you insist," he whispered and began to walk. Step by stilted step, he staggered toward the forest. Once in the trees, he leaned against a large, sturdy one to catch his breath. The pain was throbbing hard now. He looked down at the back of his leg. Blood soaked his thigh but gradually lessened toward the back of his calf. "Maybe I caught a break," he said, "and I'm not gonna bleed to death." He continued and soon came to the raft. After dropping the rifle next to the pack, he fell to his knees and pulled the first aid kit out from one of the nylon pockets. A hard shake brought a handful of Band-Aids falling to the raft floor. He dropped his head, laughing weakly. "Just what I need," he said, laughing again. After rattling the kit once more, a bottle of painkillers fell out. "That's better." The lid snapped off easily, and he shook six tablets into his mouth, put the bottle in his jacket pocket, and reached for the canteen.

He had been floating down the river for a while; he wasn't sure how long. The medication had induced a stupor, but at least the pain was a dull throb now. He knew he was in shock and was thankful for the river current that allowed him to rest. He lay on his side, cradling the pack, his head on the inflated tubing. He desperately wanted to close his eyes and sleep. But if he missed the cabin, he was finished. The cabin meant a chance at survival, even if it was a slim one.

He looked up and watched the treetops against the sky. There was more aspen now along the sides of the river. Their leaves rustled in the wind, and the warm sun that came through in scattered rays felt good on his face. The events of the morning replayed in his mind. It had been a shootout worthy of a Tarantino script. The noise was unbelievable: screaming engines mixed with the exploding gunfire. This had truly been a battlefield, even if it only lasted a minute. He was thankful he had stuck to the plan. These boys had been tough. Taking them on at the campground could have been worse than dying in a rubber boat. But, the job was done. He stared at the shore, watching the trees go by.

More time passed. Where was the cabin? He couldn't have passed it. But, it had been far too long since he had been there. He remembered a wide spot near a bend in the river, not more than twenty feet from the riverbank, impossible to miss, even as delirious as he was. He reached for the small paddle and braced it in the water. The raft drifted toward the bank he wanted.

The current slowed; it was a good sign. Soon the river began to disappear as it bent in a gentle arc. He kept the paddle in the water, forcing the raft closer to the bank. A large fir hung out over the river's edge, and as he passed the gnarled wooden trunk, there it was. The roof had fallen in, the log walls sagged, but it was the same cabin. The raft floated onto the bank, where it bounced against a dirty black shore, spinning front to back.

He grimaced hard, forcing one leg over the inflated rubber and into the river. The cold water took his mind off the pain, and once both legs were in, he stood up, the water to his knees. Dragging the raft on shore, he walked to the cabin door. It was hanging off a rotten leather hinge; the stale smell of packrat feces told him there was no point going in. He lowered himself to the ground, leaning back against the wall at the door's edge. Reaching in his pocket, he pulled out a cell phone. *This better work,* he thought and pressed the power button.

"C'mon," he whispered. "Light up good for me. Please!"

The screen came to life, but in the top corner, two words sent a pang of fear through him: No Service. He watched the screen, then rubbed it against his chest as if trying to coax a genie from a bottle.

"C'mon! Just one bar!"

On command, a sole green signal bar lit up, followed by a second. "Yes!" he hissed and began pressing the keypad. With the phone at his ear, he listened to each ring.

"Hello?" came the familiar voice at the other end.

"Thank God! Simon, it's me. I need your help. I'm hurt pretty bad."

"What happened?"

"Long story. Listen, I need you to come get me."

"Where are you?"

"I'm at the cabin. Remember?"

"The cabin? The fishing cabin?"

"Yes! The fucking fishing cabin! Listen, I'm on my way out, can't talk much more. You gotta come get me."

"On my way." The call was ended.

He dropped the phone and reached into his pocket. Most of the painkillers had spilled out of the bottle. He grabbed a small bunch, dropped them in his mouth, swallowing them dry. His head dropped back against the log wall. The river and the trees that lined it soon began to blur. The sun gave everything a fuzzy halo, with the soft sound of the current providing a lullaby. The slits of his eyes closed their last, and he slumped to the ground.

CHAPTER

15

"Looks like a gang war to me, sir. Besides these ones, there are a bunch of smaller empties near the pistol we found." The detective surveyed the carnage of bodies and motorbikes, then knelt next to the scattered shell casings lying along the yellow centerline. "You're probably right, constable," he replied after picking one up carefully to examine the calibre. "I imagine that maybe an automatic weapon of some kind was used. Someone obviously planned to do a lot of damage."

"We've blocked off traffic at the highway junction; Constables Richards and Simmons are directing local traffic back the way they came."

"Well done. Have you mapped the scene?"

"Almost."

"Good. Make sure you take a lot of pictures, then check the trees next to the highway carefully, both sides."

"Yes, sir."

He was glad the officers available today had no direct involvement in the earlier killings. Not only did he prefer to work alone, but the fact that there were now three homicides within less than a year in an ordinarily sedate area suggested a common thread was in play. He did not believe in coincidences. Even though each incident involved entirely different scenarios, his gut focused on one undeniable fact: someone was out to settle a score.

He stood up, watching the constable walk toward the farthest downed chopper. Then he took two steps back and waited. To his left was the clue he wanted. In his eagerness to point out the cartridges, the constable had missed it; a pool of blood not belonging to any of the riders had dried in a circular pattern eight feet from the spent casings. The young officer didn't make the connection that an automatic rifle would eject the brass a good distance after firing. Someone outside this group of bikers had taken a hit. Once the constable was far enough away, he reached into his pocket and brought out a small glass vial. He knelt once more, removed the cotton swab, dabbed gently at the blood, and then sealed it in the vial.

This was a desolate stretch of highway. Once again, the perpetrator had planned this very carefully. The detective had gone back and forth looking for the tire marks that would have indicated a hasty escape, but there were none. *This guy was smart and definitely has some cajones on him to lock horns with these six*, he thought to himself. *But how the hell did he get away?*

"Sir!" the constable called. "There are more over here." He was standing on a large rock near the trees' edge, pointing down at more spent ammunition.

"He spent at least one night here," said the detective.

"Sir?"

"See the piece of burnt wood sticking out of the gravel? Keep digging a little, and you'll probably find more buried underneath it. Our shooter knew they were coming and waited. He was probably dropped off a day or two earlier. But I don't know how he got away. Then again, maybe he's still here, watching us from a distance."

The constable ducked into a crouch and began looking in earnest in all directions.

"Relax," said the detective with a smile. "This man is a professional. He wants no part of us."

"So what comes next?"

"We wait for the ambulances and tow trucks to show up. They should be here pretty quick to cart away the bodies and machinery. These six are all dead, so they'll go straight to the morgue. When you get back, ask the pathologist to call me with his findings, then we'll meet with him. Do you have any other thoughts?"

"Well, sir, like I said earlier, I'd wager a rival gang is trying to tighten its grip and decided to remove the competition. This has been going on at the coast for some time now, and I think it's spreading."

"You're probably right, my good man. Why don't we start to pack up and get ready for the cleanup crew to remove this mess, then we're outta here."

"Yes, sir. I'm on it."

"Hey, wake up!"

He felt a gentle shake that brought him back to consciousness. The bright red behind his eyelids told him that the sun was in his face. He kept his eyes closed.

"C'mon! Wake up!" said Simon, louder this time. He shook his friend's shoulder once more.

"Ouch! Christ, Simon! Not so hard; I've been shot."

"What? Where?"

The teacher rolled onto his stomach. A large oval of wet blood surrounding a small hole in the back of his jacket had soaked the left side of the fabric.

"Shit! Now what have you done?"

"It's a long story," he said with a grimace. "But first, you gotta get me out of here."

Simon reached under his chest to help him up.

"Wait," gasped the teacher. "There's a space blanket in my pack in the raft. Put it on the seat, or I'll bleed all over your nice new interior. There is a knife in my pocket. Jab the raft full of holes and then bury it under rocks, branches, or whatever other shit you can find. Put the rifle and pack in your trunk, then come get me."

"Just like a teacher!" said Simon. "Always giving orders."

He heard the rush of air as Simon deflated the raft, but he still hadn't opened his eyes. With the side of his face in the gravel, he relaxed his eyelids. The bright sun hurt and blurred his vision, but after blinking hard, things came into focus. Simon was scurrying around and soon had everything stowed. He came back and helped the teacher to his feet, eventually lowering him into the passenger seat of his import. The pain in his back began to throb harder again as the car bounced over potholes and ruts. But he needed to be lucid and decided against more medication.

"So stay with me here," said Simon. "What the hell happened?"

"You'll hear about it soon. But I tried to take on a bunch of goons. For a bit, I was doing pretty well, but I got sloppy and screwed up. Listen, I'm fading again, so pay attention. I can't go to the hospital, but I'm going to give you some directions."

Steve Paulson walked along the long driveway that bordered the edge of his acreage. He was a dark, swarthy individual of average height but powerfully built. The five o'clock shadow on his face was a permanent feature, no matter how often he shaved. With a horse's bridle in his hand, he was making his way toward a large white building when the main door opened, and a young woman in a white lab coat started toward him. Her long auburn hair was tied in a braid that hung down the middle of her back, and her blue eyes highlighted a perfect set of teeth as she smiled at him.

"Hey, cowboy," she said as she got closer. "You just finishing up?"

"Why, yes I am, pretty lady. How about you?"

"I'm all done for the day; I just need to make sure the animals are secured with enough water for tonight."

"I guess that's what I love most about you," he said. "You have such patience with animals, especially the one you married."

She turned to walk back to the building and then looked over her shoulder at him, smiling. "That's right. You be a good boy, and maybe I'll rub some horse liniment on you for a special treat tonight."

He watched her walk back to her clinic, remembering how lucky he was. Four years ago, while teaching science at a local high school, he had been introduced to Allison through mutual friends at a dinner party. She had recently graduated from veterinary college and was working at a local animal hospital. To say that Steve was immediately smitten was an understatement. For the rest of that evening, he focused all his charm in her direction. She appreciated his wit, and after several dates, grew to love his gentle manner and honesty. They married a year later and decided to open a small animal clinic on a five-acre parcel of farmland they had purchased on the outskirts of town.

Steve watched her walk into the building, and as he started back himself, a small grey car pulled into the driveway, slowly approaching him. He had never seen this vehicle before, so he thought it best to step onto the mowed grass as it got closer. The car stopped alongside him, and the window lowered. The driver turned to face him.

"Can I help you?"

"He needs you," the driver said as he gestured with his head to the right.

Steve placed his hand on the car above the window and bent down to look over. He recognized the profile at once.

"Hey! How the . . ." he began but stopped when the teacher turned to face him, his face pale, eyelids half-closed, and jaw hanging loose. "Jesus Christ! What the hell happened?"

"Hey, Stevo," the teacher said with a half-breath. "It's been a while, I know, but I'm hurt. I need your help."

Steve dropped the bridle and ran around to the passenger side, opening the door. He reached under the teacher's armpits to help him out. The teacher leaned forward, revealing the blood smeared on the silver blanket.

"I'll help," said Simon, and getting out of the car, he went to the passenger side and stood by the open door.

Steve lifted the teacher out of the car, hanging on to his right side as Simon reached under his left arm.

"Owwwww! Fuck, Simon. Don't lift my left arm. It hurts like a bitch!"

"Oops," said Simon, then looked at Steve. "Okay, I'll grab his belt and support his chest, and you put his other arm over your neck."

"Let's get him inside. So, what the hell happened?" Steve repeated.

"I've been shot," the teacher said, moaning. The three of them half-stumbled, half-walked toward the door Allison had entered only minutes earlier.

"Who would do that to you? Hang on, we'll get you inside and call an ambulance."

"No, Steve, you can't do that. I can't go to the hospital."

They made it through the doorway, then into a second room, placing the limp body on an examining table.

"Allison!" Steve called. "Need some help here!" He looked down at the teacher whose ashen face stared weakly up at him. "What do you mean you can't go to the hospital? Allison!" he called again. "You gotta hurry!"

"I got into a tiff with some bad guys. Watch the news tonight, and you'll hear all about it. But trust me, Stevo," the teacher said softly, "they had it coming. And, if I go to the hospital, I'll never see the light of day again."

Allison walked into the room and stopped short near the table.

"What is this? What's going on?" she said, moving to the teacher's side. She looked over to Steve, her brow furrowed, and her lips pulled tight in a thin line.

"He's a teacher," said Steve. "He was my mentor when I first started out. You remember? I've talked about him before. He's been shot in the back."

Allison looked back down. "Help me roll him over."

Steve lifted underneath the teacher's left side while Allison lowered him onto his stomach. Then she looked across the table.

"Hi, I'm Simon," said Simon, grinning like an idiot.

"Simon, grab those scissors over on the counter and bring them to me."

The teacher was silent. His cheek pressed against the cold stainless steel of the table. The throbbing in his back pulsed slowly, but he felt a strange calm. As he watched Allison move about him, he felt no sense of urgency. He was more curious than anything else. How would a vet react to this strange man bleeding on her table? Would her sense of compassion compel her to treat him, or would she simply plug the hole and call the police?

She took the scissors from Simon and made a cut through the base of his green jacket. Then she grabbed one side of the cut fabric.

"Steve, you do the same and pull hard."

Steve grabbed the other side and braced himself. Together, they began to pull. The jacket ripped up the middle to the collar. Allison cut the remaining piece with the scissors, then repeated the procedure for his blood-soaked shirt. The upper left of the teacher's exposed back revealed a single puncture wound, the middle of which was clotted and black. The edges still oozed fresh blood. Allison pressed down on the wheel locks, pulling to roll the table through a far entrance to another adjacent room.

The teacher's mind drifted as the blur of movement and clinical noise mixed together added to his confused state. He tried to focus his senses, but exhaustion and injury had taken their toll. He simply continued to lie silently, running the events that led to this over and over in his mind. He lost all sense of time.

He couldn't tell how long everything had taken, but then he heard her voice.

"Steve, Simon, come in here."

They entered the room where the teacher lay still. What appeared to be an X-ray machine was positioned above his back. Allison stared at an illuminated image hanging in front of a bright light. She pointed at a flat bone structure bisected by a dark line with two irregular dark spots to either side.

"Your friend has a scapular fracture," she said, drawing her finger down the dark line. "In other words, he has a broken shoulder blade. These two dark areas are what's left of the bullet, which has broken into two pieces, probably the result of hitting this ridge on his shoulder blade. He's lucky. If it had entered further to the right, he'd be either paralyzed or dead. He needs to go to the hospital right now."

"I can't," said the teacher.

"Somebody had better explain something to me, and real quick," Allison said, her arms crossed over her chest with fingers clenching hard into her sleeves.

"Sweets, come into the next room. I need to talk to you," Steve replied, standing at the doorway and motioning her over. She walked through ahead of him. Steve followed her, then leaned back against the counter, resting his palms on the edge. He looked at her.

"So?" she asked.

"From what he told me, he was involved in a fight with some nasty people. I understand your concern. But I would trust this man with my life. And more importantly, I owe him. He's the one who saved my career when I was just starting out and when that prick tried to kibosh my teaching chances here because I refused to kiss ass. You know the details already. That man in there was my mentor and went to the wall to support me, putting his own job at risk. He says we need to watch the news later, which will help explain what happened. But he would never get involved in anything like this unless it was a matter of life or death. Please, for me, give him the benefit of the doubt and help him if you can."

"Do you realize that if we become complicit in a crime, we could lose everything we've worked for?" The tone of her voice was flat. Her eyes bore down on him with a brilliant intensity.

Steve looked down, pawing at the floor with his boot. Then he looked up at her, meeting her eyes. "I know. But if we just hand him over, without giving him a chance, I'm not sure I could face myself in the mirror."

They went back into the X-ray room. She went over to the side of the table, looking down at him. The teacher turned his eyes up toward her, still silent. Simon was lost in the image of the illuminated X-ray, tracing his finger over the outlines of bones.

"Against my better judgement, I'm going to treat you," she said. "We'll worry about what comes next after."

The teacher closed his eyes and feebly forced a single nod, the right side of his head planted against the stainless steel, his mouth open slightly.

"Thanks," he whispered.

"The bullet fragments aren't too deep, so there are two ways we can do this. I can use lidocaine as a local anesthetic. It would freeze the area while I operate, but you would still be conscious. Or, I could give you propofol intravenously. It would induce unconsciousness, and I don't think the procedure would take more than fifteen minutes, so it shouldn't be necessary to intubate you. After you regain consciousness, the left side of your back will be very sore. So I'd give you a shot of hydromorphone to relieve the pain."

"Knock me out," he mumbled, his lips barely moving and his eyes half-shut. "I need to sleep."

He felt the table begin to move. Then he heard Allison's voice.

"Let's get him back into the other room. Steve, you'll wash up with me. Simon, the choice is yours; you can wait outside or stand out of the way."

"I'll stay," he said

Once the table stopped, the teacher listened again as water began to run. Then a metallic sound as the instruments were placed on a tray and the shuffling of footsteps took over. *I've done it good this time,* he thought. *I always knew it could end badly. But it's okay; better to croak here than on some shitty highway.*

He felt his right arm being lifted gently, then a cold sensation as something wet and soft rubbed against his skin. The last thing he felt was a quick jab in his arm, and slowly, a wonderful feeling of euphoric weightlessness came over him. Then he was out.

It was the bright light that first lit up his senses. His eyes were still closed, but the backdrop of his eyelids were a brilliant white like a movie screen. He was on his back now, still on a hard table, but a pillow supported his head and something softer—a folded blanket possibly—supported the weight of his upper back. He clenched his left hand and could feel that his arm was in a sling. His mouth was dry. He tried to initiate some saliva by closing his lips and pressing his tongue to the roof of his mouth. It didn't help.

His thoughts were a kaleidoscope of images. He tried to focus on these memories, but his sense of time was gone. Slowly, his mind began to piece things together. The black forms on motorbikes and the cacophony of gunfire replayed first. Then he was on his back lying on the pavement, then floating down the river.

He moaned, then took a deeper breath and moaned again. He heard movement in the room and then footsteps. A door opened.

"He's waking up."

It was Simon calling to the outside of the room. He was still in this world; it was a good sign. The left side of his back was sore, as though someone had poked him with a sharp stick. His eyes opened slightly, but the light hurt; his vision was uselessly blurred. He thought he should try to get up, but there was no point in that. He knew he would just drop to the floor. A sense of urgency was beginning to creep over him. He would have to leave soon or put Steve and Allison at risk.

"I heard him moan," Simon said as the others entered the room.

The light that overwhelmed his sight was broken by moving shadows as people moved around and huddled over him.

"Man! Was that you?" It was Steve's voice almost directly over his face. "We caught the evening news. They're saying it was a gang war south of town."

"Water, please," he whispered. The need for a wet tongue blocked out all else.

"Lift his head back, Steve," said Allison.

A pair of strong arms gently raised his head and shoulders while two more pillows were wedged beneath him.

"Here. You'll feel a straw against your lips. Drink very slowly, one sip at a time." It was Allison's voice, calming and professional. The water was wonderful, cool and soothing. He started to sip faster, but the straw was removed.

"Slow down, or you'll just vomit," she said. "I'll dim the lights, then you can try to open your eyes. I got both pieces out of your back. You should be fine, but it's going to hurt soon, and you're going to be out of commission for a while. Here."

The water was back again, and he sipped slowly. The glare faded, and he opened his eyes halfway. The blur was still there, but he could make out Allison's form to his right.

"Thank you," he said.

"So was that you? Did you get into some kind of gunfight with that group?"

"Yes." He could see her arms were crossed as she stared down at him.

"You and who else?"

"No one else. Just me."

"Just you?"

"Yes."

"Didn't I tell you the guy was fucking amazing?" Steve exclaimed.

"Steven!"

"Sorry." Steve lowered his head in chastisement, then looked up smiling.

"So tell me, what would possess a pillar of the community, like yourself, someone who teaches little kids right from wrong, to shoot it out with a bunch of lowlifes?"

The teacher turned his head toward her, blinking hard to bring her face into focus. "They hurt someone close to me . . . very, very badly. The police couldn't do anything, so I did."

"So what do I do now?" she said. "You can't stay here. We're already at great risk by helping you."

"I know. As soon as I can move, Simon and I will leave, and I won't bother you again."

"What will you do for medical care? Your stitches will need to come out in about a week."

"I'll get Simon to do it. I'm sure he can change a dressing too?"

She turned to Simon. A wide-eyed look of panic and confusion spread across his face.

"I'm sure Simon could help change a Band-Aid," she said. "But stitches are out of his league. Come back in seven days, and I'll do it."

The teacher looked at her and smiled. Her head was cocked slightly to one side. Her smile and blue eyes gave him the reassurance and comfort he needed.

"Thank you," he said. "But you two have done more than enough already. Simon and I will search YouTube for what to do. And I want to apologize for putting you both at risk."

"Hey," said Steve. "I owed you one, big time. It was good to see you again. Maybe we can have a beer sometime."

The teacher reached for Steve's hand. "I'm buying," he said, then closed his eyes.

An hour later, Steve and Simon walked him to the car, gingerly placing him in the passenger seat. Allison put her right hand on the open door and looked down at him. She reached into the left pocket of her lab coat and pulled out a small plastic container, and held it up.

"I've given you a shot of hydromorphone that will keep the pain in line for a few hours," she said. "After that, you will need some pain meds that Simon can pick up at any pharmacy. I'll give these to him. They will help fight any possible infection. So take two a day until they run out. And good luck."

The teacher smiled at her once more. "You've saved my life, and I thank you. I only hope one day I can make it up to you both."

Steve and Allison watched the small grey sedan make its way down the gravel driveway, turn, and drive off. His arm was around her shoulder.

"Thanks, babe," he said. "You're the best."

"Well, now we're in this together, my man. I just hope that's the end of it."

CHAPTER

16

The coffee shop was like most scattered throughout the downtown area of the big city. They usually occupied street corners with black sandwich boards placed on the sidewalk, highlighting the luncheon specials in multi-coloured chalk. Stools inside lined the large windows, allowing bored patrons to spend far too much time savouring expensive specialty coffees while people-watching.

Most of the clientele that entered this particular establishment represented the executives, secretaries, and retail employees who spent their days earning a living in the area's concrete towers and trendy shops. But today, there was one person who didn't belong here. He was seated along a wall next to the aisle that led to the bathroom.

Eric sat by himself at a round table for two. He faced the front entrance staring at the glass door, nervously clutching a cup of black coffee. He wore a plain black cotton jacket pulled high on his wrists. His denim pants were torn at both knees, and his crossed feet sported well worn, dirty white sneakers. He sat slouched over his coffee, motionless, his stringy brown hair hanging in threads on his shoulders. Mirrored sunglasses perched on his pointed nose. The stubble on his face did little to hide the creases and sallow cheeks of a neglected body. Eric was an informant and knew that exposing himself like this was dangerous and stupid.

The door at the entrance opened, and in walked a stern-looking man wearing a blue blazer and grey pants. Eric straightened his posture, maintaining a firm grip on his coffee, watching the lone figure approach his table.

The detective pulled the chair back opposite Eric, then seated himself, placing his hands on the table, fingers interlaced. He stared at Eric without blinking.

"How you doing, Weasel?" he asked.

"You know I hate that name," Eric replied, pushing the dark glasses higher up on the bridge of his nose.

"But I hate formalities, and we can't get too chummy. What have you got for me?"

"You realize the chance I'm taking sitting here with you? My kind usually doesn't come around this part of town. But even still, if I'm made while talking to you, I'll probably end up with a sharpened screwdriver plugged into the back of my skull."

"That's not what I asked," the detective said, his cold dark eyes bearing down further.

Eric sipped his coffee and lowered his head, staring at the tabletop. "I know," he said. "It's just that the people you're interested in don't appreciate how I earn my spending money."

"Did anyone here, or anyone you know, order that massacre last week?"

"That was an ugly one, wasn't it? But it's weird. No one in these parts has a clue who did it or who might have put out the contract. Everyone is as surprised as you. Things seemed to be running smoothly, for the most part. Sure there were little bumps here and there like that kid's overdose and the one bust. But the product was flowing, and the cash was going where it was supposed to."

The detective relaxed his posture and leaned back to his side, placing his right elbow on the back of the chair. "So, nobody local? White? Asian? Somali?"

"Nope. But it has put people on edge trying to figure out what happened. Until something comes out, chances are things are going to be tight-lipped." He looked around the detective toward the front entrance, then back over his shoulder to the rear. "But listen, I'm getting real nervous here. This isn't usually how contact is made. I gotta split."

The detective continued, "I know, but I needed information now. This one is important, very important."

Eric pushed his cup to the side and leaned forward. "So when do I get paid?"

"Go see your regular contact. He'll have your cash. But if something comes your way, I'll expect to hear about it. Real soon."

Eric nodded, then stood up and continued toward the bathroom and rear entrance, where he disappeared into the alley. The detective turned sideways in his seat, staring across at the abstract artwork on the opposite wall, thinking. Three minutes later, he got up, walked to the front entrance and onto the sidewalk.

The teacher sat on the park bench, posture straight, unable to bear his weight against the backrest. The pain was less now and could be managed with simple meds. A couple of sparrows landed near his feet, looking for handouts. He watched their bouncing steps that seemed like a dance beckoning for a reward. When none came, they flew off, landing near an elderly gentleman walking slowly by with a cane.

Spring break was coming to an end in two days. He had requested two more weeks of sick leave, explaining that he had separated his shoulder in a biking accident. But in truth, he just didn't feel like going back to the classroom. This was strange for him. Even after Emily's death, he had looked forward to being surrounded by his kids. Their vitality was always a much-needed distraction, which went a long way in recharging his soul. Maybe it was just the wound that drained his spirit, and once he was back in a satisfying routine, the passion of teaching would return as it always had. But things were different; he was different. It was odd. The visceral need for revenge wasn't there. But the adrenalin rushes he'd experienced this past year were like nothing he had ever felt before. It was becoming an addiction. Not just the final acts themselves, but the detailed planning and preparation had heightened the anticipation to new levels.

For now, he just needed to heal, and patience would be the key. It allowed time for reflection, and reflection tempered the impulses that led to disaster. Sure, he had made a serious and costly mistake. But then, taking a bullet would sober him. It would leave him with a permanent reminder should he ever rush his actions again. And what of his actions? What was next? In short, nothing.

He stood up from the bench and began walking as if taking a morning stroll. It wasn't good to dwell on what might happen. Before, everything had come his way, making his decisions to act easier. Now it was best to accept this lull and boredom and not go looking for trouble. He would remain vigilant in case the police made a breakthrough, and therefore, the "way out" needed to be kept close at hand. With that in mind, he continued to walk, taking in the clean air, looking up at the sunlight coming through the branches above and listening to the soft sounds around him. At any moment, it could all disappear.

The constable came to the doorway of the detective's office and knocked. "Here you go, sir. I've cross-referenced the lists from the school district with those from the mill as you asked. Twenty-two names came up within the time frame you gave. Of those, three are dead." He placed a file on the detective's desk. "What next?"

The detective leaned back in his chair, looking up at the rookie constable's questioning face. "Now we go through each name, one at a time. Check for aberrant behaviour of any kind; criminal records, lawsuits, custody issues, marital status, tax problems—anything that would point to an individual even remotely capable of killing another person."

The constable's mouth opened, and a pallor spread across his face.

"That's right, my fine young officer," said the detective with a smile. "The person we want lives out of the norm. He—almost certainly a male—has the disposition, opportunity, and time to do something like this."

"Does that include the motorcycle shooting?" the constable asked.

"Who knows?" the detective replied. "But probably not. I'm still looking for a gang connection there."

"Okay, I'm on it," the constable said, standing erect to display an air of confidence. He turned and started to walk away.

"And get some help if anyone else can spare the time," the detective called out. With that, he stood, grabbed his jacket, and made for the exit. It was time to pay someone a visit.

Twenty minutes later, he was sitting in the pathologist's office, waiting, examining the almost bare white walls. The only items hanging on them were framed degrees and certifications mounted above the padded leather chair across the desk from him. *These people are always the same,* he thought. Their academic accomplishments were always mounted directly above their thrones, like shrines to their brilliance and hard work. He himself had worked his way up from the street level as a beat cop with no "alphabet soup" behind the name on his business card. He didn't begrudge these people their titles or whatever, but the inherent vanity that went with it always struck him as ridiculous.

He was anxious, drumming his fingers on the armrest of the plain office chair he sat in. But hopefully, the information he was counting on today would crack his investigation open a little wider. He had virtually no evidence to date—no witnesses, no fingerprints, not even a consistent pattern of method or motive.

It was only his gut instinct that kept driving him to find the link that would connect these crimes.

The office door opened, and in walked Dr. Robert Henderson, a tall, thin man with receding blond hair and wire-rimmed glasses sitting on a hawkish face. He came around the detective and stood beside his leather chair with a file folder in his hand.

"Hi, Bob," the detective said. "We spoke on the phone after the bodies were brought in. Have you got anything for me?"

"You betcha, and sorry to keep you waiting," Robert replied. "I wanted to get the bodies out for you to look at before you got here. Come with me, and I'll show you. You won't need the camphor ointment under your nose today. We've had these boys on ice since they came in; no rotting smell to ruin your supper."

The two of them walked out of the office and down to the end of a white corridor, where Robert opened a metal door with a small square window placed at eye level. There may not have been the smell of decaying flesh in the large room, but the odour of disinfectants was overpowering, causing the detective to squint and blink hard several times.

"Don't worry, you'll get used to it quickly," the pathologist said matter-of-factly. "As you can see, I have them lined up for you."

The pale white bodies were laid out on stainless steel tables. They were illuminated with bright incandescent lights that hung from the ceiling, shrouded in aluminum covers. Robert motioned him over to the farthest table.

He continued, "We'll start with the first five, from left to right. Notice this first one. There are two gunshot wounds close together in the upper torso. He was probably dead before he hit the pavement." He stepped to his right. "Now look at the next one. Once again, two similar bullet wounds, again in the upper torso, and certainly fatal. In fact, the next three have almost the same bullet pattern imprinted on them, except the fifth one, who took two in the throat. And, considering that these were moving targets, whoever the trigger man was, he was one hell of a good shot. We removed all the slugs. They were all 5.56-millimetre military rounds, all fired from the same weapon, probably an assault rifle of some kind."

The two of them continued slowly past each table. The detective examined all the wounds as they walked, marvelling at the marksmanship involved. At the sixth table, Robert stopped and opened his file folder. "Now here's where things get interesting," he said. "Have a close look."

The detective leaned in closer to the body. The dead man was large, not only tall but barrel-chested. One side of his face was almost completely missing, the flesh torn and ragged as if blasted by gravel. Leaning in even closer, the detective could see the road grit that hadn't been washed away. But the worst of the facial injuries impacted the man's mouth. Only little more than half of the goatee remained, and the right side, where the upper and lower lip normally joined, was gone, revealing broken and bloody teeth. The detective grimaced and stood up to examine the rest of the body. The right thigh had one bullet wound, then five more bloody points of entry arced across the torso, starting near the hip and ending six inches short of the left shoulder, near another wound that had shattered the collarbone.

The pathologist stuck an index finger in the file folder as he closed it. Then he pointed his other index finger at the dead body, tracing the bullets' path as he spoke. "This boy was tough," he said. "These two bullets probably took him down, but they weren't fatal. But for him to get up, as wounded and mangled as he was, took a lot of hate and strength. Then we come to the other six in the diagonal pattern. They were fired at an upward angle. If an assault rifle was used, then the shooter was on his back and very close to this man when he finally went down for good. So can you see what happened here?"

"Oh, yes," said the detective. "Our shooter came out from his vantage point after they were all down, maybe to admire his handiwork or maybe to finish off any that were left alive. But this gorilla caught him by surprise and sent him to the pavement with a bullet of his own. Then they squared off at point-blank range, with our shooter coming out the only survivor. But I can tell with your finger in that file folder that there's more to the story."

"Yes, there is, and I'm sure it's really why you're here." The pathologist opened the file once more. "The blood sample you sent me doesn't match any of these six. Most likely, your assassin left a pool of his own on the pavement."

"And?" asked the detective.

"The DNA profile gives us more," the pathologist said, looking at the pages in front of him. "He's male, no secret there. But more importantly, he's Caucasian, probably of western European descent. His eyes are blue and with that, most likely on the fair side in terms of hair and skin."

"Anything else?"

"Nope, not really anyway. Except that his blood type is O-positive, but then half the population is O-positive."

The detective extended his hand. "Thanks for your help, Bob. And all your hard work."

"Ha! Are you kidding?" the pathologist said. "This one was great! I never get anything like this around here. Finally, something fun."

"Bob, maybe you should buy yourself a dog," laughed the detective. "When you get a chance, send me a copy of that file." He turned and walked toward the windowed door.

The constable sat bent over his desk, covered in pages of information. He was writing notes on a lined pad when he heard footsteps approach him from behind. He sat up and turned, looking at the face of the detective.

"Sir?"

The detective leaned in, putting his hand on the desk. "I want a complete physical description of everyone on that list. Pictures would be even better."

It had been nine days since his return to work. The teacher sat in the chair behind his desk, flexing the fingers of his left hand. There was no problem with sensation or strength, but he still needed the support of the sling. It would take some time yet, but he could now bend his elbow without pain but not much more. If it were only his arm that was the problem, he would be much happier. It was being here that was the hardest. The kids weren't in class yet, and alone in his room, he surveyed the walls, the desks, even the tiled floor. It was the same as he had left it. The posters of reptiles that made up their last assignment covered the wall nearest the windows. The fluorescent lighting was adorned with mobiles dangling grammatical rules and definitions written on circular card paper. Even Charlie's cage was the same, neatly cleaned with the ageing gerbil making the best of his confinement. But here he sat, a stranger in his own room.

Since his return, he had simply been going through the motions. There was no vibrancy in his lessons, and smiling became a struggle. His mind often drifted to the events that had, without exception, changed him. He tried from the onset, but every day, the monotony would build to the point where anxiety began to creep into his psyche. As the end of each day approached, the best he could do was fidget in his chair and watch the clock. His colleagues noticed the change in his mood as well. They tried to offer support for his malaise but eventually wrote it off to his injury and left him alone. Constance knew something was very wrong. She had visited him several times at school, but each visit saw her approach him more and more cautiously. After her attempts to break the ice, he would engage in the necessary chit-chat that was simply a façade, concealing the emptiness she felt in him. Her last visit ended with an expression of sadness, followed by a comment referring to the "teacher zombie." He simply nodded.

The class this day would start in five minutes. The teacher stood up from behind his desk and slowly meandered among his students' desks. Everything was in order. The assignments that had been photocopied were placed on the counter against the wall. The theme for the day was neatly written in coloured pen on the whiteboard. His preamble was memorized and ready to go.

When the clock on the wall made its way to eight-thirty, the school buzzer signalled the start of classes. Within minutes, the students wandered in, greeting him, then walking to the side of the room to place lunches and backpacks on the floor beneath the counter. He returned the courtesy, greeted each by name, smiled obligingly and made his way back to his desk.

The day seemed to progress well enough, but after lunch, a sense of restlessness made its way over a corner of the class. As if on autopilot, he reminded the group to stay focused, but the tension began to grab him. His leg started to bounce uncontrollably, he grabbed his right wrist with his left hand, and his upper and lower teeth began to chew at the inside of his lip. One student, Malcolm Stewart, became the catalyst that would end it for him.

Malcolm was a typical ten-year-old. He was a sandy-haired boy with freckles, dressed in the plain T-shirt and jeans he wore almost every day. Although an imp on occasion, a simple stare after calling his name was usually enough to settle him. But today was different. The corner of the class began to focus on Malcolm. The volume of chatter increased as heads turned. Malcolm was grinning, his hands busy on top of his desk.

The teacher began to breathe heavily, sweat forming on his brow. "Malcolm," he said sternly. "Is there a problem back there?"

"No, sir."

"Good. C'mon, gang, you know what you should be doing."

The volume in the class decreased, but Malcolm was undeterred. He had fashioned a small spear using his pencil that he rolled inside a piece of paper. He whispered to the blond-haired girl in front of him.

She turned in her desk. "You better not!" she said aloud.

The teacher looked up. His right hand clenched into a fist. "Malcolm, maybe you need to spend some extra time after school today. The counter needs cleaning."

Malcolm simply smiled innocently as the volume of chatter decreased once more, but within minutes, it reached a crescendo with all surrounding eyes on Malcolm. He picked up the paper shaft and stuck the sharpened pencil into the blond-haired girl's shoulder.

"Owww!" she screamed. "Ow, ow, ow." Her hand reached up to the top of her shoulder, and tears streamed down her face.

Without further thought, the teacher stood erect, the back of his legs knocking the chair to the floor. All colour left his face. He raised his fisted right hand and slammed it onto the desk.

"Jesus Christ, Malcolm! Stop being such an asshole!"

The class froze. There was complete silence, except for the sobs of the young girl. Malcolm sat motionless, his mouth open. All eyes were on the teacher. For a moment, he simply continued to stand, staring at the back wall. No eye contact was made with any student. Then he turned and walked out of the room.

With quick strides, he made his way down the hall, ignoring everyone he passed. Opening a door, he passed the secretary, not saying a word, and approached the principal's office. Walt's door was open, and the teacher stood at the opening. Walt was seated at his desk and, sensing a presence, looked up.

Walt put down his pen. "Hey, what's up?" he said.

Without expression, the teacher looked at him.

"I'm done."

CHAPTER

17

Jimmy Takada kissed his wife Sarah goodbye before making his way to the car in the driveway. Once behind the wheel, he took a deep breath and looked up at the blue sky. It was a great day, and he indeed was one of the lucky ones. He was on his way to work this Monday morning. Dressed in a casual jacket, slacks and tie, he drove his new Lexus calmly through the suburbs on his way to the Ministry of Environment building at the center of the city. He had been at his new job for a year now. It signified all he had worked so hard for. The years spent as a field technician were the grooming that had brought this all together. But he could not discount the self-discipline that came with being raised in a Japanese immigrant family. Hard work had been the family mantra. His devoted parents were as loving as all good parents, but laziness was not tolerated. Along with his older brother and sister, he had learned the value of diligence and honour.

He had recently moved his family to the best neighbourhood they could afford. The new home and vehicle had been something of a financial stretch, but he knew he deserved it. His daughter was in her final year of high school this year while his son was on his way to finishing his first year of university. As the week ahead was in order, his next big project was already in the works. Jimmy's life was coming together as planned.

He pulled into his stall at the top of the eight-floor parkade, up against the short barricade that bore his name. The perks of his position, the status that went with it, and the significant salary increase were well deserved. He adjusted his tie in the mirror, made sure his hair was still in place, then grabbed his briefcase and headed for the elevator. Reaching the sidewalk, he stopped. It was busy this morning, a good time to pick up his favourite specialty coffee, then round the corner to his office building.

The main doors to the Ministry of Environment opened automatically to the main foyer. It was a bland entranceway as most government buildings were. The beige tiled floor and cement walls echoed his footsteps on his way to the main elevator. Several potted plants sat in the corners, but he felt that the large framed pictures of the coastline needed to be replaced with some contemporary art. He would suggest this to his supervisor at the next staff social. Scanning the directory was a favourite habit as he waited for the elevator doors to open. His was the office of environmental policy on the fourth floor. It was much nicer than the rustic, poorly heated field offices he had worked in over the years. He sipped his coffee and smiled. There were no mice in his filing cabinets now.

When the elevator doors opened, he walked down the hall to the reception area.

"Good morning, Donna," he said, smiling at the young, brunette secretary seated behind the counter.

"Hi, Jimmy," she replied, looking up. But he noticed her smile was weak, and her eyes seemed sad. *Probably boyfriend issues,* he thought and continued down the hall. The office seemed empty, and there was no one at the coffee station, as was the normal situation on Monday mornings. He walked farther, noticing that the door to his office was open. At the entrance, he saw that his supervisor, Carl Wilson, was seated to the side of his desk. Another individual that he recognized but couldn't name was seated behind his desk.

"Hey, what's up, Carl?" he asked. "It's a little early for our Monday morning meeting, isn't it?"

"Have a seat, Jimmy," Carl replied. He motioned Jimmy to a third chair that had been placed in front of Jimmy's desk. His face was pale, and his lips were drawn in a thin line. His appearance seemed dishevelled like he hadn't slept well and had dressed in a hurry. Jimmy sat down in the empty chair, placing his briefcase at his side.

"You may remember Miles Carson from human resources?"

"I do," said Jimmy. His chest tightened, and, reading their faces, he could feel his pulse quicken. "Is there a problem?"

Miles looked at Jimmy. He wore a tailored slate grey suit with no tie, and his brown eyes were framed with black, thick-rimmed glasses. His appearance exemplified that of a university professor, but there was no emotion on his face.

"Jimmy," he said. "I'm afraid I have some bad news, so I will cut to the chase. The premier is holding a press conference later today. She's going to announce extreme cuts to the civil service in almost all ministries and at all levels. Your job has been declared redundant as of today. I'm sorry, Jimmy. You will receive two months' salary as severance, and your benefits will carry on for sixty days. You will receive your pay for today and have this morning to collect any personal items."

Jimmy sat motionless, his lips slightly parted. His mouth began to go dry. "I'm being fired?" he said, looking over at Carl, whose head was lowered, staring at his clasped hands in his lap. "I know I've only been here a year, but my work record is exemplary, not to mention that our department has several projects that need my input."

"I know, this is very difficult for all of us," Miles continued. "But this comes from high up, and I have the ugly job of being the messenger."

"Is there nothing else for me anywhere?" asked Jimmy in a pleading tone. "You are both familiar with my skills. I'm sure I can be useful somewhere."

"Jimmy, all field operations and other project operations are going to be handled on a contract basis. Several consulting firms have already been contacted. We anticipate tenders to come in within the week. You could possibly approach one of them. Of course, you can count on us for excellent references."

Jimmy could think of nothing else to say. He could only stare straight ahead, his mind unable to focus.

"We'll leave you alone to collect your thoughts and belongings," said Carl.

An hour later, he had the diplomas from the wall, his desk pen set, and the framed eight-by-six photo of his family packed into a small cardboard box. He placed this under his arm and picked up his briefcase. Looking out over the city through the window, he scanned the horizon, then looked up at a plain blue sky. A lump formed in his throat.

Slowly, he walked down the hall. He stopped at Donna's counter. "Did you know about this?" he asked.

She looked up from the keyboard of her computer; her eyes were red and swollen, her lips trembling. "The notice was on my desk when I got here this morning," she said softly. "I'm so sorry, Jimmy. Carl and Miles are making the rounds now. There are others."

Jimmy nodded slowly, "Bye, Donna. You take care of yourself."

"You too, Jimmy."

At his car, he put the box and briefcase down before pulling the fob with his keys out of his pocket, unlocking the Lexus. He ignored the brief honk of the horn and flash of lights and simply looked up at the city around him. "What the hell just happened?" he said.

He sat in the car, the motor still silent. *Now what am I going to do?* he thought. *I'm up to my ass in debt with no job.* Consultants that handled his responsibilities were scarce, and his chances of landing anything soon were just as slim. The standing joke was that their field personnel made peanuts for wages.

He couldn't go home yet. He needed to think. Driving out of the parkade, he made his way through the streets, and after a short time, he stopped at a community park that overlooked the ocean. It had been a favourite place for him and Sarah to visit. Soon he found himself sitting on a bench, replaying the morning's events in his mind. It was important to stop this, he decided. There were more important issues to consider. The well-being of his family came first. They could sell and move, but the disruption to his wife and daughter would be terrible. *Think, Jimmy, think!* he said to himself.

He wandered through the park, making his way along the sidewalk, pausing every so often to sit on a bench. His appetite was gone, the thought of food non-existent. There was always his co-workers' favourite bar. Maybe a stiff drink would settle his mind, but it was Monday. Coming home today with alcohol on his breath would set off alarm bells. He kept walking.

Four o'clock came and went. He got into his car and started home. It was too early to break the news to Sarah, not before he had some idea of what to do next. He just needed more time.

Pulling into his driveway, he reached for his briefcase, looked in the mirror once more, and gave his smile the best effort he could. He made his way up the stairs to the front door and into the hallway. Sarah was standing near the entrance, smiling as she always did at the end of his workday. He smiled back.

"Hey, handsome," she said. "How was your day in the pits?" Her brown hair was fashionably styled, combed like it always was. In a blue T-shirt and jeans, he was still awestruck at how beautiful she was.

The pits, he thought and smiled weakly once more. Now there was an appropriate word for this day. "It was okay, you know how

Mondays are." He walked over and held her, breathing in her wonderful smell, holding her longer than usual.

"My, my, my," she said, giggling. "Did you get a raise or something?"

He shut his eyes hard since the pit in his stomach almost made him retch. This was going to be a difficult evening. Gaining his composure, he relaxed and stepped back. "Is Ashley home?" he asked.

"Yup, upstairs on her computer. Soccer practice was cancelled today, so she's home early."

He put his briefcase on the floor and walked up the stairs to his daughter's room, stopping at her open door. "Hey, sunshine," he said. "What are you up to?" She turned in the chair in front of her desk. *She looks so much like her mother,* he thought.

"Hi, Daddy," she said, smiling. Her perfect teeth and healthy glow intensified the angst that held him. "Just yakking with the gang online. We have a big tournament coming up in a couple of weeks. It's a road trip too; gonna be a blast."

He walked over and put his arms around her, kissing her softly on the head. "Yes, my soccer superstar," he said quietly. "You're the best, and I love you so much."

"Aw, I love you too, Daddy."

The rest of that night passed painfully. At dinner, he ate what he could, but hunger refused to return. Sarah commented that he seemed a little distant. He tried to initiate what conversation he could, saying apologetically that his new project took up most of his thoughts. Sleep was almost non-existent. Their bedroom had a pale glow from the street lights outside. He stared at the ceiling, then nodded off to sleep for a short while only to wake up with his fears and shame consuming every part of his being.

Mercifully, the alarm went off at six-thirty. Sarah stirred as he rolled onto his side next to her back and held her. She cooed sleepily while he nuzzled her hair and kissed it softly. After a few minutes, he got up and began his normal workday routine.

Just before eight o'clock, he said goodbye to Sarah and Ashley, kissing them both, and left the house for his car. During the drive, an idea began to take shape in his thoughts, helping the trepidation that had consumed his night dissipate. At eight twenty-four, the silver Lexus rounded the corner into the parkade and made its way to the top. He pulled into his empty place and smiled when he saw that his name was still fastened to the short concrete barricade. As he sat in the plush seat, he thanked his Asian heritage for the discipline in his being that always saw him through.

Jimmy reached for his briefcase, opened the car door, and stood quietly for a few seconds. Then he smiled once more; he knew his life insurance policy was ironclad and very generous. He walked to the barricade and stepped up the short distance to the top.

Jimmy Takada closed his eyes and took one more step into nothing.

The library room in the heritage house was large and finished in copious amounts of oak. The shelves of the south wall were filled with volumes of classic literature and academic texts that hadn't been read in years, if at all. But in this house, proper appearance was crucial. Visitors needed to see the surroundings of style and intellect. Several plush, upholstered reading chairs occupied the center of the oak floor, and antique area rugs added the finishing touches of good taste.

A dimly lit hall located at one end of this room was also finished in oak wainscoting, a patterned burgundy wallpaper above the polished wood. Various ornately framed oil paintings and family portraits lined the walls that led to an open door at the end. Through this door was a bedroom, where a crystal light fixture was centred on the ceiling, lighting the room completely and highlighting a large canopy bed against the far wall, and an immaculate Persian rug lay on the floor. A walnut roll top desk was placed next to a window, and two five-drawer chests stood against the third wall. The center of the fourth featured a large antique armoire with a full-length mirror.

The premier stood in front of the mirror. She was dressed in a beige business pantsuit and white blouse. Self-conscious of her short stature, her outfits were often completed with distinctive heels as they were today, reflected as part of her strategic stance in the mirror. She was an attractive woman with a cherubic face, blue eyes, and shoulder-length blond hair. Standing as she was, in front of the mirror, was a nightly routine. Her image was everything. Every look, stride, and personal nuance had to be carefully crafted and maintained. The press followed her every move, and now that her career was about to reach its apex, mistakes were to be avoided at all costs.

The premier was single and had never married. She had been raised in a devout Christian household, her father a charismatic minister at the local Pentecostal church. She adored her father. He had provided the most important education she had ever received. As a minister, he was an evangelist. With a Bible in hand, he delivered his sermons every Sunday with passion and power. Working the room like a trained thespian, he would make piercing eye contact with as many in the congregation as he possibly could. His right hand held the worn Bible high as he spoke, the brightly coloured, tasselled bookmarks flashing as he shook it feverishly. The left hand held a microphone that delivered his most powerful tool, a baritone voice that could hold a crowd spellbound. The qualities of tone and volume, hesitation and emphatic outbursts put the fear of God in all his parishioners. The message was always the same: they all had a choice to make—either Heaven or Hell.

As a child, the premier could not remember ever having missed one of his sermons. As she grew older, she knew that with a voice like that, she too could influence the people she needed to climb to a position of importance. Being in such a position was what she dreamed of, and the adoration that went with it was even better.

She had had a younger sister once, but it was difficult as there just weren't enough resources and attention to go around. The tragedy at the lake the summer she was eleven changed all that. She invited little Helen to come swimming with her, and when they were far enough from the rented cottage, challenged her sibling to a breath-holding contest. Sadly, poor Helen never surfaced, even after putting up quite the struggle. Several minutes after all movement stopped, she came screaming out of the lake to her parents, crying that her baby sister was in trouble. Life was much better as an only child.

In high school, she was the student council president, captain of the debating team, and the student leader who led the most important assemblies. She was forbidden to date, but that suited her just fine. Her ambition was her passion. It was easy to toy with the affections of several men during university, but the idea of a constraining emotional relationship was impossible to embrace. Naturally, rumours of her sexuality, or lack thereof, surfaced on occasion. However, she simply smiled and deflected the comments by explaining that her academic life was her prime focus.

And now, she had all the skills she needed. The political maze had been easy to navigate. Within five years of receiving an undergraduate degree, she had won a seat in the legislature and had become premier within eight years, winning the past two elections handily. While most considered such a rise to the top meteoric, it was the use of the most important political hammer that garnered such success—fear. Just as her father had, she delivered her own dire warnings of what would happen to the masses if the Left gained power. In her mind, democracy was easily manipulated because it had two inherent flaws: stupid people were allowed to breed, and stupid people were allowed to vote. It was the second of these that she exploited with a mastery that would make her father proud. Issues didn't matter to most. People had been raised on television and the media, where looks and a convincing delivery could sell anything.

Now it was time to sell the last piece of her plan that would secure her future. Tomorrow night, she would speak to the people via a live broadcast, one in which she would outline her plan to streamline government, saving everyone from the nightmare of bureaucracies and red tape. They needed to know that there were far too many on the government payroll, collecting inflated salaries, benefits, and burdensome pensions. She would eliminate such waste and privatize as many services as possible, making everyone's life much easier. Of course, there would be collateral damage, probably a lot of it, in fact, like the young man who had recently taken his life. Such a shame. But in her world, it all boiled down to success and whatever it took to get there. She would convince the masses that the tax savings would create prosperity. Hidden from everyone was the one component that would make her rich.

The Consortium, a group of wealthy individuals, approached her several years ago. If she could put a rigged bidding process for government services in place, they would secure the contracts needed to further line their pockets. Never mind that any tax reduction was not going to happen. They would simply hire workers at reduced wages while pocketing the lion's share as "operating needs." The premier had been guaranteed a percentage of all contracts to be placed in an offshore account. She would also be given a lucrative, paid seat on several corporate boards once she retired from politics. This was too good an offer to pass up. Once she left office, it would be possible to live the life she felt she deserved. Free from any financial burden, she could enjoy the trappings of wealth and any lifestyle she chose. Daddy might not be thrilled with her choices, but he would just have to accept it. Money changes everything.

Now she stood in front of the mirror. Everything was in order, save for one last detail—the laugh. In a world where one had to attend far too many fundraisers, stumping for the party, it was necessary to tolerate countless idiots and feign sincerity without hesitation. She had taught herself to smile like an angel, followed with laughter at a moment's notice that appeared as genuine as homemade apple pie.

Once again, looking in the mirror, her smile in place, she threw her head back, laughing as if she had just witnessed the funniest event of her life. Repeatedly, she practiced this, the sound reverberating off the bedroom walls.

"Hey, Simon! Dammit, open up! It's me." The teacher had been waiting impatiently for his friend to show his face. He knew Simon was in the house, but an obsessive loner could attend to only one issue at a time. This was pretty much his routine now; contemplative walks, exercise, and visits to his friend. It was a good way to heal, physically, at least. But at some point, he was going to have to move on and become useful somehow. What that might entail, he had no idea. His skill set (wouldn't that look good on a resume?) had evolved, and along with it, the realization that his lack of tolerance had gone from bad to worse. So he waited, flexing his left arm. The strength had almost completely returned, and what little pain remained was endured as a badge of honour. Finally, the door opened. Simon stood there in his robe, looking as dishevelled as he always did on mornings.

The teacher smiled and shook his head. "You realize it's eleven o'clock in the morning, and I still have to stand here waiting for you to open up?"

"But Kitty needed to be fed and have his box cleaned," replied Simon, running his fingers through his hair, then adjusting his glasses. "The poor little guy was starving."

"You know, Simon, when I die, I want to be reincarnated as your cat—just sleep in the sun all day, carouse all night, eat gourmet food, and crap in the sand."

"But Kitty's been neutered."

"Good point. Okay, negate that thought," laughed the teacher. "Could you just change the bandage one last time and have a close look at my back, just to make sure nothing serious is growing near the wound?"

"No problem."

They walked up the stairs and into the bathroom. Simon turned the light on while the teacher removed his sweatshirt.

"Speaking of carousing," said Simon, "when's the last time you bedded a woman?" He adjusted his glasses once more and pulled at the strip of the bandage covering the teacher's shoulder blade.

"It's been a long time, a very long time." The teacher sat on the counter next to the sink, his head looking down at the floor.

"What about that foxy counsellor at your school? You've mentioned her and what a looker she is more than once."

"Not gonna happen. I also came to tell you that I've been put on indefinite leave, so I won't be back at school for a while, if ever."

"No way! You? What the hell happened?"

The teacher raised his arm to shoulder level while squeezing his fingers into a fist.

"Popped my cork in class. Just some stupid kids goofing off at the back of the room, and I lost it. I guess I'm lucky they didn't fire me outright."

"Shit, that job meant everything to you."

"I know. But, to be honest, since I've taken it upon myself to clean up the world, the old routine just became a bore. It's kind of a funny feeling when I think about it. I keep waiting for a sense of loss to set in, but it doesn't. Shame, maybe, but not loss." They both went silent for a moment. "So what about my back?"

Simon leaned in closer, squinting with his mouth open, tongue in his cheek. "It's healed up pretty good, but there is an indent where the bullet went in like someone used your back for a golf tee and the nine iron hit a little low. I'm pretty sure this missing divot is something you're going to have for the rest of your days. But the stitches came out well, as I did a masterful job if I don't say so myself. As long as you can move your arm okay, I guess you'll be fine. Maybe you should go see that vet again, just to be sure."

"Thanks, 'doc.' But no, those two did enough just sticking their necks out for me. I won't put them at risk again."

"So what comes next?"

"Financially, I'll be okay for a while. They're paying me until someone decides what to do. I've got a nest egg stashed, so I'll be good for a long while yet. But I feel different now. Who knows, maybe a new career path is in order."

"Says the serial killer."

The teacher laughed. "Touché."

"Well, maybe you should plan ahead before you throw in the teaching towel. After what the premier said last night, things are going to be a little tough job-wise for some time to come."

"What? I missed it. What happened?"

"Same right-wing bullshit; massive job cuts in the public sector. It was all over the news last night. She's going to save us from the commies and keep the tax demon at bay. We've heard all this kind of crap before, but this time, she's gone nuts. There's a lot of nervous, upset people out there right now. Apparently, some poor guy on the coast snuffed himself after getting the axe. They're worried things might get worse."

"Shit," the teacher said, sitting silently for a moment before reaching for his sweatshirt and pulling it over his head. "Okay, I'd better get going. Listen, Simon. I really have to thank you for all you've done."

"Hey, what are crazy friends for?"

"No, really. You've pulled my ass out of the fire big time on this one."

"Not to worry. I envy you. Your actions have been noble, even though most would disagree and prefer to lock you up. But you've lived more in this past year than all the other poor schmucks out there who stumble through each day only dreaming of such thrills. And just to be a small part of it is a vicarious rush for me."

"Maybe you've got a point," he said reflectively. "Okay, I'll keep you posted. See you later."

He walked down the steps to the door. Once outside, he walked with his head down across the lawn to his truck, got in quickly, and drove away.

He never noticed the black sedan parked two houses away, a figure slumped down behind the wheel with a camera on the seat beside him.

CHAPTER

18

The premier paced the floor of her official office. Dressed as usual in her pantsuit attire, she walked in deliberate thought, her head down, oblivious to the lush trappings that lined the walls and floors of the spacious room. Two days ago, she had gone on air to outline her plan. Almost immediately, the response was less than enthusiastic. This was going to be a challenge. The backlash had been worse than she thought. Organized labour was planning to mount a series of protests, and the press had not been as sympathetic as initially hoped. Priorities now lay in bolstering her popularity to keep her objectives intact. The election would be in late October, and only a complete victory would ensure the plan's safety. Her top advisor had been summoned. Alecia would save the day. Alecia was smart, with enough talents to help her navigate any political minefield.

"Looks like you need some help, and we have some work to do."

The premier looked up toward the open door. Alecia stood at the entrance. Lean, with short red hair and a pale complexion, she appeared almost masculine. If not for the green pantsuit she wore, her feminine voice and black, round-rimmed glasses, one could not be faulted for making such a mistake. She was the premier's most important aide and confidant. Without question, her loyalty was unwavering. Alecia almost always accompanied the premier to public events, often seen at a close but safe distance to ensure that every detail was handled without problem or incident.

"Close the door and have a seat," said the premier. "The election will be this fall. I need to sell this package well before then. Did you read the morning paper or catch the latest newscast?"

Alecia took the seat across the desk from the premier's. "Yup. There are a few out there who did their best to carve you apart," she said. "But we've got lots of time yet. With steady pressure, we can soften these people up. Remember, it will all be old news soon enough. So I wouldn't worry."

"What do you have in mind?"

"First, we handpick the data we need; exorbitant government wage increases, decreased household income due to taxes, etc. Then we run a series of commercials explaining how dire the situation could be if spending isn't restrained. Finally, and here's the best part, we take you on tour. You can prepare a staged sales pitch for a series of public forums. It's what you do best. By the time the election nears, the numbers will be on your side."

"Sounds simple enough."

"It is. We pound the message home and scare them silly."

"Alecia, what would I do without you?"

The air was warmer now. The leaves of the trees lining the boulevard had fully flushed, and they moved back and forth softly in the breeze, using the sun to cast a mosaic of shadows on the sidewalk. He had been running for more than a half-hour now. Sweat ran down the sides of his face; his tracksuit was dark with moisture down the center of his back, hidden by the snug pack he wore. This was much easier now. The stamina had fully returned; in fact, it was the best it had ever been. His body was lean and strong, the muscles contoured along his upper body and legs. After the stitches and sling were no longer needed, he had purchased a set of weights, which fit easily in his empty basement, near the gun cabinet. Two ten-pound weights, wrapped in a spare jacket, lay at the bottom of the pack together with a plastic water bottle. He looked at his watch. To date, the best time for this eight-kilometre run was an average of five minutes per kilometre. But with the weight carried today, it would take longer. There would be no stops, and the pain that came with exhaustion was exhilarating. Ten minutes later, the teacher rounded the last corner before he was home.

Once inside, he stripped, showered, and threw his tracksuit into the laundry hamper. Next, he pulled an old grey T-shirt over his wet hair. It clung tightly to his upper body, hanging loose below his chest. It was funny to think that almost all his school clothes didn't fit properly anymore. He put on his faded jeans and opened the fridge to prepare a protein shake. The run had been good for the soul. But of late, he had been feeling restless, anxious to experience the adrenalin rush once more, something that only a brush with disaster could accomplish. For now, he had other plans. The afternoon would be devoted to research. It was essential to find out as much as possible about the political storm Simon had talked about.

The rest of the shake was placed on the table, and he took a seat in his usual chair. Flipping open his laptop, he waited for the screen to light up. "Okay, Madam Premier," he said aloud. "Let's see what you've been up to." It didn't take long for the results to line up. Government site after site displayed pictures of the premier followed by lengthy articles describing the "right path for the future," "need to rein in government excess," or "fight to preserve prosperity." He had heard it all before and kept scanning. Soon the pretty pictures disappeared, and gloomier predictions from a variety of sources began to fill the pages. Words such as draconian, merciless, brutal, and financial slavery began to repeat themselves. The opposition parties joined the labour unions to mount the best defence they had, but the consensus was that they didn't have the money or political strength to fight for long. He continued his search for a while longer but stopped abruptly. His eyes narrowed, focusing intently on the screen, and he began to read slowly. Again and again, he scrolled over the text, blinking only when he had to. His heart beat faster, a broad smile took shape.

"Well, well, well," he said with a chuckle. "It looks like Goldilocks is taking a trip into the forest again."

The rest of the afternoon was uneventful, but only in that it was necessary to attend to the needs of living a normal lifestyle in a normal house. However, his mind was working overtime, scheming once more. Maybe it was time to stop thinking small and take down a much bigger fish. It was amusing to think that most people considered puzzles, novels, or other hobbies a mental exercise. To spend the same amount of energy planning another person's demise was something altogether different. For him, it was becoming a craft.

Shortly before six, a rumbling stomach signalled the need for dinner. After putting on some jazz, he poured himself a glass of wine. Bordeaux had replaced scotch now. He had decided that a well-aerated red wine was healthier than glass after glass of hard liquor. He walked over to the fridge, only to be interrupted by a knock at the door. This was unusual. He had no plans for company and rarely got solicitors. Worse possibilities flooded his thoughts. Could it be that the police were close now, or had the remnants of the Demons somehow found him out? He stood without moving. There was another knock. The nine-millimetre was in the bedroom, tucked under the mattress near his pillow. The magazine was full, but the chamber was empty. Still, he might be able to reach it if he had to. He went to the door, hesitated, then opened it.

"Wanna buy some girl guide cookies, mister?" It was Constance. She was dressed in jeans and a white cotton blouse, her long dark hair styled in waves over her shoulders. Her perfume flooded his senses, the fragrance soft and exciting.

He laughed. "Sure, little girl. Why don't you come in and show us what you have?" came his mischievous reply. He caught himself; it was a dangerous invitation, one that should have been avoided. Opening the door wider, he stepped aside, motioning her toward the kitchen. Constance stepped past him and walked over to the kitchen table, surveying the area in slow circular steps.

"I like what you've done with the place." The hint of sarcasm made him chuckle again.

"My interior decorator calls it 'minimalist *moderne*.'"

"I bet she does."

"Could I offer you a drink, maybe some old leftover scotch in a coffee cup perhaps? Or even better, a decent Bordeaux? I'm sure I have another chipped wine glass around here somewhere."

"Oh . . . give me the wine, Mr. Fashionista."

"I don't see you carrying anything chocolate or vanilla under your arm. So what brings you here?" He thought it best to dispense with the flirtatious overtones.

"I just thought I would see how you're doing. You left suddenly and have been gone a while now. I hoped you might call to clear up what happened. Walt is being evasive, as he should be. But that doesn't stop the rumours. Really, I'm not trying to be nosey; I just want to make sure you're okay."

"It's pretty good," he said. "I'm pretty much healed now, just trying to stay fit."

Constance stared at the teacher's hard pectorals hidden behind his T-shirt and his veined forearms. "Yes, you have," she said, her eyes wide and bright. "So what brought all this on?"

He continued. "I lost my temper in class and swore at a kid. Even though he was being a little jerk, I should have dealt with it better. But to be honest, at the time, I just didn't care." He looked down with a touch of shame, then went to the cupboard for a glass. Returning to the table, he poured the Bordeaux, topped up his own, and passed over hers. "Here's to better days," he said. They touched rims.

"You just didn't care? Please explain."

She deserves an explanation, he thought. But limits had to remain in place. There was nothing to be gained by spilling his guts. "I'm not sure. It would be easy to blame it on the events of a year ago, though I think it's got to be more than that. Maybe I'm getting older, or just changing in some other way." He hoped that would be enough. It wasn't.

"Well, beyond the shock value, you haven't committed a crime. With some discussion and an apology, I'm sure things could have been smoothed over."

"Like I said, I'm not sure, Constance. Maybe call it apathy or boredom. I've just lost that pizzazz. You know, that flair for the classroom. Those kids deserve better." He looked down toward the floor again. "But it's not easy. I invested so much time, so much of myself, and now I'm a little bit lost."

She looked at her wine, nodding silently. *That's better,* he thought. The statement was true enough. With luck, his humility combined with a touch of remorse should satisfy her curiosity.

They both drank deeply from their glasses. She stared into his eyes, the piercing blue colour locking him in place. Maybe it was the counsellor in her, she thought, that strengthened the urge to want to hold him, but she stood still as well. There was silence in the room.

Then she continued. "There's something else, isn't there? You're different now, something beyond the virile frame that I'm looking at in front of me. Even with what you've said, you're not afraid or unsure of your situation. Most people would be." She reached up and brushed his chest softly, causing his muscles to shudder. Her hand moved slowly to the side of his shoulder and then slid down his arm. He blinked several times but didn't speak. She stepped closer, took the glass from his hand, and placed both on the table.

Still frozen in place, he opened his mouth to speak but stopped when she touched his bottom lip. She stepped closer still until he could sense her warmth near him. As he looked down toward her, she raised up on her toes, opened her mouth, and kissed him softly. He felt unsteady on his feet.

"This is not a good idea, sweetie," he said in an exhale.

Constance grabbed at his T-shirt, pulled him tight against her, and kissed him again, stroking his lips with her soft tongue.

"No, really. Please don't."

"Shhhh," she said. "It's all good."

He reached up in a pathetic defence, but his fingers touched her breasts, her nipples hardening instantly. A desire he had long forgotten consumed him, and he kissed her back, her mouth soft against his.

She stepped back, unbuttoning her blouse, exposing the lace of her white bra. Her teeth flashed in a smile as his eyes lit up wider, like a child in wonder. She undid the clasp between the cups, which hung loosely, then fell to the sides. "Now aren't those better than Oreos?" she said, smiling and reaching for the hardness in his jeans. The teacher said nothing; he simply stood motionless. His hands became fists at his sides, the knuckles white and shaking. With his top teeth, he began to bite down hard on his bottom lip. Soon his eyes welled up, and blood started to build in his mouth. A red trickle spilled out and oozed toward his chin.

"Hey, no . . . stop," she said, reaching for his arms. "I'm sorry."

"Don't be; it's not you," he said, lifting the bottom of his shirt and pressing it to his lower face. Then he pulled the fabric away and stared at the bloodstain. "I should explain," he continued, "but I can't, not now. I'm tired; I need to lie down."

"C'mon," she said, and holding his hand, pulled him toward his bedroom. "Let's just lie together for a while." With her help, he pulled off his T-shirt, let it drop to the floor, and then made his way onto the bed. She followed, removing her blouse and refastening her bra. Then she joined him, face to face, softly stroking his hair while he closed his eyes.

Shortly after midnight, she woke up. A soft glow from the street lights outside filtered through the window and faded curtains. Turning onto her side, she propped herself on her elbow, looking over at him. The teacher was sleeping soundly on his stomach, his head turned away from her, his arms at his sides. The contours of the muscles in his back were highlighted, but she noticed something on the left side. Leaning over, it was easier to see the conical indent not far from his backbone. It was a large scar, one that appeared to be freshly healed. She softly traced its shape with her finger, careful not to risk waking him. Obviously, something had hurt him worse than merely a separated shoulder. It was a penetration injury, like something a spear might make. For a time longer, she stared at it, curious and puzzled, then decided it was really none of her business. Maybe she would ask him in the morning.

By seven o'clock, he was showered, dressed in his jeans and T-shirt, sitting at the kitchen table again. His laptop was lit up once more as he scanned over the information from yesterday. Even though the screen would not be visible from the bedroom entrance, he listened intently for any sounds of stirring. The clock on the kitchen counter showed seven forty-five when he heard Constance get up. Closing the web browser, he waited for her to come out. While attempting to cover up with her jeans, she peeked around the door jam and smiled at him.

"Hey, you," she said. "What time did you get up?"

"Just after six. You were sleeping soundly; not even my shower woke you up. So I decided to surf the net until you got up."

"Find anything interesting?"

"Just my usual morning porn."

"Bonehead," she said, laughing. "Okay, let me have a shower, and I'll be right with you. And no peeking."

He watched her scurry around the corner into the bathroom, her smooth, shapely buttocks jiggling ever so slightly. *What a prize,* he thought. *I must have rocks in my head. But I'm screwed. It's too late now; I'm in too deep to put her at risk.*

Soon he heard the shower stop and the curtain slide back. "There are fresh towels hanging to the left of the mirror and sink," he said. "I'll get some coffee started." He went to the sink to prepare the machine. Minutes later, she came into the kitchen, wrapped in a white towel, her combed damp hair parted, resting on her shoulders. She came over to him, and they embraced with a kiss.

"Have a seat," he said, "it won't be long. How did you sleep?"

"Really well, but I woke up during the night for a bit. I looked over at you and couldn't help but notice the fresh scar on your back."

"It happened when I fell onto my shoulder," he lied. "Somehow, I wound up on my back, lying on a broken beer bottle." It was the best he could think of.

"Really?" she asked, the tone of her voice carrying a hint of disbelief and condescension. "That crater came from a beer bottle?"

"Yup. Actually, a piece broke off, and the doctor had to dig it out, which took some doing."

"Does it hurt?"

"Only when I drink beer," he said, pouring the dark liquid into two cups.

She laughed. "Such a witty boy. Come sit down for a bit."

He placed one mug in front of her and moved closer to her, holding the other in his hand.

"I'm sorry, but I don't have any cream."

"S'okay, black will be fine." She placed one hand on his arm after he sat down. "Listen, I was somewhat forward last night. I hope it doesn't put you off."

"I'm fine. You are beautiful, and I'm something of a lost cause." He smiled, leaning in closer. "It would be easy to fall hard for you. I've thought of it many times. But things in my life are complicated right now, and I just can't let that happen. I just want to be honest."

"I know, I know," she said, looking down at her cup. "It's just that you are such a mystery, more so than you ever were before. It's hard for a woman to resist a mysterious man. Of course, the toned body doesn't hurt either."

He smiled and blushed. "That's sweet." It was all he could think of to say.

"But I don't suppose a crystal ball would reveal anything for me to look forward to?"

"Constance, I can't even go there now."

"So . . . what? Like you have some kind of terminal illness or a personality disorder?"

He laughed. "Even if I did, I couldn't tell you. Trust me, please. It's better this way."

"Boy, you are a tough nut to crack, even for a counsellor. But you're not going to disappear on me, are you?"

He gripped her hand tightly. "No," he said in a half-lie, the need to be evasive forced it out of him. "On your birthday, I'll do my best to plan for something special."

"Promise?"

"I promise."

They chatted idly for the next half-hour, then she dressed in the bedroom. After coming out, he followed her to the door. She put on her shoes and moved against him one more time, kissing him softly on the cheek.

"Stay close," she said, looking into his eyes.

"I will," he replied and kissed her hand.

The teacher watched her drive away and, after closing the door, stood at the kitchen entrance for a moment, closing his eyes. The events of last night had been amazing yet terrifying. "Please, don't let me ruin her life," he said quietly, then walked over to the table and his computer.

It was time to get back to work.

CHAPTER

19

He would go north. It would be his best opportunity for success. Time was not an issue now, even though the distance to the target was significant. It would be possible to carry out a reconnaissance before the event and still have at least a month to travel a second time to seal the mission. But now, the planning had to be perfect. Once again, Google Earth had provided an "eye in the sky" to confirm the best location. Initially, there were two. Willingdon was a small community some six hundred kilometres north. Unfortunately, the venue was going to be indoors, limiting target exposure, and the opportunities for any kind of escape were slim at best. Port Arthur was better. Located another five hundred klicks northwest of Willingdon, the premier was planning to hold a rally outdoors there, speaking from a covered stage. As well, this was a seaside community with better options for a clean getaway. Still, he guessed his chances of survival were at fifty percent at best. Not great odds.

The teacher ran over everything in his mind as he sat outside on the steps leading to his front door. It was another beautiful day, one that soothed his being and calmed the doubts that crept through his thoughts late at night. He looked up at the sky as he did most days. There was nothing there or anywhere to guide

him; no omen, no dreams, zilch. He was on his own now. Worse
yet, this would involve killing a woman. Some would think that
anyone that killed a woman was beyond redemption. But being
female played no part. This was about the bullshit that kept people
on their knees. As far as he was concerned, it went beyond the
extreme right or left. Someone, and probably others, were planning
an economic coup, one that was hidden in the media crap that was
sold to the unwary. *Well, look at me now,* he thought. *I've become
an idealist.* It was probably wishful thinking to imagine that an
assassination could stop this ugliness. But at the very least, it
would make everyone involved look over their shoulder and think
twice about what they were doing.

He had been on the road for five hours. It wouldn't be that
far to Willingdon now. For the most part, the drive was boring,
passing farms and ranches mostly. There were the pine trees as
well. They lined the highway, separating the pockets of civilization
along the way. The traffic was minimal, mostly transports and
logging trucks heading in both directions. The radio was turned
off, and only the hum of the tires on the pavement and the droning
engine made any sound. He preferred it that way. It was easier to
think without any distractions. If he pushed it, he could make Port
Arthur by late tonight, but it would be best to decide on that after
a meal sometime soon.

After a while, an uneasy feeling slowly came over him. He was
alone on the highway but was certain that someone or something
was watching him. Checking from side to side revealed nothing.
The rear-view mirror showed only a large vehicle of some kind far
back in the distance. Then he saw it, a small dark shape flying
in the sky ahead of him, just above the treetops. He suspected it
was a crow or a raven, but to think it might be "his" raven was
silly speculation on his part, something the mind conjures up
during periods of boredom. Yet it seemed to wait in the sky as he

approached. When it looked as if it would simply pass overhead, the bird dove straight toward his truck.

"What the hell are you doing?" he muttered under his breath. It was now clear that it was a large raven, wings folded back slightly to increase speed, showing no sign of breaking from its dive. In a panic, he hit the brakes.

"Jesus, you stupid bird. Stop!" At the last second, the raven spread its wings wide, pulling up just before impact and gliding over his vehicle. He exhaled a sigh of relief. "Well, you keep looking for some kind of omen, you dumbass," he said out loud. "Be careful what you ask for next time."

Once composed and back up to speed, he continued, trying not to dwell on what just happened and paying more attention to the trees and farms he passed instead. Still, the dark feeling wouldn't go away. He looked in the rear-view mirror once more and noticed that a large vehicle was gaining on him. It was an eighteen-wheeler—a common sight on this highway. After another minute, it closed the distance further. In the rear-view, he could see the black cab with the hump of the silver trailer behind it. The grill was lined with orange running lights, as was the top of the cab above its windshield. But this one also had a wedge-shaped sunshade above the glass, giving it the menacing appearance of a furrowed brow.

The teacher looked at his speedometer, reading slightly above the speed limit. Still, the black rig closed in on him slowly but steadily. The dark feeling increased, and soon no more than twenty feet separated the two vehicles. *Jackass,* he thought to himself, looking in the mirror once more. The situation was becoming dangerous. The easiest remedy would have been to pull over and let this moron pass. A year ago, he would concede the situation to avoid confrontation, but those days were finished. No, he would continue and see how the cards played out. Several more minutes passed in this standoff, with the trucker pulling up closer two more times until the vehicles almost touched. The teacher never flinched; he just continued as he had, as though he was the only one on the highway.

A few more kilometres passed. In the distance, a neon sign appeared along the side of the highway. It was a truck stop with a restaurant and gas station. He slowed, signalled right, and turned off into the parking lot. The black rig did the same, waited for him to stop, then pulled alongside him, with no more than a car width between the two of them. The teacher turned off his engine, got out of his truck, and stood beside his open door. The diesel engine of the semi continued to idle. He heard the cab door close, and he waited.

The driver walked around the front of the rig and stopped, staring at him with the sides of his mouth turned down and his lips set together. He wasn't a tall man, maybe two inches shorter than the teacher, with a mat of curly dark hair and a thick moustache. But he was broad across the shoulders, wielding a beer belly that pushed his dirty T-shirt to its limits. The image of a monster truck of some kind across the chest area was faded and difficult to make out. He wore a pair of faded jeans, the cuffs rolled up to reveal black leather boots. They were scuffed, dirty and stained with grease. A piece of chain hung from one of his belt loops and disappeared behind his back. *Probably for his monster wallet*, thought the teacher. The trucker took another step forward, opened his mouth, and spat on the asphalt.

"What are you looking at, fucko?" the trucker said, the disdain in his voice evident.

The teacher didn't move, standing motionless, without expression, and blinking only when needed.

"Maybe if you didn't drive like such a pussy, I could make some decent time."

No comment.

"A pussy and a retard mute, too," said the trucker, now taking measured strides toward him. The teacher kept his hand on the top of the open door and shifted his left foot ever so slightly forward.

178

That's it, keep coming, he thought to himself. The trucker had balled his fists at his sides, leaning forward as he walked. They were no more than a foot and a half apart when the teacher lunged forward with his upper body, pushing off his right foot for extra force. Lowering his head, he drove his brow into the bridge of the trucker's nose. He could feel the bone give way with an audible crack. He stood up and back, looking at the contorted face of his adversary.

The trucker's eyes wrinkled shut with tears streaming from the corners. The tips of his fingers formed a closed tent that covered his nose and mouth. A bright red ribbon of blood flowed from the bottom of his chin. He took a step back, bending over and lowering his head.

"Owwww . . . fug!"

Still silent, the teacher stepped toward him again, grabbing his hair in both hands and bringing his knee into the man's bloody face.

"Eeeeeeeeee!" the trucker screamed, falling onto his hip and holding up a hand with fingers splayed, the other one covering his face. "Stop! Stop! No moh," he moaned, the blood pulsing from his mouth with each attempt at speech.

The teacher bent down on one knee and pulled the man's hand away. The trucker offered no resistance. His nose was grotesquely pushed to one side, his eyes swollen shut now and beginning to turn black. The teacher leaned in further until his face was inches from the beaten man's ear.

"Now listen to me very carefully," he said in a soft, almost melodic voice. "If you ever come near me again, it had better be to kill me because I will do the same. You see, I don't give a shit about anything anymore. And I take offence to anyone who tries to make my life miserable. Do you understand?"

"Yeah, yeah. No moh."

"Good. Now stay down until I drive away."

The teacher got up, walked back to his truck, and started the engine. He shot a quick glance over to the restaurant, where a handful of patrons and a waitress holding a coffee pot were standing at the windows. No one moved.

"I'd better go find a McDonald's," he said, then circled back onto the highway and drove off.

Early the next morning, he was sitting in the diner attached to the motel he'd spent the night in. He was in Port Arthur now, having driven all day the previous day. No one had bothered him or called the police as far as he knew. He easily fit in with the few other patrons who preferred the stools along the counter to the tables at the windows. It was easy to remain inconspicuous here. Roadside accommodations in this area dealt almost exclusively with a transient clientele staying one or two nights at best. Except for the facial injury, he looked no different than any other loner just passing through. The mirror in the bathroom of the cheap room had revealed a swollen ridge above his right eye. It looked almost simian in appearance and the redness that accompanied it was tender to the touch. A small cut had also opened, but the desk attendant found an adhesive bandage in one of his drawers and offered it up along with an extra washcloth.

The elderly waitress came to his table with a menu. After pouring a cup of coffee, she stared at him for a moment.

"Thank you," he said, smiling. "If you could give me just a minute, I'll flag you down for a good meal."

She continued to stare at his damaged brow and said, "Let me know if you need an aspirin or two. We keep them handy up by the till. Usually, it's the bikers that pass through that need them after a night of tequila and trading punches. But they're not the only ones prone to a dust-up now and then."

He touched the area gently. "Oh, this. It's from a fall. I tend to be a little clumsy at times."

She smiled back. "Of course. That's the second reason why we keep a good supply upfront." Then she turned and walked back behind the counter.

He ate a full load for breakfast: eggs, bacon, ham, and a large side of hash browns. His appetite was fueled by the long drive and the leftover exhilaration of his incident with the trucker. A year ago, in his wildest dreams, he could never have imagined locking horns with such a character. Now it was almost as if he had baited him, hoping the halfwit would offer a challenge. Maybe it was simply luck, a blow directed at someone who was only hoping to intimidate. But he felt battle-tested. Best of all, it helped convey to this hapless cretin the need to behave himself. Maybe he still was a teacher at heart.

The sports field was like most that small communities had for their events. The grass expanse was oval-shaped with a lined area for either football, soccer, or both. At one end, there was a backstop for local ball teams; the other held a large covered stage that opened out onto the field. Its roof was well above the floor of the stage and sloped back gradually. There were no walls, only the large wooden posts that kept the roof in place. Two sparse trees bordered the structure, one on each side. The teacher stood in the middle of this field, with a black sports bag carrying the tools he would need, slung over one shoulder. He glanced at the sky, then west toward the ocean. It was a grand fall day. The multi-coloured leaves had begun to fall, and the sun was warm and comforting. The air had a distinct humid odour that evoked images of waves and seabirds. Looking around to see if anyone else was in the area, he saw that the entire field, as well as the parking lot next to it, was empty. But that was to be expected. It was the middle of the afternoon on a Wednesday, and most would either be at school or work.

He made his way to the stage. There were wooden steps at one side, and once he was on the plank surface, he walked the perimeter. The entire structure was made of wood and quite sturdy. West Coast Douglas Fir was often used for such purposes as it was strong and held out well against the elements. Another set of stairs served the back of the stage with an electrical panel mounted on the large round post nearest them. This was where most of Port Arthur's outdoor performances were likely held. It would be simple to set up quickly, and the area was easily maintained with no need for chairs or lighting other than the stage itself.

He walked to the middle of the stage, standing where most performers would. More importantly, it would probably be where the premier would stand. In this spot, he imagined her smiling while waving to the crowd with her entourage and local officials surrounding her. He turned and looked west, past the field and the large parking lot next to it. On the far side of the parking lot stood a large building. He estimated it to be at least forty or fifty feet tall, maybe the size of a school gymnasium. It had a flat roof and siding painted with a light stain that had long since faded from its original colour. But it was the windows that he was most interested in. Two rows of four faced in his direction, one for each level of the building. The entire structure looked to be a warehouse of some kind, hopefully, unoccupied or abandoned for now. He had driven past it earlier and seen that the property it sat on was surrounded by a high chain-link fence topped with barbed wire. The entrance was on the other side, protected by a metal gate on rollers that could be slid open. The gate was closed and padlocked with a length of chain. The supports for a sign of some kind were still attached to the top of the building over the main entrance, but whatever had been mounted to them had long since been taken down.

He lowered himself with one hand on the stage, then jumped onto the grass, the black bag still hanging from his shoulder. He looked back to the windows. The shot would be clear. There were no obstacles between where he stood now and the windows of the warehouse. But the distance would be critical, as would be the wind that blew across the field. Reaching into the bag, he pulled out a short piece of red ribbon. Walking over to the nearest tree, he reached as high as possible, tying the ribbon in place and letting it hang. It wasn't the best wind gauge, but it suited his needs. Once back near the front of the stage again, he closed his eyes briefly and took a deep breath. *You've got to get this right,* he thought and began to pace in a straight line toward the building, taking relaxed steps, counting as he walked. At two hundred yards, he stopped, scanned the area once more, then focused on the old building. It would probably be another two hundred yards to the windows. A slight breeze blew across the field, but it only came in brief gusts directly at his face. He nodded; this was good. As long as there was no crosswind, it would be necessary to calculate only the bullet drop over this distance. He kept walking, crossed the parking lot, and stopped at the fence. Four hundred and ten yards. With another ten past the fence to the wall, the entire distance was four hundred and twenty yards. He sat down with his back against the fence, looking at the stage. This was going to be one hell of a shot, and he would only get one. The possibility of hitting someone else once the commotion started was too great. This was not to be taken lightly. Either the margin of error was as close to zero as possible, or he would walk away. The teacher put on his black gloves and walked to the gate.

The bolt cutters cut the padlock with ease. After one last look around, he slid through the open gate, replacing the lock with one of his own. Quickly, he made his way past the main entrance toward the rear, close to the windows and a small access door. It was the same colour as the building, almost invisible to those not looking for it. Taking a small crowbar from his bag, he pried the locked door open, gaining access into the building.

None of the lights were on, but the numerous windows made visibility easy. Sunlight streamed through the windows, creating a spotlight effect, and the stale smell in the air was a good sign that the place hadn't been used in a long time. He walked along the concrete floor and looked around; it was open like an arena, and incandescent lighting hung from the ceiling. Several of the bulbs were broken, and the power source had most likely been disconnected long ago. Near the main entrance, a metal set of stairs led halfway up the building to a metal walkway against the wall that traversed the entire perimeter of the building, creating a second level of sorts. A small room in one corner of the upper level had a large glass window that overlooked the entire floor area. He guessed it was an office of some kind. Set into the wall below this office was a large roll-up door that closed to the concrete floor. The entire area was barren, save for a few empty wooden crates resting on the concrete and several others stored on the walkway above. This had to have been a warehouse.

He made his way to the stairway, up to the walkway. It was surprisingly wide; he estimated six feet at least. He walked around a corner to the east wall to the row of windows. The first pane of glass was covered with grime from the outside elements, but it opened easily outward, resting on hinges like a door. He pushed it halfway open; opening it any further might raise suspicion from the outside. Looking out, he could see the playing field but not the stage. He closed it and moved to the next. His luck was better this time as it opened in the opposite direction. The entire stage was visible after opening it only a third of the way. This was perfect. He imagined the rifle muzzle resting near the edge. The field of fire was at least two hundred feet on either side of the stage.

He walked on to the office. Except for an empty filing cabinet lying on its side, there was nothing else in the room. However, there was another door opposite the one he had walked through. This second door was not locked and opened easily, leading to a roof extension above the office's large metal door beneath. Resisting the urge to walk through it, he peered into the opening. The tar and gravel roof had a raised edge built to a knee-high level around it. From the positioning of the roof, he guessed it would be possible to see the stage from this vantage point as well.

He walked back to the window he had decided on and realized that the roof was not a good choice; it would leave him exposed to detection. The window was still the best. Five minutes later, he had set up two of the old crates beneath its opening. He placed one on its side, serving as a rest for the rifle, and he would use the second to sit on. He looked at his watch. It had been twenty-five minutes since he had entered here. It was time to go soon, but he wasn't quite finished. If an escape was going to be successful, he needed a place to stash his weapon together with anything else he wasn't going to carry. Unfortunately, this place was simply a big box with no nooks or crannies to hide anything of size. He continued to look, noticing a vent covering an opening in the wall near him. *Air conditioning of some kind,* he thought. There had to be a larger one with sizable ducting somewhere nearby.

He surveyed the area again, walking as he scanned the walls and ceiling. Then he saw what he was looking for through the office window. In the corner of the room near the floor was a large grate set into the wall. How had he missed it the first time? Moving past the filing cabinet, he got down on his knees, peering through the slats of the grate. "Be still, my beating heart!" he whispered. Past the grate, a silver expanse of ducting led away from the wall for a short distance and then made a sharp turn toward the other side of the building. But the grate and duct were large, at least two and a half feet wide and almost two feet tall. The grate was hinged at the top and secured with two screws at the bottom. He looked into his bag, moving his collection of tools from side to side, but he already knew the answer.

"No screwdriver. Unbelievable!" he moaned. "You brought everything else but forgot a fucking screwdriver! Dunce!"

Reaching into his pocket, he splashed around what coins he had until he found a dime. It fit both screws. After breathing a sigh of relief, he swung the grate open. This would be it. Once everything was tucked in here, he would make a run for it. After loosely putting the screws back in the grate, he made for the exit. Now there was only one piece left in the plan.

Later that afternoon, he was standing at the foot of a long dock at the ocean's edge. The drive here had been slow and methodical, winding through streets that almost seemed like alleys in what appeared to be an industrial area with sparse traffic. The signs he could make out on the buildings indicated a nautical trade: "Northwest Salvage," "Port Arthur Marine Repairs." Green dumpsters set up against the walls were propped open, and pedestrian traffic was minimal as he passed only three locals on foot, none of whom paid him any attention. Some things never change.

The dock was T-shaped with two three-hundred-foot sections jutting out at opposite right angles from the main landing on which he stood. It was made of wood, large planks set on a frame of timbers. These were loosely attached to pilings that allowed the entire structure to flex with the tides. It was beautiful here. The rustle of the small waves on the shore and the smell of the sea air flooded his senses. He couldn't remember if he had ever explored such an area before. It felt calming, and when he closed his eyes, the breeze blew his hair to the side. He felt fresh again. Best of all, there were no people.

The teacher walked along the dock, examining each boat carefully. Most were smaller pleasure crafts, but there were larger commercial boats as well, their netting and small white floats rolled onto large drums. He turned right at the junction and saw what he was looking for: it was an aluminum fishing boat, maybe twenty-five feet long. It seemed to be in reasonably good shape, but then he knew nothing of boats. Taped to one of the cabin's windows was a For Sale sign, handwritten with a phone number below it.

Stepping on the side of the craft, he jumped onto the deck of the boat. There were several compartments set into the sides and flooring. Much of what he stood on was stained with dried fish blood. He walked over to the cabin and peered through the glass on the door. Two fishing rods were leaning near one window, and a series of small steps at the front led down to a storage area of some kind. This would do just fine.

He pulled his cell phone from his pocket, dialled the number listed on the sign, and waited.

"Yello!"

"Hi, I'm standing on your boat, hoping that you might sell it to me."

"Mister, this is your lucky day. I'll be there in ten minutes."

Twenty minutes later, they had exchanged pleasantries, and the teacher and Freddy Stewart were pulling away from the dock in the aluminum fishing boat. He stood at the entrance to the cabin while Freddy manned the wheel and throttle. Freddy was the blue-collar sort. His baggy faded jeans were tucked into rubber boots, and he wore a heavy red plaid shirt—untucked and unbuttoned—over a plain grey T-shirt. Grey stubble covered his face, and, like the patrons of the diner, he wore a dirty ball cap, symbolic of the working class that inhabited most rural areas. The teacher put his age at around fifty, but he could have been younger. The lines on his face told a story of hard work and exposure to the elements.

"See how good she runs?" Freddy said, staring straight ahead through the cabin glass toward the bow. "Yessir, I bought this darlin' brand new and babied her ever since. Sure, there are a few scuff marks here and there, and she's a little grimy from the fish guts, but the engine is what keeps you alive out on the salt chuck, and this one couldn't have gotten better care from anyone else."

"I haven't been around a whole lot of boats," the teacher said. "But she seems fairly easy to operate."

"Of course," Freddy replied. "Here, take the wheel and play with her for a bit."

The teacher traded places with Freddy, holding the wheel in one hand and the throttle in the other. He sped up, heading out farther from land. He smiled. In another life, he could have easily lived on the ocean. There were no streets or highways or other noisy intrusions that stained the soul. He turned his head toward Freddy slightly but kept his eyes forward.

"So I have to ask, why are you selling her?"

Freddy stared forward, seemingly focusing on something in the distance. "The cancer got me, in my liver. I been fightin' it for a year now, and the doc says I got about a year if I'm lucky. Rosie, my wife, says we need to enjoy the time left as best we can. So we're gonna take a trip. I want to see the Grand Canyon, then the redwoods in California: somethin' I always wanted to see but never made the time. Stupid."

"I'm sorry," said the teacher.

"Don't be," Freddy said. His eyes were moist as he kept his stare forward. "I loved it out here too much and thought I would live forever. But like a lot of other people, life slapped me in the face before I could plan for retirement."

The teacher thought Freddy might ask why he had come all this way just to buy a boat, but it didn't happen. "I haven't seen many people around today," he said in an effort to change topics.

"It's like that most weekdays around here," Freddy said. "But everyone's getting kinda excited and all stirred up about the premier lady that's comin' soon."

"Is that good or bad?"

"Both, I guess. It don't really matter to me; I've worked for myself my whole life. But I'm kinda suspicious. When I hear someone push that hard in the newspapers and on TV, I get a sense that there's bullshit in the wind. But we don't usually get politicians out this far unless they want somethin.' So people are gonna come see just for somethin' to do."

The teacher left that part of the conversation behind and began a slow turn toward the shore. "I like the boat," he said. "How much you want for her?"

"Thirty-five thousand. I know that sounds a little steep, but I know this is a damn fine rig. And I'll throw in the fishin' gear for ya."

"Sounds good," the teacher said and offered his hand. "Let's go back into town and find a bank. I can transfer the money to you."

CHAPTER

20

"I'm going away, Simon."

"Again? Are you coming back?"

"I hope so."

The teacher was standing in the middle of Simon's living room, looking at his friend. Simon was seated on the couch in his usual spot with his cat asleep on his lap. Once again, he was still dressed in his robe, holding a newspaper in his hand with his index finger marking a page.

"Are you going to need some help?"

"Maybe, but I'm headed up the north coast. If I get into a jam, it will probably be a done deal before anyone can save my ass. But I'm hoping you can do something for me."

"Sure. What do you need?"

The teacher was holding a sealed white envelope in his hand. He stepped forward, leaned over, and dropped it on the coffee table in front of Simon. Simon reached over and picked it up. The cat stretched slightly but then curled back up, still asleep.

"What's this?" asked Simon.

"It's my will. I scribbled it out last night, so it hasn't been professionally prepared. But, it explains why it's handwritten, and it has my signature. Under the circumstances, it will have to do."

"Does it have any special requests?"

"Just those that involve Constance. You remember, don't you? She's the sweetheart I worked with."

Simon smiled while looking at the envelope, turning it over several times. "Yes, I do." Then he stroked the cat's head. "Did you leave Kitty anything?"

"Not a chance. You should make that useless animal earn its keep, like maybe catch a mouse or something."

"Now, now, I told you to be nice. Who else am I going to able to talk to once they plant you?" He looked back up at the teacher. "But seriously, it sounds like you're going for broke this time."

"I guess. But it's not a suicide plan. Things kind of have to come together, or it's not going to happen. I'm hoping to make it out alive."

"Okay. Well, even though I'm the last person qualified to judge anyone's actions, I understand you have your reasons. I've not tried to stop you before, so I'm in no position to try now. Be careful, okay?"

"Thanks, Simon."

With that, he walked back down the stairs, then stood at the open door for a moment, and called back to Simon. "And read the will! It's cremation; don't stick me in the ground!"

It was a Tuesday morning when the bus pulled into the curb at the depot in Port Arthur. The teacher was the fourth person off. He slung his black bag over his shoulder, then waited for the driver to open the storage compartments. When the second door had been lifted, he stepped to the side of the driver, who was unloading various bags of luggage and backpacks, and reached for a long grey ski bag.

"It's okay, I've got this one," he said, smiling at the driver.

"A little early for skiing, isn't it?" said the driver.

"Fishing rods," replied the teacher. "Very expensive ones too. Heading out tomorrow for three days. Gonna be the trip of a lifetime."

191

"Good luck," said the driver, interested only in reaching for the next suitcase.

The teacher carried his bags farther up the curb toward the main ticket office. A lone white taxi cab was parked near the entrance. The driver was sitting behind the wheel with his head back and eyes closed, his window half-open. The teacher walked up, set the black bag down, and tapped the window.

"Got time to give me a lift?"

The startled driver jerked himself upright and turned to face the teacher with eyes wide. He was older and very thin. The hand he placed on the wheel was boney, the tips of the fingers stained yellow. The teacher surmised he was a smoker. Judging by the grey pallor of his sunken cheeks, it was a habit that had consumed him most of his life. His slicked hair, combed to the back along the sides in a fashion not seen since the fifties, was dyed brown and had the appearance that it was done with shoe polish. He blinked a couple of times, then cleared his throat.

"Yeah, sure. Where ya goin'?"

"To the main dock."

The driver shifted to open the door, but the teacher held up his hand.

"S'okay. I can put my rods and bag in the back seat myself. Then I'll come around."

They made their way toward the ocean, making the obligatory small talk. The driver related his life's story of having lived in the area for as long as he could remember. Then the conversation changed to the weather and how lucky the teacher was to go out fishing this time of year. Ten minutes later, they pulled up to the dock. The teacher paid the fifteen-dollar fare, thanked the driver, and waved with a smile as he pulled away.

He walked along the wooden planks, taking in the ocean breeze and sunshine with a complete sense of calm. Once he arrived at his new purchase, he threw the black bag onto the deck, the heavy clunk of the metal tools muffled by the bag. However, he held onto the long grey ski bag, and when he had successfully hopped over the side, pulled out his key for the cabin.

He opened the door and walked ahead, then down the four stairs to the sleeping area under the bow. He left the tool bag on the floor but opened the ski bag slowly, sliding out the meticulously padded rifle. The bubble wrap came off easily, and he held the scoped rifle up for inspection. It was as pristine as when he first removed it from the cabinet more than a year ago. This time, however, there was a nylon cartridge carrier strapped to the side of its butt. One cartridge was held in each of the five slots. He wasn't sure why he brought five when it would be one or nothing. Just a habit, he guessed.

He placed the rifle on the sleeping bag lying on the bunk and looked around the tiny space. The rest of the floor area was covered with plastic bags and enough provisions to last weeks. Jugs of water lined the wall together with a bottle of scotch. Finally, there was a green duffle bag that contained fresh clothes and a shaving kit. This was the last task on his list before he had left Port Arthur more than three weeks ago. If he made it this far after taking the shot, he would head south along the coast for as long as his supplies and gasoline held out. But he wasn't worried about that. There were plenty of small ocean communities farther south. In time, he could moor this boat somewhere and head home. Hopefully, Simon would be available to pick him up instead of probating a will.

After stocking the black bag with a handful of protein bars and two bottles of water, he decided that a long nap was in order. He would sleep as long as possible and then, at midnight, navigate the streets to the warehouse.

"Did you sleep well, Madam Premier?"

"Alecia, are you telling me that with all your talent, the best motel you could find in these godforsaken backwoods was that fleabag dump we slept in last night?"

Alecia smiled as the premier walked toward her. She looked at the puffy areas under her boss's eyes and, even though the premier's makeup was the very best, it couldn't hide the fatigue in her face. "I'm sorry, but the accommodations available in this area are sketchy at best. I had some of the other staff go over the room to make sure bed bugs were not a problem or any other vermin for that matter. The plumbing and lighting were adequate. Then again, if you had been willing to take the floatplane to Port Arthur, it would have made things simpler."

"I get airsick in those glorified kites," the premier said. In truth, she was terrified of flying. It hadn't always been a problem, but as she got older, she found it almost impossible to board an aircraft without a stiff drink first or a dose of anxiety medication. This was as good a reason as any to move onto the next stage of her life, a luxurious retirement where everything was first class, and travel was kept to a minimum.

Alecia held the door of the black limousine open for them to enter the back seat. They would drive to Port Arthur today and hopefully find a better hotel. Early tomorrow evening she would sway the townsfolk with her charm, shake hands with the local politicians, then tell the limo driver to get back to the big city as fast as was legally possible. There she could rest up for more of the campaign grind.

At midnight, the teacher donned a black hoodie, black sneakers, and gloves, and after loading the handgun, he placed it in the black bag. He shouldered his equipment once more, picked up the ski bag with the rifle inside, and stepped onto the dock. A single light mounted on a thin metal pole where the docks diverged lit up the surrounding boats with an eerie glow. A partial moon shimmered off the water with only the brightest stars visible. He began to walk. Once on the streets, he would have to be patient and careful. Fortunately, it was a weekday, so traffic of any kind should be minimal at best. Using shadowed building entrances, vacant alleys, and even dumpsters, if necessary, would make his chances of getting to the warehouse undetected much better.

At the first street, he stopped and listened. Tonight, his biggest asset would be his hearing. Hopefully, it would provide enough advanced warning to hide or stash his equipment out of sight. From doorway to doorway, he walked silently, stopping every few minutes to listen to the sounds of the night; now there were none. He kept on. The air was cool, and the sky was clear. Over the ocean, the crescent moon offered some light, just enough to contrast his surroundings. Ten minutes later, he stopped, standing motionless, the sound of an engine rumbling in the distance. He looked to both sides. The second doorway across the street was set into the building. It would have to do. He sprinted across the pavement and into a doorway, leaning the ski bag upright in the corner with the second bag next to it on the tiled entrance. Streetlights were few and far between in this area of town. There were no lights or shadows here, only the darkness softened slightly by the distant moon.

The sound of the engine grew louder. To his right, headlights reflected off the side of a building and turned the corner toward him. The shape of a car made its way down the street. It was becoming louder, the exhaust obviously modified for effect. He pressed himself into the corner as best he could. It was probably a muscle car or street racer of some kind. He held his breath as the driver accelerated, and a black sedan shot past him without hesitation, the sound system blaring "Paradise by the Dashboard Light." *Probably off to the ocean to park with his girlfriend and lay waste to a bottle of hooch,* he thought. *Gotta love these small towns where the kids own the night.*

He needed to move faster. Jogging now, he made his way along the dark side of each street, avoiding every light possible. Fifteen minutes later, he put the key in the lock, slid the gate open, and locked up behind him. The side door opened easily. Once inside the warehouse, he stood to let his eyes adjust to the light as best they could.

It was different here at night. The light from the parking lot came through the windows, casting a dull haze on the far wall that reflected it back throughout the floor space. It wasn't great, but it was enough and would have to do. He made his way up the stairs to the stacked boxes next to the window of choice. Placing both bags gently on the floor, he sat a moment longer, then reached into the black one and began to search with his hand. Out of the bag came a small silver flask holding a few ounces of scotch. He unscrewed the cap and took a generous sip. He was here.

Yes, he was here. His meticulous planning had brought him this far, but what was he doing here? Sure, he had exorcised two significant demons from his past. Clyde and Ted were rotting in whatever afterlife waited for them. Emily's killer was still walking the streets, but he would probably waltz through life and simply bury any remorse deep within, out of mind. Or even worse, he would, over time, create an alternate scenario, one where the young girl had ridden her bike into the street without looking, making it impossible to avoid the accident. Like many others, he would let the roots of this lie grow until it was the only vision that came to him when he thought of that day. But the result was still the same. There was nothing he could do to avenge the girl, not even if he laid waste to every drunk driver or drug dealer he could.

So why not just go home? Why not start fresh and try harder to be happy with what was left? Months ago, he had watched a fictional TV program where a disillusioned rich man decided to help everyone he could by giving all his wealth to the poor and unfortunate until he was destitute. But the world still had plenty of impoverished and suffering souls that he couldn't help. In frustration, he slashed his wrists, the moral being that anyone who thinks he can save the world by himself is a fool. Was he a fool? Maybe. But he had "crossed the Rubicon" long ago. Only a fool would think it possible to reset the clock. The teacher that once was no longer existed. A new purpose and a new resolve had taken hold. Now he would take this to the end if he could.

He stood up to open the window far enough to see the stage in the distance. Two small security lights kept the floor lit with the help of a larger street light behind. He pulled a small penlight from his pocket, placing it between his teeth; it would serve as the only extra illumination. Using a flashlight would be too risky. Bending down, he carefully removed the rifle with both hands and inspected it once more. The stock was smooth, the metal of the barrel and scope unmarked. He closed his eyes and ran his fingers along the weapon, re-familiarizing himself with every moving piece. The light was put away. From now on, everything would be done by feel or with what surrounding light was available. He unfolded the bipod and allowed the rifle to rest on the higher crate near the window.

The end of the muzzle was flush with the window frame, and through the scope, he scanned the target area. The field of view was excellent. He sat on his left calf to elevate himself enough to continue this scan and hold the crosshairs steady. If his calculations were correct, at this distance, the bullet would drop nineteen inches. The top of an average head to the bottom of the chin was nine inches. He assumed the premier's head would be no different. Two vertical head lengths would be his guide. He pivoted the barrel slowly to the left, searching through the scope viewer. There it was. The small piece of ribbon he had tied on a tree branch hadn't come down, and, even better, it hung limp. There was no wind.

The chamber was empty, and he lifted the bolt, cocking the rifle. Aiming at one of the light bulbs, he breathed calmly, then slowly squeezed the trigger. The loud click of the dry fire was fine; the crosshairs never wavered. He did this three more times until he was certain he could pull the trigger and keep the bullet true. He closed the window, placing the rifle on the walkway, resting on its bipod.

One more sip drained the flask. Now it was time to wait.

He sat with his back to the crate, his knees pulled to his chest, rubbing his face and eyes. It was now noon. The night had been long and uncomfortable. He thought he should have been used to it by now. The time spent in the forest waiting for the Demons had been longer and indeed more frustrating, but it felt worse now for some reason. Maybe it was the stale air or these barren surroundings; he wasn't sure.

He was alone with his rifle. The rest of his equipment was in the ducting that came into the abandoned office. The screws to the grate were loose. When it came time to make a run for it, he would stash the rifle as fast as possible and then make for the streets. If the ensuing chaos gave him a head start, a dead run could get him to the dock in just over twenty minutes. His pistol is all he would take; it was tucked into his jeans at the small of his back, and it wouldn't slow him down. If needed, there were three recessed door entrances along the route back and one open dumpster. They would be his last chance if the hunt came his way.

Seven hours to go.

The sun set at five-thirty. At six-fifty, the premier and her aide walked up to the open door of the black limousine. Twilight was long gone now; only scattered stars gave any indication that there was anything beyond the darkness. The premier smiled at Alecia as she held the door open.

"Last night was much better."

"Yes, Madam Premier," said the dutiful aid. "We had the hotel replace all the bedding and completely scrub down every surface they could. You seem very well rested and looking your very best."

The premier smiled, putting her hand on Alecia's shoulder. "Like I've said over and over, what would I do without you?" she said and lowered her head to sit at her place on the finely leathered seat.

The limo was led out of the parking lot by a black SUV that carried three more of the premier's support staff. It would be a short, ten-minute drive to the venue. The premier knew she would have to deal with some brief formalities, including an introduction from the mayor, but she felt on top of her game tonight. She wore a red skirt and blazer; it was power attire at its best. At her request, portable stage lighting had been put up this afternoon to highlight her performance. There was no need for a podium or notes; she had everything memorized, and she would remove the microphone from the stand, working the stage better than any act these bumpkins had seen in a long time. *Yes,* she thought to herself with just a hint of a smile, *Daddy's got nothing on me tonight.*

At six-forty, the teacher opened the window a third of the way with a slow, even push. During the mid-afternoon, he had heard vehicles, closing doors, and hammering sounds. Now he could see that the stage had been prepared for the evening. Larger lighting hung over the front, and a microphone was in place, as were nine chairs, maybe nine feet back. A surprisingly large crowd of about a thousand people had gathered on the field. More were still making their way onto the grass. He didn't think that many in this town would be interested in something like this. But Fred had told him earlier that any celebrity in town went a long way in breaking up the boredom.

Bending down, he opened the rifle breach, pulled a cartridge from its holder, and chambered the round. He placed the rifle as he had earlier and, from a standing position, began to scan the target area. The lighting was better than he expected. He could clearly make out the slender microphone. To the left of the stage, the ribbon still hung without moving. Then he saw what he had hoped he wouldn't. A police cruiser pulled in to park behind the structure. As two officers got out, another cruiser drove slowly past the parked one as if on patrol.

"You didn't honestly think it was going to be that easy, did you?" he said softly to himself. His chest tightened, and he forced himself to breathe slowly but continued to look through the scope. The officers walked onto the stage, where they stood, one at each side of the row of chairs. The other police car had driven on. "I didn't think there were that many cops in this whole town," he whispered facetiously.

Then came more headlights. Three vehicles, a black limo, a large SUV, and a smaller sedan pulled in beside the cruiser. He could hear the murmur in the crowd intensify. Now four individuals emerged from the sedan. He focused the scope on each of them, in turn, three men and a woman. The lead male wore a black suit with a chain of office shining in the surrounding light. *The mayor,* he thought. He led the three others onto the stage, where they took their seats in the chairs furthest to the left. The doors of the SUV opened and two more women and a lone male exited. They were very well dressed, their grooming suggesting a degree of sophistication not found in a town like this. He focused on the women as they walked—both brunette, neither of them his objective. It was close now. He put his shin on the crate and sat on his calf.

Finally, the limo's back door opened and out came another woman, this one a redhead dressed in green. She held the door open for the last to emerge with the distinctive blond hair he had seen in so many photos and on TV. The red attire caught his attention immediately, an inviting and easier target. He gave it only a moment's consideration—the shot needed to be fatal. An eloquent, wounded martyr could easily garner sympathy, appearing as the brave victim. She was moving as well. This had to proceed as planned, with her sitting or standing in one spot. He tracked her, with the scope moving in a slow arc as she ascended the stairs, her ever-persistent smile on display for the crowd. Her entourage had taken the seats to the right. The premier waited for the redhead and then, as the last one standing, gave a quick wave to the crowd before sitting in the middle chair.

The teacher looked at the ribbon one last time; it did not move at all. He then looked back to the center chair. The crosshairs were his guide now. He felt a calm come over him, and with measured breath, he elevated the thin black cross above her head, directly over her temple. One head length, now two. His index finger moved to the trigger. The premier turned to her right and said something to the mayor, who then stood up and walked to the microphone.

The teacher relaxed his finger ever so slightly. *Easy, easy,* he thought. *Patience.* Then he sighted on the mayor. The mayor tapped the microphone, then spoke to the crowd. The teacher's ears blocked out whatever was being said, but he registered the word "introduce." The left side of the scope picked up the bright red colour that moved into view. The mayor moved to the side as the premier came to the microphone, faced the mayor, and smiled. The crosshairs moved smoothly again. One head length, then two. His finger set against the trigger. He took one more breath, exhaled slightly, then began to squeeze.

The premier had taken her place at the microphone, her sparkling teeth and blue eyes facing the mayor. They clasped hands as the mayor leaned forward.

"I hope your room was better this time," he said. "I put on my best apron and cleaned it myself!" On cue, the premier threw back her head to laugh.

The crack of the rifle filled his ears, and the stock bucked against his shoulder. At that instant, the image in the scope blurred suddenly. "What the . . .?" He tried to refocus, but frantic movement was all he could see. Quickly, he pulled the rifle back and closed the window.

"Shit!" he cursed. "What the hell just happened?"

CHAPTER

21

"**G**otta move!"

The teacher removed the spent casing, tucked it in his pocket, and ran for the office. On his knees, he opened the grate, pulled out the ski bag, and tucked the rifle in. Once it was back inside, he pushed everything in the duct as far in as possible. He turned each screw several times, but that was it and bolted out of the office and along the walkway. At the door, he stopped briefly to look carefully outside and listen. There was yelling and screaming coming from the field, but here, no one was in sight. He ran for the gate. Frantic and clumsy, he fumbled with the key. Finally, when the gate opened, he started to run again.

A siren. He stopped in his tracks. Then another one. He turned in their direction, listening intently. They were coming closer. *Damn! They're fast!* he thought. *I'm not gonna make it.* No amount of panic would solve this. He lowered his head, staring at the pavement, his thumb rubbing the opposite palm. Like a statue. he stood there, waiting. "C'mon! Think!" he said. He looked up. The door was still open. "Okay."

Running back the way he came, the teacher went through the door, then ran up the stairs. He stopped at the window, pushed it open, then placed the empty casing on the walkway. *With luck,* he thought, *they'll find it and think I've gone.* Running to the grate, he went to his knees. Loosening the screws, he held the grate open with one hand and slid on his back into the aluminum duct, the pistol digging into his skin. Lowering the grate carefully with his foot, he slid farther along, pushing both bags with his shoulders. This was too slow. The sound of the sirens was very close now. He managed to get onto his right side, but the other shoulder jammed against the top of the duct. He pushed with his right hand against the opposite side. The top of the duct moved slightly. He pushed harder, and it began to buckle upward. Finally, with a metallic warping echo, it gave enough, and he was on his stomach. The duct turned sharply left in front of him. The sirens came to the open gate and stopped. He pushed faster until he was completely around the corner and hidden, the bags resting near his head and along his side. He looked into the darkness, breathing softly and listening.

Feet pounded quickly up the stairs.

"Wait, you stupid ape!" a voice yelled from below. "If he's here, he's got a gun. Find some cover!"

The teacher slid farther and stopped. It was possible to make out voices, but not how many there were. They were searching but not close yet. Minutes went by in silence. He tried to think like they would. Whoever had called out first was obviously smart enough to exercise caution. If they were systematic, they would sweep the main floor area first. But there couldn't be that many police available in a town like this, even with the premier's arrival. They would have to search quickly, then move on to prevent him from leaving town.

Now, more voices, but still, he couldn't make out what they were saying. The footsteps clattered against the stairs again. "Up here!" a voice called out, followed by someone ascending the stairs, more than one this time. He slid farther alongside the aluminum, then stopped, straining to listen. "Look at this; it's from a rifle. He took the shot from here." The voice was loud. They were being called closer, but one of them had found the spent casing. Good. Now if they would just turn around and leave to look somewhere else. There were more erratic footsteps and murmuring, but he could only make out the odd word. "Keep looking. Over there." It was the first voice he heard when they came inside. This guy was calling the shots.

Again, he pushed himself further but stopped instantly when a searing pain flashed along the side of his ribs. He clenched his teeth, closed his eyes hard, and reached back. A nail, a stupid nail! Somehow it had come through the bottom of the duct during construction, probably when they were framing the wall. He took the glove off with his teeth and felt his side. The hoodie near his ribs was wet with his blood. The sound of footsteps came closer. Once again, more than one. He closed his eyes, breathing soft and shallow.

They were in the office now. Carefully, he looked back at the duct he had come around. Light reflected off the aluminum, but it was not direct; it was only reflected light from the walls or whatever else they were shining flashlights on. If they saw the loosened screws on the grate, he was finished. His heart pounded hard in his chest, and sweat ran down his brow.

"Check the door," said a different voice.

One of them walked to the door and opened it.

"C'mere. Check this out. It's a roof." More footsteps, heading outside, then the voice again. "There's nothing here; he's gone. Let's go back to the corporal. We'll seal the place off. He can send someone in tomorrow morning to look for prints or whatever else might have been left behind."

The sound of footsteps trailed away. He swallowed hard, breathing deep. Sweat ran into his eyes, stinging them, but he refused to move a muscle, only blinking hard. Then he heard voices again, but it was impossible to make them out. Finally, he heard the clatter on the stairs and the sound of a closing door. He had to be very careful now. The slim chance was his, but if he was going to make the best of it, every movement from here on required deliberate forethought.

Time passed. He wasn't sure how much, but it had to be at least an hour, maybe longer. The strain of confinement had taken its toll. He was tired, and the lack of any fresh air was becoming unbearable. But the bleeding had stopped, and so had the voices or any other signs of the police. It was time to get out. Reaching into his pocket, he pulled out the penlight to look at his watch. It was ten forty-seven. He aimed the light along the duct. It continued for some distance, but at an arm's length ahead, another shaft went straight down. Avoiding the nail, he made his way to the edge, pointing the light down. It was bigger, and at the bottom, it branched in three directions.

"Don't be stupid," he whispered. "It's a twenty-foot drop at least." Even worse, it would wind up being the world's longest coffin if he got stuck. He looked back the way he came, but it was too far and slow to go backwards. "If I don't get out of here soon, I'll go crazy or die." He turned off the light, lying there in the silence, resting. He thought about dying, right here in this miserable shaft, in this miserable building. It would be easy enough to use the pistol, end it quickly with a bullet. Easy—now there was the operative word. It would have been just as easy to have avoided all this in the first place. *Christ!* he thought. *Stop already! How many times do you have to go over this? What's done is done. Now, move!*

He leaned his chin over the edge, looking down. His eyes widened and strained to their limits. "No way!" The words escaped his mouth in a gasp from his own weight on his chest. "I couldn't see it before because of the stupid penlight." A bluish glow came from one of the shafts at the bottom. "It has to be from outside." It was an epiphany. The ducts lay alongside the building's outer wall. The light, probably from a streetlight, had to come in through another vent, an intake vent. He just needed to find a way down. Less than a minute later, a desperate idea became his only way out.

Grabbing the equipment bag, he rummaged through it until he found the screwdriver. With one hand on the shaft's opposite edge, he reached down and drove the screwdriver through the thin sheet of aluminum. It stopped against something solid after penetrating a couple of inches. *Wood framing,* he thought. Again, he rammed the screwdriver as hard as he could and felt it penetrate the wood slightly. If it could hold his weight, he could lower himself to the bottom in stages. Like a dying man who had been given a reprieve, he started moving with urgency.

He dropped the equipment bag down the shaft, where it clambered against the metal. *Just in case I have to beat my way out of here.* Ignoring the pain in his side, he squirmed across the opening, then lowered himself until he hung by straining fingertips. Front and back, he braced himself with his sneakers, hoping the rubber soles would grab enough to bear at least some of his weight. Reaching down with one hand, he began to put his weight on the handle of the screwdriver and lower himself farther down. It held. Again, he braced himself as hard as possible, pushing with his front foot to keep his back against the metal. He pulled the screwdriver out, then rammed it in again as far down as he could. Slowly, he put his weight on the handle again. It didn't hold.

The blade broke free of the wood, and he fell, still clutching the handle. Landing with his right shin hitting the bag, his left foot smacked the bottom, driving his kneecap into the upper shaft edge. A flash of pain exploded behind his eyes and spread through his knee. "Shit!" he grunted through clenched teeth. He knew he had done a good job of hurting himself this time. Sitting as he had when he took the shot, his weight was on the back of his right calf. But this time, his left leg was bent, his foot on the floor and his knee six inches from his face. With teeth still clenched, he pressed into his thigh. No pain, good. He did the same with his calf. Again, no pain. At least he hadn't broken any long bones, but his knee was a different matter. Gently touching the top of the joint, he could feel the torn jean fabric. Worse, he could feel more blood. As if his side wasn't bad enough, at the very least, his knee was gashed, and his kneecap was possibly broken. But the agony was a small price to pay for the good news. Twelve inches in front of him was the vent he had hoped for.

Gotta rest, just for a bit. He leaned his head against the side of the shaft and closed his eyes. He needed water, but all his was gone. He thought of the boat; the boat had lots of water. It also had a bed and lots of food. Best of all, the boat was on the ocean, the wonderful, beautiful ocean. It was only a half-hour away, but it might as well be ten miles. He was lame, and more police would be on the way soon. It would be like running the gauntlet. He had no choice.

Sizing up the grate, he figured a couple of good kicks would break it open. With hitching breaths to fight the pain, he wrestled the bag from under him and pushed it into the duct to his left. He cocked his right leg and kicked at the grate. Another breath and he kicked again. A screw gave way. Two more kicks in quick succession, and the rest broke free, and he slid out into the cool fall air.

He was lying on the gravel of a parking lot next to the wall he had come through. A single LED lamp on a tall wooden pole in the middle of this lot had been his beacon. Exhausted, bleeding and damp from his sweat, he'd be in Heaven if he could just sleep for an hour. But the dial on his watch read almost midnight. *Keep moving.* As he struggled to his feet, the pain was intense. He lifted the front of his hoodie and tore a strip off the T-shirt underneath, then tied it around his knee. He limped toward the gate, the pain shooting through his leg with each step. Yellow tape stretched across the opening, but there were no other signs of the police. He continued.

Twenty minutes later, he was sitting slouched in a dark doorway, breathing hard, sweating again, grimacing. The throbbing was fierce and unrelenting, but it kept him awake. A half-hour later, he was sitting in another, the same one the teen lust-birds had driven past the day before, not noticing the dark shape pressed against the door. But this time, there were no cars or sirens. The street was completely deserted with only the hum of the lone streetlight near him. Leaning forward, he looked up, then to the top of the light standard—nothing, only the stillness in the black sky and the dull glow above the streetlight.

I guess I'm on my own this time, he thought. *But I could use some inspiration in the worst way.* He got to his feet for the third time and hobbled onto the street, this time using his left arm against the nearest wall to take the weight off his knee. Even slower now, he plodded from building to building, his head down, looking every bit like a drunk trying to make it home after a hard night. He wasn't sure how much farther he had to go, but what strength was left was giving out. The scuffing sound of his sneakers against the pavement was erratic, and his breathing was loud and hard. He kept going.

"Mr. Shit-hot-jogger-stud," his voice spat out after a while. "Fuck the good guy crap! Shoulda had at least one good romp with Connie-babe. Twit!" Then he stopped, breathing deeply, a faint scent drifted on a soft breeze. "It's saltwater!" It couldn't be that far now. In his fatigue, he had lost his grasp on time. But that didn't matter now. This inspiration had no feathers, but it gave him a surge, and he limped faster, slapping at the wall with each step.

Then the walls were gone. The sea was in front of him now, the water calm with only the odd light casting a shimmer on the surface, the heavenly smell of the water strong and comforting. Standing there, he wanted to jump and shout with his hands in the air to pay homage to the exhilaration. *A stupid idea,* he thought. *Get a grip and go get some sleep.* The dock was there, and the lone light near his boat was still shining. He looked around slowly; nobody, not even a stray dog or cat, had crossed his path since leaving the warehouse. Gingerly, he put one foot after the other. At the end of the pavement, he made his way across the short stretch of sand, then stepped onto the wood decking. His eyes fixed on the light as he started the last stretch. He passed the first boat, then another. At the light, he stopped to give his knee a short rest.

There it was, his boat, the most beautiful thing he could remember seeing, and all he could focus on. Fifty feet to go. He started to walk again.

"You've been a busy boy, Mr. Emerson," the voice came from behind him.

The teacher froze in place. Instinctively, he reached behind for the pistol tucked into his jeans.

"I wouldn't do that if I were you." The voice was calm and measured, sending a wave of panic throughout his body, as though he had just lost the biggest gamble of his life, with a pile of insurmountable trouble ahead.

"It's not for you," he said.

"I know," the voice replied. "But still, I'd prefer to err on the side of caution."

"May I turn around?" The question reminded him of a small child asking permission.

"Yes."

The teacher raised his arms slightly from his waist and, with his fingers loosely spread, lurched in a circle, pivoting on his good leg. Then he saw him, a figure in partial shadow sitting on the bait container of a boat on the opposite side of the light. The shadow from the cabin covered his upper body, but he could see the badge in his left hand and the gun held loosely in his right, resting on his knee.

"You don't look so good."

"Been a rough night."

"You're bleeding."

"I lost an argument with a nail and some nasty metal."

The teacher was confused by the statements coming his way. So far, there were no questions, and he couldn't figure out why he hadn't been knocked to the decking and cuffed. Probably, this officer was simply toying with his prize for now.

"Like I said, you've been busy this past year."

The teacher paused, the statement igniting the flashbacks of his actions. "Just 'taking out the garbage,'" he said.

"One might say that's correct. But your methods aren't very subtle." The figure leaned forward, out of the shadow, and put his badge in his jacket pocket. He was a heavy-set man, dressed casually in tan pants and a brown bomber jacket. His round face was highlighted by a full head of jet black hair with a sheen brought on by the light.

"But they're complete." He noticed the chit-chat was over. It was time to cut to the chase. "You were smart enough to find me, so I gather you've done your homework and pieced together my motives."

"And that gives you the right to commit murder?"

"For me, it does."

"Their sins are so egregious that they would cause a respected teacher to become an assassin?"

"Maybe if the police had worked harder to track down a lowlife who ran over a small girl, leaving her to die in the street, things might have played out differently."

The teacher's statement hit home, and the detective's expression became one of reflection. A long silence ensued. They looked at each other, waiting to see who would flinch first.

Then the detective broke the silence. "I must admit, you're very good, one of the best I've ever come across. I can only imagine the amount of effort and planning that went into your work. It was very difficult to track you down."

"But you did. May I ask how?"

"Well, you see, I'm pretty good at what I do myself. Long hours, basic police work, and intuition go a long way when it comes to finding someone like you. And, of course, a vial of blood helped seal it. After that, you were easy to track. By the way, where did you take a bullet?"

The teacher said nothing. He simply looked at the detective smugly. He was tired, but there was no point in handing himself over on a platter.

"So what happened tonight?" the detective asked.

"What are you asking me for? You're the cop."

"Not here I'm not. Not tonight. My business with you is down south. Tonight, I'm just a spectator."

Maybe it was the fatigue, but the teacher could not make any sense of the conversation. The man was not being glib or cocky; he was simply stating a fact. The whole thing struck him as a casual conversation between professionals.

"I don't know."

"You don't know?"

"That's right. Something went wrong, and a run-for-it was the best I could manage."

The detective put his elbow on his knee, brought his hand to his face, and stared off, seeming deep in thought. Then he looked back at the teacher, and they both stood in a long silence once more, not moving, simply staring at each other.

"So what now?" the teacher asked.

"Go . . . beat it," the detective said. There was no emotion in his voice. But the teacher's eyes became narrow and questioning.

"Excuse me?"

"Yup. Hop on your boat and get lost."

"I don't understand."

The detective paused, then got to his feet. He holstered his pistol and stood up straight as though at attention. "Let's just say I owe you one. But don't worry, I'm sure our paths will cross again."

The teacher tried to process this but decided it was best to take the offer. He started to turn, still maintaining eye contact, not sure if this was a ruse. Then facing his boat, he began the final stretch to his refuge. After several steps, he stopped, looked down at the decking for a second, then back at the detective.

"You know, I don't know your name."

The detective showed a hint of a smile. "Takada. Detective Inspector Karasu Takada."

"Thanks, inspector," said the teacher. Then, cocking his head to the side, a flash of recognition came to his eyes. "I understand," he said, looking up. "Karasu? Really?"

"Yes," replied the detective.

The teacher smiled and nodded. "Good name," he said, ". . . for a bird." Then he turned once more and limped toward his boat.

EPILOGUE

The Herald – September 30th, 2016

The police in Port Arthur are reporting that the assassination attempt last night on the premier was unsuccessful. However, Premier Collins did sustain a serious facial injury, the extent of which is unknown at this time. Extra law enforcement officers were called in immediately, and an extensive search for the gunman, who is still at large, is continuing throughout the town and surrounding area. Several crime scenes have been cordoned off, and forensic specialists continue to work through the day. At this time, the motive for this attack is unknown.

There are times when one should think twice about feigning sincerity, as it often causes more pain and suffering than intended. The premier probably meant well, but her choreographed laugh at the mayor's attempt at humour caused her head to move back, elevating her chin as she opened her mouth. The bullet, which was initially intended for her temple, struck her lower jaw, removing an inch of bone, eight teeth and half of her tongue.

Speak no evil.